BEHIND

THE

IDOL

A K-POP ROMANCE

BY

★LUCY GOLD★

DEDICATION

For those everywhere still looking for their Only One

종진
JONGJIN
ONE MONTH PREVIOUS

"Jongjin, I'm surprised you don't feel like you've missed out on life."

The fake-blonde interviewer leaned forward, crossing one high-heeled leg over the other. She was looking at the five of us as we sat straight-backed on the hard vinyl sofas of the show's filming room.

She continued, her tone unconvincingly worried. "I mean, Jongjin, you trained for nine years! The longest of everyone in Tr3sure. And then, of course, with your *explosive* popularity, you're facing *so* many expectations and demands. Don't you ever get tired of any of it?"

I looked right at the camera with my most brilliant smile. "Of course not. What more could I want?"

종진

JONGJIN

1

The noise of the plane buzzed in my ears as I opened my eyes. I blinked groggily and glanced out the tiny window over Laon's lolled head, seeing bright blue sky.

Welcome to America.

I was trapped in the middle seat, wedged between Laon and Tae-X. My other two Tr3sure brothers, Seojung and Sun Chi-Ho, were in the same row on the opposite side, also asleep. I was the only one awake.

I managed to maneuver my arm out from where it was pinned under Tae-X's to check my watch. It was 4:56 American time, so we would be landing in about an hour.

Tr3sure had never been here before. We'd done Asian and European tours, but never the U.S.A. We'd been excited when it was first announced where we were going, but the management had decided to make the most of this trip, and that meant we'd be doing more than just California concerts—we were staying an entire month so we could also film a reality TV show at the same time. It had put a damper on the initial excitement, since we knew there would be no pause button. After working constantly on our upcoming album for weeks, we'd been hoping for a small break.

I watched the flight attendant slowly make her way down the aisle, offering people snacks, and I zoned out. The last day of our trip, July 1, was when we flew back to Korea—which was just a day after my twentieth birthday. I couldn't decide if that meant I'd have more or less time to just relax. For months, I'd been thinking about it— usually Tr3sure just set up a birthday live for our fans, but this year felt... different. I wanted to do something more. It was the end of my teen years, my supposed childhood. It was the break I'd been craving. A time to just have fun and not worry about work—not worry about what I was supposed to be feeling, what people wanted me to feel.

"Would you like anything?"

I blinked back to reality. The flight attendant had arrived at me now. She was holding some sort of cookie-like sweet.

It took an awkward second for my English to kick in.

"No thank you," I said, and she moved on with her cart.

There's no way I would've been able to eat that sweet. I was the main vocalist for Tr3sure, and sugar was bad for vocals. I was banned from it most of the time. The same thing went for dairy—which made my favorite dessert, ice cream, virtually *forbidden*. It had been almost a year since I'd had it last. Just another sacrifice that came with being an idol—nights craving cold, luscious ice cream.

I glanced across the row at the other sleeping Tr3sure members. I was right not to wake them up for free snacks. We probably wouldn't be able to eat anything anyway, sugar-free or not, since we were on comeback diets.

I sighed and ran a hand through my messed-up caramel-espresso hair, pushing it out of my left eye. It was the newest style they had chosen for me, which all the fans seemed to like. But what *didn't* they like about me? Most of Tr3sure's fan base, GOLD, preferred me for some reason. I was the favorite, and the one with the (true) underdog story. *Jongjin trained for nine years before debuting! He was passed up so many times! He dedicated his whole life to his dream! Just look at him now!*

Seojung, Tae-X, Laon and Sun Chi-Ho deserved the attention more than me. That was one reason I sometimes wished I wasn't the favorite. But I knew they didn't mind as much as I did. It was a blessing and a curse to be the most popular member, and they knew it. The fans' adoration ranged from cute to violent, and JNP was even tougher on me than it was on the other Tr3sure members. It was an exhausting upkeep of demands from everywhere—the fans, JNP, the relentless media.

It's not like the other members had it easy, though. We were living our dream by sacrificing other parts of our lives, and sometimes that meant working almost every waking minute. I'd even heard Tae-X mumbling the fan greeting in his sleep a couple times.

That was something I'd kept secret, not even telling Seojung, our leader. Tae-X already struggled with the separation of his idol identity from his personal identity. I didn't want to make it worse.

Maybe a trip to California, U.S.A. was just what he needed. Tr3sure wasn't as wildly popular here as we were in Asia and Europe, so people probably wouldn't recognize us. He—and the rest of us—would get to enjoy some anonymity.

I suddenly felt very energized, my foot starting to tap. I couldn't wait to land. One would think that busy idols would relish the relaxation time on an airplane, but now I was itching to get up and do something after waking up on this horrendously long flight. Getting a break this long during comeback season was unheard of, so I'd much rather be spending it outside in the sun, maybe sprawled on the grass. Not trapped inside a stuffy plane.

I glanced around for something to do.

Maybe I could practice my English on unsuspecting passengers. Casually, I turned around to look at the seat behind us, where a brunette teenaged girl sat, earbuds in and eyes glued to her phone.

I paused, wondering, doubting whether I should talk at all. But it was too late— she had already noticed me. *Oh no.* She looked up at me, surprised, and then yanked out an earbud. "Sorry, was I kicking your chair?"

Come on, English....

"No, you weren't, it's..." I wracked my brain, but couldn't think of a reason of why I'd turned around.

She squinted, confused.

Just act normal.

"It's... *um*," I finished conclusively, as if arriving at some great point.

Speaking English was the only time I ever started to feel anything close to panic. Most of the time it was great if I didn't think about it, but as soon as I was focusing too hard, everything I knew just flew out of my head. I could feel my face turn hot as I tried to find a way to finish that sentence.

The girl was giving me a slightly wary look usually reserved for crazy people. What should I say?

And just like that, I felt the idol Jongjin click into place. "Have you heard of Tr3sure? They have good music." I smiled, and flicked my eyebrow up smoothly, which fans went crazy for. Her expression turned to startled, then she blushed. Now there was something I knew how to react to. I swept my bangs slightly away from my face as if unconsciously, putting on a pleasantly amused face.

"Anyways. That's all." I gave her a nod and turned lazily around, leaving my arm still propped up on the back of the chair and silently thanking Tae-X for the English slang he had taught me.

After a hot second, I shrunk in my seat, suppressing a groan. So much for normal.

You panicked, there wasn't much else you could do. Did I even *know* how to have a normal conversation without my instincts kicking in?

I pushed a hand against my forehead, giving a silent groan. I could practically feel the girl behind me eyeing me hopefully now, burning a hole in the back of my head, and it was completely my fault.

I hadn't really gotten a normal life, and constant flirting—relished by our GOLD—was just a side effect of that.

I couldn't wait to get off this stupid plane.

Think about something good. Something you can actually solve.

Something good....

Like my birthday.

I wanted it to be different. Maybe it was possible for me to squeeze some fun in between all the things we had to do. I could probably fit something in with just one hour of extra free time.

I quietly ripped a blank page from Laon's travel songwriting notebook without waking him up and borrowed the pen too, pulling the cap off with my teeth, feet still tapping incessantly.

If you were just any normal guy having a birthday, what would you do?

Number 1: Eat ice cream.

That would be an amazing start. Excitement bubbled in me as more possibilities started whirling around my brain. Maybe we could have a picnic somewhere!

I shook the thought off, trying to ignore the way my light, happy feeling was fading like someone had popped a balloon inside of me. The staff would never go for something that took up hours.

What if you asked for extra time?

I mulled this idea over in my head. It wasn't such a bad one. If there was any day of the year to get extra hours off, it was my birthday. The other members would also be ecstatic to have some extra free time. We could go together.

The cheering thought was something to hold on to. It was going to be one busy, crushing month, with all the things we'd have to do. But if I could just have some birthday time off, I would be recharged. Energetic again. It would be worth it.

I checked my watch. Only fifty minutes left. I kept writing.

레일라
LEYLA
2

I stared out the window of the car at the setting sun, which was glowing a feverish orange, glinting off of the silver buildings in the distance. Palm trees studded the scene, silhouetted against the sky.

"Almost there, Leyla," my father said cheerfully. I glanced at him.

The truth was, we weren't *almost there*. He'd picked me up from the airport, lonely and disheveled with earbuds firmly in and lugging a gigantic rolling suitcase that held all the possessions I dared bring, just as rush-hour traffic had hit California.

We'd spent the rest of the evening in a crawl, the ridiculous number of lanes all clogged with cars. I knew it'd been at least one hour, but it was starting to feel like five, and there wasn't an end in sight.

When I still wasn't giving any sign of making conversation, my father piped up. "This is normal," he commented brightly. "Can take two hours to get somewhere that should be fifteen minutes away. Terrible, really terrible traffic."

By the tone of his voice, you'd think he was describing something great. I fought the urge to put my earbuds in again and close my eyes. "Wow."

We spent the rest of the car ride in near-silence, except for his occasional questions about my long flight, what I thought of the Southern California scenery, and whether I was excited to see the house.

I'd never been to my dad's house, though he'd owned it for over a decade. I hadn't even visited California before. My older sister Amanda was the one who'd flown out to me and my mom's house in Michigan a few times, and when I saw my dad, it was when he and Amanda picked me up for a couple weeks during summer vacation to go camping or stay at a hotel somewhere between the two states.

In the past year, both my parents had suddenly decided that I needed to go live permanently with my dad. I strongly suspected it was because of me and Amanda—we'd hardly gotten to spend any of our childhoods together, except for a few weeks of vacation each summer.

Now Amanda, at eighteen and a half, had announced her intention to eventually stay on university campus once she'd saved up enough money. Which basically made this my now-or-never chance to live with Amanda, and for us to be normal sisters.

I hadn't lived with Amanda since I was about five. That was when Mom and Dad had divorced, and Dad and Amanda had moved to California.

"Are you okay, Leyla?" my dad asked, and I gave a start, returning to reality and turning my head away from the window —where I'd been watching the scenery zip by with a dead, dull stare— to look at him. "You're normally so talkative and energetic."

That Leyla hadn't existed since my mom told me that I "was going to California, no arguments". Ever since I'd been told that I'd be ripped away from all the people I knew and my entire future. And anyway, how did he know what "normal" was for me?

"I'm fine," I lied with a smile. "The plane just tired me out, that's all."

He seemed appeased, cheerfully turning on the radio, and didn't bring it up again.

I numbed my fingers in the too-cold air conditioner blasting from the vents and turned to look out the window again. It was growing steadily darker outside, the city lights emerging. Once upon a time I would've oohed and aahed over the magic of it, but nothing seemed to excite me these days.

I thought of Aaron and Jackie back home. Ran it over yet again in my head the way we'd excitedly planned triple-dating at the senior prom next school year. The way Jackie had teased me about a guy I was already planning to invite, a green-eyed boy in my math class I'd never talked to but crushed on from afar. The way we'd always said we would go to the same university together. The way our parents and teachers had always told us how lucky we were for the three of us to just be best friends, without any dating drama or anything. Saying how lucky we were to be so close.

And most of all, I remembered the look on their faces as I said goodbye to them, with no idea when I would see them again.

When we finally pulled up to the house, it was dark. Dad parked in the street and I got out, stretching, the warm night air hitting me in the face. It felt soothing after a long day of being artificially blasted by air conditioners. My sneakers scuffed the concrete and I rubbed my eyes, trying to wake up all the way from my bleary state.

The neighborhood was absolutely packed with houses all crammed together. Many people had lights on, the bright yellow filtering through their closed blinds. Far down the street, people were talking as they got out of their car, slamming the doors. The taillights flashed as they locked it and went inside their house, the sounds of their voices and the scuff of their shoes on the concrete fading. Crickets chirped and the warm breeze swept against my skin, rustling the leaves of the palm trees high above us. There was a crispiness to the sound I wasn't used to. Everything seemed so *alive.* Far off, there were sirens.

I took a deep breath, fingering the earbuds around my neck and turning back to my dad, who was opening the car's trunk and dragging out my gigantic suitcase.

"What do you think?" he asked hopefully.

I turned and looked all around again. My dad's house was nearly identical to all the others, right down to the tiny square of struggling grass in the front that was supposed to be the yard.

"It's... different from Michigan," I said.

I could think of some more words, but I didn't say them. *Dirtier. Smaller. Water-parched. No personality. Predictable.*

Dad took his key and unlocked the front door, flicking on the yellow light in the entryway. I followed him as he carried the suitcase, puffing, through the hall and started up a flight of very narrow wooden stairs. It was a tight squeeze. I paused at the bottom, looking around, seeing the living room on the opposite side and the kitchen ahead, right across from the front door. There was no dining table, just some barstools shoved up against the high counter. Beyond was a sliding glass door that led to their postage-stamp-sized backyard, which had a trampoline shoved up in the corner. Weeds snaked up the legs and the poles were rusted, at least from what I could tell from the shining backyard light. It obviously hadn't been touched in years.

"There's a trampoline!" my dad said eagerly, seeing what I was looking at. "Amanda used to love that when she was younger. You could have some fun on that!"

I felt tempted to tell him I was seventeen, not five. There's no way I would ever feel compelled to start jumping on that deathtrap. Instead I smiled and said "Yeah," which made him look very pleased.

The house didn't exactly look new and fresh, although there was no clutter. The air smelled a bit stale like no one had been home all day, mixed with the scent of some kind of ocean-scented air freshener. Pegs in the hallway held a neon pink bag that was obviously Amanda's, and I felt a thrill of excitement in my stomach.

Dad caught me looking at it. "Amanda's out working," he said. "She won't be home for another few hours at least. But she's been getting your room all prepared for you in the past week! We never used it, so she said it was dirty."

The way he said "she said it was dirty" made it obvious that *he* hadn't seen any dirt. I breathed a silent thank-you to Amanda.

I followed my dad up the narrow wooden stairs, to where he was paused in front of what was obviously my room, looking uncertain. "I'll just... let you get settled in, then?"

"That sounds great, Dad," I said, relieved. He hastened down the stairs, and I watched him go, finally turning back and stepping through the doorway, hauling my suitcase with me.

My new living space was —in a word— small. There was barely enough room for a bed beneath a small rectangular window, with a small bedside table slash mini dresser, complete with a small closet with a sliding door. I inspected that, sliding back the door to reveal that it was empty save for many clothing hangers dangling off the wooden bar. It was clean and dust-free though, with shelves for shoes.

I turned back to face the rest of the room, noticing a (again, small) succulent in a cute pot perched on the windowsill. It had a note underneath it that said *From, Amanda.* I smiled to myself. She'd tried to make this place more livable. There were also some narrow shelves hugging the wall that looked like they'd been freshly installed.

The walls looked like the same white they'd probably been upon building. The comforter on the bed, which was new, was the only splash of color in here. Amanda must've remembered that I liked mint green.

I shoved my suitcase out of the way and shut the door, collapsing onto the unfamiliar bed and fumbling with my earbuds around my neck. I plugged the jack into my phone, inserted them in my ears, and closed my eyes as the bassline washed over me. It was *Iceland,* Tr3sure's latest song. The opening, sparkling notes rung satisfyingly clear, and then Seojung's calm voice chanted the first line.

The beat picked up a notch—and then Jongjin's distinctly sunny voice cut in, the sound floating around me, and it was as if a heavy weight on my shoulders had been released, sending my head into a dizzyingly light spiral. I let out a soft sigh, my limbs relaxing on the bed like I'd been melted.

I held my phone in front of my face and studied the album picture that was on the title track of the song. All five of them were wearing pale blue suits with silver thin chains wrapped around them like cobwebs, the glittering white trim on the cuffs and collars looking just like magical ice. Jongjin was standing in the middle of them all, his face tilted in an almost lazy expression, his arms crossed over his strong chest. Yet there was a slight smile on his face, a sparkle in his eye that made him look alive, full of mischief. He was tall, strong but very lean, with a slimness to his figure that suited his height. He was the second-youngest and the main vocalist of Tr3sure—a spot that had made him the most popular of all the members.

Or maybe it was his inherent charisma, his easy smiles, jokes, and buoyant laughs. Or his nicely shaped lips and natural bronze-brown eyes, softened by straight dark lashes.

The song climaxed, Jongjin's voice —like vanilla butter and sunshine— carrying it all the way to a strong finish. *Iceland* was the perfect example of Tr3sure's two main subgenres, dance pop and ballad, mixing together like a good drink. Part invigorating, part wistful.

I sat up and swung my legs over the bed, feeling recharged. It was time to tackle unpacking.

There wasn't much to do. My huge rolling suitcase held all the possessions I couldn't do without—though I'd still had to leave much more behind in Michigan. It had been difficult choosing what to bring when space was so limited, especially when I didn't know when —or if— I would be coming back. I had a small bag of bathroom and hair items, my most essential clothes that I hung up in the empty closet, and one pair of shoes (besides the ones on my feet). Next came my laptop and stack of origami papers, which I had to put on the mini dresser beside my bed for lack of a desk. With the energizing notes of Jongjin singing in my ears, I also set a few of my favorite books on the wall shelves, put my sticker-covered thermos on the floor near the doorway, and tossed two small pillows on my bed. One was a kawaii mango named Aam. The other was square with a swirled blue-and-gold paint pattern.

I also hung up a Tr3sure poster of Jongjin next to my bed with pushpins, displayed some of their photo cards on the shelf and put two albums on my mini dresser, next to my laptop. They were the first two Tr3sure albums—one purple-and-gold, the other lime-and-silver.

Lastly, I plugged in a night light. Darkness made me anxious.

And that concluded the entirety of the things I'd brought. At least the room barely looked like it had personality now. I looked around, wondering what else I could do, but there didn't seem to be anything at the moment.

I paused the Tr3sure song I was in the middle of and took out my earbuds, checking the time. It was 10:06 at night, which meant in Michigan, it was already one in the morning. Even though my mind was awake and buzzing, my body was lagging.

I changed into shorts and a T-shirt, brushed my teeth, took off my glasses, and slipped under the covers of the unfamiliar bed, staring up at the ceiling.

It was weird that I'd just unpacked and settled into a room that I'd never even seen before. I missed my own bed and my own covers, and my own ceiling. I missed the large window positioned just-so across the room instead of a tiny one right above the middle of my bed. Even the color of the night sky outside was wrong. Instead of being gray-toned, the tone was almost... dusty.

I wondered what Jackie and Aaron were doing right now. I rolled over and fumbled my phone from off the bedside table, sending a quick text in our group chat.

Anyone awake?

There was no response, even after several minutes. I heaved a deep breath, a weight feeling like it was being pressed onto my chest. Of course they were asleep. I was all by myself, now.

I was filled with a sudden rage that I hadn't even realized I'd been suppressing. I hated change. I hated having to move away from everyone when I didn't even get a choice. I hated the fact that my best friends' lives were now on separate tracks from mine.

I let out a strangled sound, on the verge of throwing something. I raised my hand, ready to punch the covers.

But then my fury deflated and my hand fell limply down again. Cold, aching loneliness flooded me instead, and my eyes stung.

I didn't want to cry. I wouldn't. I hauled myself up to a better sitting position and switched on the light, dragging my laptop onto my crossed legs and propping my pillow behind my back. I put my glasses back on and reached for an origami paper, using the laptop as a flat surface to fold on. My hands automatically started smoothing out the paper, making crisp lines that turned into a crane. I reached for another one, which turned into a three-pronged crown that looked like the one in Tr3sure's logo.

I looked at it displayed next to the crane on my bedside table, feeling calmer. Some people might have thought it odd that Tr3sure seemed to be such a large part of my life, but I'd been stanning them for two years. It was more than just a music thing for me. I knew their personalities and mannerisms, and now Tr3sure had become the only thing that stayed the same in my life, comfortingly stable.

And then there was Jongjin. His small, quick smiles, his sparkling gaze, the way he was introverted underneath his laughs and flirting. The way he always hid his negative emotions like sadness and anger. The depth I saw underneath his warm eyes, the thoughts I could never hear, no matter how much I longed to.

I reached for another flat paper, but just rested my hands on this one, not sure what to do next, thinking.

Before I knew it my head was snapping up. I blinked my bleary eyes, disoriented, my glasses crooked on my nose. My neck felt stiff and my laptop, origami paper and all, had slid off my legs and onto the bed. My gaze flicked to the window, and I stared at it for a second anxiously, afraid I'd slept until morning. But it was still dark outside. What had woken me up?

There was a thump downstairs. My heart sped up to double-speed. *Amanda.* I clumsily slid off the bed and tiptoed to the stairway landing.

Amanda had just turned off the downstairs light and was coming up herself. I could see her illuminated from the dim light of my bedroom leaking from behind me.

"Amanda!" I whispered.

Her head snapped up, surprised. Her eyes were wide underneath her glasses. Her skin was the same color as mine, but her thick black hair was cropped short. She was so much older than when I'd seen her last. *She already looks like an adult,* I thought with a pang. I'd missed so much of her life.

"*Leyla!*" she whisper-squealed. "Oh my gosh, Leyla, I didn't know you were still up! It's been so long since I've seen you!"

She quickly cleared the last of the stairs and joined me on the landing, wrapping me in a tight hug. "I'm so sorry! I wanted to be there to greet you home, but my boss is so scatterbrained! I couldn't leave her like that, and she begged me to stay. She's way in over her head."

I laughed a little, still holding onto her tightly, my eyes prickling with tears for some reason.

"I'm so glad I got to see you before I went to sleep tonight!" she said. "I'm exhausted. How was your trip?"

"The plane ride was long but the drive here felt even longer," I said as we broke apart.

Amanda winced. It was distracting, how adult she looked. Not at all like the round-eyed teenager I'd remembered her to be, with shoulder-length hair and pink lipstick, always taking selfies. "Yes... the traffic's one thing about living here. Sometimes it's not so bad though! You should come visit me at Ginger Bakery sometime! And tomorrow I only have to go to work in the evening. We can spend the day together!"

I let out a little groan. "Not *all* of it together. Apparently a high school is having some sort of freshman event. And Dad says I have to go." I refused to say *the high school I'll be going to next fall*. That's what Dad wanted, but that didn't mean it would end up happening.

I'd avoided thinking about the event tomorrow for as long as I could. I even hated having to bring it up now.

It sounded miserable. Crowded with people who I would never meet again and maybe some current students who had been threatened into it by their parents, or worse, around to mess with freshmen's heads. I'd probably be the only junior there.

I didn't understand why Dad thought it was a great idea to dump me in this event right after I arrived. Maybe he was hoping I'd just walk in and go "Wow, this looks great, Dad. I'd love to stay here in California just for the opportunity to walk in these outdated beige-linoleum halls that smell like stale mac'n'cheese."

But it didn't matter. I didn't want to be here no matter what anything looked like. I wanted to be back in Michigan, laughing with Jackie and Aaron in one of our living rooms, sharing rumors about how the fancy neighborhood gave out Tootsie Rolls wrapped in twenty-dollar bills on Halloween. I wanted to be able to cross the street without worrying about being steamrolled by sixteen lanes of traffic. I wanted to go sledding with Jackie and Aaron and their siblings when it snowed. Here, it would never snow.

Amanda winced again. "Yes... Dad told me about that high school, um, event." She patted me on the arm. "It'll probably be short. Just survive and see if you can flirt with some cute guys."

Apparently time hadn't changed her boy-craziness.

"I'm *really* tired," she said, rubbing her eyes, which did have dark shadows under them. "I need to go to bed. See you tomorrow?"

"Bright and early," I sighed.

I watched her go into her room to change. As she flicked on the light, I could see that her walls had been changed from light pink to a more serious navy blue. After she closed the door I still stood there, a lump in my throat.

I swallowed it, hard, and turned back to my own room, latching the door softly behind me. Everything was changing. Everything *had* changed. It felt like the world was spinning and I was powerless to do anything except float there, pushed this way and that by people who actually had control over any of it.

I wouldn't let myself cry. I sat back down in bed, turning off the light and plunging myself into dimness lit only by the small night light.

After a few quiet seconds, I fumbled for my phone and opened up the most recent Tr3sure live replay, putting in my earbuds. Jongjin's familiar, handsome face filled the screen. He was smiling and waving, his eyes looking much more energetic than I felt. My heart did a little skip.

"Anyonghassayeo," he sang quietly, and I set my phone facedown under my hand, listening. Then he was ambushed by four other voices sabotaging his live, laughing as they said the familiar chant. *"Hello! We are Tr3sure, and you are GOLD!"*

Jongjin continued talking, a smile in his voice and occasionally interrupted by the other members, though I couldn't understand more than a few words.

I turned the volume down slightly and lay down in bed, pulling the covers up over me, the sound of his soft, pleasant voice filling my head so that there was room for nothing else. I let out a sigh.

I drifted off to sleep like that, full of peace, his voice a lullaby. Everything else was changing, but Jongjin stayed the same, the one safe place in my life.

레일라
LEYLA
3

It was morning. The sunlight streaming in through the tiny window was unnaturally bright, shining right on my face. I groaned, stretching my stiff limbs and yanking the earbuds from my sore ears. It took me a second to remember where I was.

And what the day held.

Amanda's door was still closed when I went out into the hall to shower. I did it quickly and got dressed in a plain t-shirt tucked into loose jeans, with the platform sneakers I'd worn yesterday. They had extra-thick soles that conveniently added a few more inches to my short stature, plus I just liked the style.

I didn't bother looking too closely at myself in the mirror. I wasn't trying to impress anyone today. I'd just go to that stupid high school event, put in my earbuds, and come back the same as before. It wasn't like anyone would care or notice me—I hoped. I brushed my hair and gathered it in a quick ponytail loop, going downstairs.

All the windows were open, and the air was already warm. It just *screamed* "summer". It was empty, with no sign of Dad, though there was something on the counter. I walked cautiously towards it, seeing a bowl of cubed watermelon with a note underneath.

For your breakfast, it said in Dad's messy handwriting. There was a little smiley face next to it, though he'd done it sloppily and it kind of looked like a grimace. *Cereal's in the pantry - bowls are on the top-left shelf - eggs are in the bottom drawer of the fridge. Frying pans are in the cupboard under the bowls. There are also frozen pancakes and breakfast sandwiches in the freezer. Help yourself to anything you want.*

I popped a cold cube of watermelon in my mouth as I looked in the fridge. There was a lot of other food in there too, like leftover lentils, jars of chutney, and rice. I went for cereal and milk instead. I had to hunt down the spoons, though, since he'd forgotten to tell me. He might've been in a rush as he left for work.

There was a large thump from the stairs. Amanda had come down, still in her pajamas, yawning with her short hair sticking every which way and frizzing around her face. She smiled when she saw me and then her eyes widened at the bowl of watermelon. "Wow. Dad never does that." She yawned. "I'm driving you to high school this afternoon."

"You won't let me drive your car?" I said, putting my bowl of cereal on the counter and hopping up onto one of the barstools. The warm breeze from the open window behind me gently moved my hair as I tucked my feet under the stool's metal bars. "I have a license."

She smiled. "I'm going to see how good you are at not crashing into things first."

The mention of the high school event had made me miserable again, even though it was an unfairly gorgeous morning. I poured some more fresh cereal into my bowl, since most of it had turned soggy.

Amanda left to shower and I finished eating. While I waited for her to get out of the shower, I retreated back into my room to check my messages for Jackie and Aaron's responses.

They'd both replied to my *Anyone awake?* text.

A: sorry! I was totally out like a light. how are you doing today?
J: Yeah, me too! Tell us about California though! 🖤

I blew out a breath. It just wasn't the same as being there—responding to obligatory polite questions.

I typed it anyway, telling them all about the traffic, palm trees, how the color of the sky had even changed, and about the miserable trip to high school today.

No response.

They usually did it right away. I kept refreshing it, but no typing and no message appeared.

"Have you already forgotten about me?" I whispered.

☆ ♡ ☆

Amanda drove me around for most of the day while she showed me cool places she liked. Sometimes we just parked and talked. I learned more about her in just half an hour than I did from our year of sparse texting.

"I can't believe you didn't want to move here," she said, shaking her head as we sat outside the stupid high school with its stupid event no one wanted to go to, in the far side of the parking lot under some palm trees. There was hardly anyone here, since everyone was parked in front. And we were early anyway.

"I mean really," she continued. "It's K-pop central! You love K-pop! This is where things *happen!* There are K-pop shops! You can buy merch! You can eat out at Korean restaurants! You'll finally have a chance to go to a Tr3sure concert and meet Jongmin!"

I stared out the windshield at the too-bright black asphalt glowing in the sun. It was afternoon and hot outside, and we had the air conditioner blasting as the car idled. I ignored the way she called Jongjin "Jongmin". It was actually one of her closest guesses yet.

"The Tr3sure concerts were sold out less than ten minutes after tickets were released," I said quietly. "So no *seeing Jongjin* for me anytime soon."

I'd gotten over that months ago, but it was extra-frustrating knowing that I was *here* and I actually could've gone—knowing that this could be a once-in-a-lifetime chance that I'd missed.

"They actually are having a concert here?" Amanda said in surprise.

"Yeah, three. You didn't know that? You just said—"

"I was referring to the hypothetical future. When are they? Is the band already here?"

"Five days from now, seven days from now and ten days from now. And how should I know if Tr3sure's already here? They mentioned something about maybe filming a TV show, so if they are here, they probably haven't told anyone. It'll be top-secret so that they aren't mobbed by fans."

We sat there in silence for a bit.

"Well, at least you can still go out to Korean restaurants and K-pop shops and stuff," Amanda finally said.

"Yeah," I said absentmindedly. A year ago, I would've given anything to be able to go to some authentic Korean restaurants and K-pop shops. But Jackie and Aaron weren't here to share anything with me. I would be doing it all alone.

I glanced down at my phone—it'd been hours, but Jackie and Aaron still hadn't responded—and then at the ugly brown high school building. I didn't want to make friends here. What, so I could just leave again?

Amanda was looking at me in worry, seeming to read my thoughts. "Wouldn't it be nice to have a few acquaintances here? They don't have to be your *best* friends. Just so you're not bored this summer."

"I'm not going to be bored," I said stubbornly. "Anyway, how could I be, knowing that Tr3sure could be hanging around somewhere close by?"

Amanda rolled her eyes. "A boy band is not a life, Leyla," she said. "You're so weird and mature half the time and so young and clueless the other times. I want you to go out and live. Not act like a turtle."

I'd sincerely forgotten how annoying Amanda could be. I laughed, feeling cheered by this for some reason.

"What?"

"Nothing."

Amanda sighed. "Anyway," she said. "I should take you to a K-pop store after this. Your room is so bare. You only have one poster of Jongjee."

I craned my neck to look at her, shocked. "You *recognized* Jongjin? I thought you said they all looked the same!"

She waved a hand. "Well, he's the one you like the best, so I kind of figured you wouldn't be cheating on him with someone else's poster."

I made a *ch* noise in the back of my throat, not bothering to hide my smile.

"Well," she said, looking meaningfully at her phone, "it's time."

The smile dropped from my face. "Right," I said. I pushed up my glasses resolutely, grabbed my sticker-covered thermos and swung my body out of the car. I closed the door before I could think twice. Amanda smiled, leaning over and rolling down the window. "I'm just going to be at the Starbucks near here. The guy at the front is sooo cute. See you in an hour?"

"I thought /was supposed to be the boy-crazy teenager," I sighed. "See you in an hour."

Amanda drove away. I watched her go, the heat from the asphalt radiating on my face. I shielded my eyes from the June sun, then turned and marched to the school.

I made it through the front entrance and sliding-glass doors to the first hallway, which was stuffed with freshmen and their parents—and more comfortable-looking high schoolers standing, sitting, leaning, and all chattering loudly with their friends.

I could feel my face go hot as I walked down the hallway, trying to blend in as much as possible. I was white-knuckling my water bottle as I found the front desk, for the lack of anything better to do.

"Excuse me," I said loudly. The woman there looked up with a smile. "Yes? How can I help you?"

"I'm wondering—"

She leaned forward. "What?"

With extreme regret, I raised my voice to be heard over the din. "Is there a tour or something for next year's students?"

I could tell the people around me were listening. My face went hotter. I could feel a burning resentment towards my dad spring up in my chest. Why, oh why did he make me do this?

"No. Just look around for yourself."

"Right," I said, turning abruptly back around and avoiding all the eyes watching me. I continued down the hall, having absolutely no idea where I was going, my gaze frantically flicking back and forth for any signs. I just wanted to be out of there and somewhere quiet.

Instead, somebody stepped around a corner I was passing by and I nearly collided with them.

It was a guy. I had just one second to take in his red shirt, square jaw and gelled hair before he stepped back, face contorting in anger.

"Watch where you're going," he snapped.

"Sorry," I said automatically.

He didn't continue on his way, but eyed me coldly. "Rude and ugly isn't a good combination."

My mouth actually dropped open in shock as he walked away, vanishing among all the people, leaving me frozen.

I could feel my whole head heating up in humiliation and fury. Rude and *what?*

The noise and motion around me seemed to blur into a buzzing that filled my ears. Instantly, I thought about what I looked like. I wasn't the best-looking person who ever lived, but *ugly* was an overstatement, wasn't it? And then I hated myself for even being insecure enough to think about what he'd said. That guy was just a jerk. A jerk who I'd be going to school with this fall if my family had their way.

I looked around me at all the strangers passing by, a sea of strangers who didn't give a care about me. Most of them didn't even glance my way; I might as well have been invisible, nonexistent, not there. And I thought of Jackie and Aaron and how no one had ever called me ugly there and how I recognized most of the people in the halls and how I wouldn't even be alone in the first place for someone to pick on me.

It became too much. I started walking back the way I'd come, faster and faster, the corners of my eyes prickling, until I'd shoved past all the strangers and burst into the warm, open afternoon air.

I sucked in a huge breath and strode quickly back to the side of the building where Amanda had dropped me off, but of course she wasn't there. It was much, much too soon. I stumbled in my haste, my platform sneakers dragging on the asphalt, as I leaned against the school's wall, out of sight of the main entrance.

I took several more shaky breaths, my back completely pressed up against the hot concrete of the building. I fumbled for my earbuds, jamming them in my ears as I put on 'Jongjin's 3 best vocal performances', my special calming playlist.

Just breathe, Leyla.

I closed my eyes. Instantly California faded away. Where I was didn't even matter. I couldn't hear a sound besides Jongjin's sunny voice in my ear. I had watched this video so many times I knew exactly what was going to happen next.

This was an audition for a show Tr3sure had been on, and Jongjin was doing a solo and was up against one of Korean popular culture's hardest judges: Daeshim.

Jongjin was in ocean-blue jeans, dress shoes and a dark brown leather jacket. His hair was dyed gold at the tips and kept falling into his eyes. His expression I could remember perfectly: a soft, bittersweet longing as he paced the stage, chest rising and falling with each note he sang.

And by "sang", I mean absolutely slayed it. When he sung, you could tell he did it with his all. His voice climbed in sorrowful waves until I could scarcely believe it was still coming from him. It was the kind of voice that lifted you up in the clouds as everyone stopped to listen.

I actually did open my eyes now, looking down at the scene I was so familiar with. Jongjin's head tilted downward, and his body tensed as he finally hit the high note of the song. And then he went another note higher, his eyes scrunched intensely, in complete control of the attention of every single person in the room.

The famously stone-still judge Daeshim's eyes widened, his eyebrows shooting up on his forehead.

Jongjin's voice came to a soothing stop, finishing off with a soft waver that broke my heart and mended it at the same time.

Static silence hovered in the audition room for five agonizingly long seconds, Jongjin breathing heavily as he stared at the judges' table, awaiting Daeshim's judgment.

And then the spell broke. Waves of thundering applause swelled. I never knew or found out what happened after that, because the video always ended there.

I paused the playlist and closed my eyes again, letting out a fluttering breath. I didn't need to tell myself to calm down anymore; I *was* calm, my heartbeat erratic for a different reason now.

I sat down, back still against the hot concrete building, warm air dancing across my face and stirring my hair, and gazed out beyond the school parking lot at the stores and palm trees. *Rude and ugly isn't a good combination.* I wished with a burning desire that I could say the same, that I could sneer at him like he had at me, but he hadn't been ugly—just rude. Did the fact that he was good-looking give his opinion on other people's attractiveness more weight?

Maybe he really was right, though. It's not like I had a track record of guys lining up for my number. My love life had been zero. Was that because I wasn't pretty enough?

No, there was nobody you wanted either. It's not like there had been a guy I'd seriously liked. Even the green-eyed boy Jackie and Aaron had teased me about going with to prom had just been someone I'd admired from afar, having no idea who he actually was or anything about him. Even Jongjin was someone I would never truly know.

I had yet to meet someone, in real life, that I actually liked—*really* liked.

I was still silently arguing with myself when I became aware of a group of teens heading in my direction. They'd rounded the corner of the building and I hadn't noticed them. I felt myself tense up as all ten or fifteen of them started walking towards me, apparently on the way to somewhere.

I looked down at my phone and tried to tune out their loud laughter as they passed by, hoping they wouldn't notice me, hoping they'd leave me alone, but then a voice suddenly cried *"Tr3sure!"*

Well, that was the last thing I'd been expecting. I looked up in surprise. They'd all stopped around me, looming over me since I was sitting down. I stood up quickly, seeing a girl in the middle pointing at my sticker-covered water bottle.

"You're a Tr3sure fan!" she said with a huge smile.

"Oh," I said, leaning over to pick it up and giving her and her friends the once-over. "Yes." The girl had blond-and-blue hair and neon red shoes. Somehow I could immediately tell by her ease that she was one of the most popular students here. Her friends, a mix of genders and appearances, were all as trendily dressed and comfortable as she was.

"I'm Carolyn," she said, sticking out a hand for me to shake. "I was just volunteering with a bunch of other juniors—sorry, I mean *seniors,* or we will be this fall anyway—to welcome the freshmen."

"I'm Leyla." Only popular students would come back to this place to volunteer instead of escaping. The hairs on my arms were practically tingling as I glanced around at them all again. They were the social rulers, the in-crowd.

A lot of people said hi. I mumbled hello. A blonde boy was looking at me with a strange expression on his face. A broad dark-haired guy in a football shirt was watching him, and then his gaze flicked back to me. I looked down at people's feet (which were mostly Vans and Converse), fingers still tight on my water bottle.

I didn't belong here. Not with these people, not at this school, not in California.

Everyone was looking at me. My cheeks prickled. There were so many of them— maybe ten or fifteen—that Carolyn didn't bother saying their names as introduction.

"I rarely meet other Tr3sure fans!" Carolyn was saying excitedly. "It's awesome you're advertising them! Have I ever seen you before?"

"I just moved here," I said. The feeling of awkwardness was creeping up my neck, and I felt self-conscious and out of place. Though Carolyn was a GOLD... so at least I wasn't completely in enemy territory.

Carolyn's eyes got wide. "You just moved here? You should join us on Saturday night! We're going out to eat and bringing dates. I'm sure one of the guys could take you!"

The blonde boy who'd been eyeing me opened his mouth nervously, and looked right at me as he started to say, "D—"

"I would gladly take Leyla out, if she would be willing to go with me," the broad dark-haired guy cut in smoothly.

For a second I was shocked into silence, utterly disbelieving, my face heating up. Was he serious? I was about to say no—almost automatically—and excuse myself, saying goodbye to these people forever.

But then *Rude and ugly is not a good combination* flashed through my head. Obviously *this* guy didn't think I was ugly. I didn't know if it was out of spite or the need to prove myself, but the words came to my tongue.

"Sure," I said firmly.

"Awesome," he said, smoothly stepping forward and offering his hand for me to shake, which I did, still in numb shock from what I'd just said. "I'm Milo." He held my hand for much longer than necessary, and I could feel my cheeks heating up, relieved when he finally let go.

"Ooh," one of the girls said in a teasing voice, but as I glanced past Milo, I noticed some other girls trading snotty glances. The blonde boy, too, was looking at Milo darkly.

Carolyn, on the other hand, was beaming. "I'll just get your number then," she said.

I was stunned in disbelief, looking around at them all, and at the blonde boy. Wait... had *he* been about to ask me before Milo interrupted him?

Just then a familiar dark red Kia pulled up beside us, and the window rolled down to reveal Amanda. She took in the mass of students and me with a baffled expression. Pure relief shot through me at the sight of her.

"Amanda!" I said, hopefully not sounding *too* pleased, and then faced Carolyn again. "Sorry, I have to go."

"I'll be quick," said Carolyn, staring at her phone. "What's your number again?"

I recited it, and she typed at lightning speed.

"Great," she said, sticking it back in her jeans pocket. "See you Saturday, Leyla!"

"Yeah! See you!" I said with a smile that matched hers, walking around Amanda's car and getting in the passenger seat, slamming the door quickly behind me and leaning back against the seat so that I was out of view.

"Get me out of here," I said to Amanda in a low voice.

Amanda, a loyal sister, complied.

Once we were on the highway, safely far away from the school, I groaned and buried my face in my hands. "What have I *done?*"

"What *did* you do?" said Amanda, confused. "Did you make all those friends? What was going on?"

"A guy asked me out!" I shrieked. "And I said yes!"

Amanda squealed.

"No!" I said. "That's not a good thing!"

"Who was it? Was it the guy in the blue t-shirt?" she said eagerly.

"I don't know!" I groaned. "I don't remember what he was wearing. His name's Milo and I only said yes because earlier some other guy called me ugly. It was stupid!"

"Some—*what?* A guy called you *ugly?*" she gasped.

I fell silent. Even now, it stung way more than I would ever admit. I could feel heat rushing to my face.

"Was it the guy in the hoodie?" Amanda said. "I should've run him over!"

"It was nobody there," I groaned, leaning back against the seat and putting my wrist over my eyes. "Some guy in the halls. I went outside and then Carolyn and Milo and all their friends attacked me."

Amanda giggled. *"Milo* apparently doesn't think you're ugly."

"That's why I said yes. I was so *stupid!* Now Carolyn has my number because she seemed like she was in charge of the whole thing and they expect me to come on Saturday night when they go to a restaurant!"

Amanda put on her turn signal and looked over her shoulder as we merged into another lane. Traffic was slowing down. "Poor you," she said. "A date with a guy and a night out with friends. I don't know how you survive such *suffering."*

I sighed and peered out the window at the other cars, which were all continuing to slow down. "Is there an accident up ahead or something?"

Amanda looked at me blankly. "No. Why would there be?"

I just shook my head silently at SoCal natives. Traveling at half the speed limit was, apparently, normal.

"Anyway," I said. "I wish I had just said no and then left."

"Why?"

"Because... because I'm not actually attracted to Milo! He seems too smooth. Slimy. And you should've seen the looks some of the girls were giving me when he was shaking my hand all smarmily."

Amanda pulled a face.

"And I don't even know all those other people and they're the *popular* kids, Amanda!"

"Horrifying," she commented dryly. "Popularity. I wouldn't get too close to them, Leyla, you might catch it."

I rolled my eyes. "They just don't seem like people I can see myself being friends with, and I don't even want any friends. I already have them."

"...In another state," Amanda said slowly.

I glared at her. "I don't need more," I snapped. "I'm already dealing with enough right now, I don't need to go to some sort of stupid Saturday thing."

"Okay, fine," she said indifferently, staring out at the road.

I fell silent. *Rude and ugly.* Maybe he was right. What had I done since I arrived here but grouch and complain? I was even rude to Amanda.

And as for the ugly part, I couldn't even say he was wrong there either. It was flattering to be asked out by Milo, and my emotions had gotten whiplash. But now that that feeling was fading, I was left with the impressions I'd really gotten in the moment. The truth was that I had the feeling that Milo didn't actually like me in any way. It was more like he thought I should like *him.*

Amanda dropped me off at home and headed to the bakery. "I won't be working too late, probably," she said. "See you tonight."

I agreed and then trudged to my room. I glanced at my metallic Tr3sure albums that normally made me so happy and then collapsed onto the bed, putting my arm over my eyes.

I was exhausted and felt like crying, but I wouldn't. I didn't want to. I'd been holding it in since I'd gotten here, and I was going to keep doing it.

Instead I put my whole day on repeat inside my head, cycling through it endlessly. California. My tiny room, nearly bare. The school I was supposed to be going to without Jackie and Aaron. The guy who'd called me rude and ugly. The sense of *invisibleness* I'd felt in the halls. Jackie and Aaron, who hadn't texted me at all today, like they'd forgotten I even existed now I was gone. Milo asking me out and me saying yes, even though he seemed smarmy.

The *ping* of a text notification interrupted me. I let out a low moan and felt around the bed for it, finally finding it and bringing it up to my face.

It was Carolyn.

Hey Leyla!

I didn't feel like typing back, but she was already doing more.

I'm so excited, I hardly ever meet fellow Tr3sure fans! Can't wait to hang out this Saturday. Milo is pretty popular but hardly asks girls out. He seemed quick to ask you!! I

was just going to go to a cheap fast food place, but now I'm tempted to make Saturday night extra-fancy :P

I stared at it for a long time. Something about it wasn't sitting right.

Not just the "pretty popular" part—because things like that never happened to me—but just in general. Milo hardly asked girls out? Then why was he so smooth and smarmy and *experienced* doing it to me?

I let my hand fall back to the bed and rubbed my eyes. Sitting here stewing wasn't going to get me anywhere. I got up, retied my ponytail loop, and went to see what Dad had planned for dinner. It was a long day, but it wasn't over yet.

종진
JONGJIN
4

I wasn't ready for the alarm that went off on Tae-X's side table. I groaned, rolling my stiff neck on the pillows of the unfamiliar bed and hearing it crack. I sat up, rubbing it. It took me a second to remember where I was—a hotel, because we were on tour. Tae-X, Sun Chi-Ho and I had taken one room as usual, then Seojung and Laon took the other—sorted according to how much we annoyed each other. Or got along, as an optimist would look at it.

It was still dark outside. That meant a little more time to myself today, besides whatever we usually got. Of course, "time to myself", like this instance, usually meant the slashing of my sleep time. That was fine, as long as I didn't do it too often. I was used to it.

We'd gotten reminded of the tasks we had to do last night. This month in America, we were going to be doing three L.A. concerts, two fansigns, countless interviews, and the TV series, not even counting the weekly content we had to come up with. Filming took up most of our busy schedules, and the "free time" —which didn't count eating breaks and the end of the day— was never prescribed at a specific time, or duration. It all revolved around the sporadic filming schedule, which made it impossible to plan *anything* in my personal life.

I wished I could forget all the things we had to accomplish this month and go minute-by-minute like I had to with my "free time". Knowing everything we had to do was like a weight pressing down on me.

Today, though, I'd ask for birthday time off.

I took a deep breath, turning off Tae-X's annoying alarm, rolling out of bed and nearly tripping on Sun Chi-Ho, who had a temporary bed close to the floor at the foot of mine, as I went to the bathroom. I waited until the door was closed to turn on the light, trying not to wake the others.

There were dark shadows under my eyes and my skin looked dull. I ran my hands under the faucet, fixing my messy hair, then slapped my face with the cold water. A little color returned there.

I gave my reflection a winning smile. A little better, but not perfect. The makeup team would need to disguise all of our tiredness with lots of concealer.

The smile dropped off my face as I brushed my teeth, showered, went through my skincare routine that involved some expensive new serum JNP had given me, and got dressed. Filming wouldn't start today, but there would be lots of meetings and practice for our concerts. They were going to show us around the stage so we had time to get used to it. There was a possibility we'd be glimpsed and photographed in public, so we were supposed to wear our sponsored Michael Kors clothing today, like we would be doing all month.

I shrugged on my typical style—slacks, dress shoes, and a crisp-casual white button-up with obviously designer styling. The media didn't call me "the best-dressed idol" for nothing. With my hair dyed warm caramel-espresso brown instead of a garish color like Tae-X's, I could've passed for a professional man. Except for the ring I slid onto my finger and the single diamond stud earring I put in.

I did an experimental eyebrow-flick in the mirror.

I stopped posing. Did I have to do that all the time? It was automatic, unconscious. *See what looks best for the fans. Practice your expressions.* It's not like we had a new music video coming up. We'd done that months ago.

Annoyed at myself, I frowned and started washing my hands. I swept my hair just-so with a little water and gel, spritzed on my favorite cologne, and then came back out into the hotel room, feeling a lot fresher and more awake.

"Morning," I said in Korean with a dazzling smile, yanking up the hotel blinds so light flooded the room. Tae-X and Sun Chi-Ho, both still in their respective beds, groaned miserably.

I yanked the covers off Tae-X, who curled up defensively like some kind of hedgehog. "Your alarm went off half an hour ago."

"No," he gasped, sitting bolt upright with his orange hair sticking up in the back. "Why didn't you wake me up? Did you turn it off again?"

"Yes I did. You needed your sleep. Besides, I was using the bathroom anyway. You couldn't."

Tae-X mumbled something under his breath I couldn't hear that involved the words "Jongjin" and "nasty". It was probably rude, so I ignored him.

Tae-X, out of all of us, needed the most sleep. He had a bad habit of staying on his phone watching American shows at strange hours and suffered from sporadic insomnia. Not to mention the late nights and odd hours where he "just had to" write song lyrics because he was, as he said in English, "*in the zone*". I still had no idea what that meant, but I could probably guess. Or sneak a peek from the thick English Slang book he always carried with him. He didn't really need it—he was practically fluent, but he always wanted to sound cool.

I didn't have the memory to keep up with all the slang and fad words. They seemed to change all the time, and often made no sense. I fell somewhere in the middle with Tr3sure's English skills. Sun Chi-Ho was better at it than I was, Laon was worse, and Seojung knew hardly any—though he knew Japanese and Spanish, so he deserved some slack.

Tae-X swung his legs over the bed, orange hair still sticking up, grumbling. Sun Chi-Ho, who'd already showered the night before, pulled his covers tighter over his dark pink-sunset head at the noise and rolled over sleepily.

I checked my phone, flipping it out of my pocket gracefully and giving it a jaunty little spin. "We're supposed to meet Assistant Manager Son downstairs in exactly twenty-five minutes."

We'd get breakfast there too. Since we were filming and on a concert tour, the diet was extra-strict. Nothing but protein avocado smoothies for breakfast, nuts and detox juice for snack, and salad and chicken for lunch. Dinner was the one variety, but it was decided for us and usually low-calorie. We'd be eating fun American foods on the TV series and had to make up for it in the rest of our meals—we had to look as muscular and lean as possible for the concert, with sharp faces.

At home we weren't so restricted and had to come up with food for ourselves, but since we were abroad, management controlled everything we ate. I was used to this from our Europe tours.

My phone rang, distracting me. I answered it and brought it to my ear smoothly. "Hello."

"Jongjin," said Manager Jeon, shuffling something in the background. "OK, so I just got a call. Apparently you've been invited to a Gangnam variety show."

"Oh," I said, taken aback.

"They'd need you in two months, so it's not like it'll interrupt anything right now. You'll do it, right? It's a great opportunity."

I didn't say anything for one second, quiet, standing there in the middle of our hotel room.

It's a great opportunity. Being an idol was like a debt I had to repay. Not everyone got to debut. Not everyone got to have the same chances I did, the same luck I did, the same label I did. Now I had to take every opportunity, no matter how it impacted my life.

Don't complain. Don't want anything. Don't need anything. Do what they say. Give them what they want. Give the fans what they want. Make everyone else happy. Just one smile, Jongjin. That's all it takes. Just one smile.

Of course Manager Jeon didn't expect me to say no. For the briefest moment I wondered what would happen if I did. But it had been two years of this, and nine years more before that. Why would I suddenly do something different now?

"Of course I'll do it," I said with a cheerfulness I didn't feel.

Manager Jeon's voice perked up audibly, even though, if I'd said no, he still could've legally forced me to do it. "Great! I knew you'd say yes. I'll give them a call back."

And he hung up without saying goodbye.

I rubbed my temples, sighing.

Think of your birthday. It was the one thing I could hold on to, the one thing that kept me from splintering from the stress and pressure. *Think of getting time off, to just relax.* If I could get even half the day off, everything would be okay. *Just hold on until then.*

"What's wrong?"

I turned around, seeing Sun Chi-Ho sitting up in bed and awake now. I'd briefly forgotten he was there.

"Oh," I said, my voice bright. "I'm going to be on a variety show. It'll be a really great opportunity."

Sun Chi-Ho blinked, then smiled. "That's awesome, Jongjin!"

I nodded. It was time for a subject change. "You should really get dressed. Who knows how long Tae-X will be in the bathroom."

Twenty-five minutes later we were all gathered downstairs, in a private conference room JNP had rented, the five Tr3sure members all sipping our protein avocado smoothies. Normally at this time in the morning we'd be practicing our dancing for hours, but everything had changed due to being on tour. We were also doing emergency English lessons (except for Tae-X) to brush up since we'd be going live at the concerts and fansign with mostly English-speaking fans. Manager Son organized all this; we were told where to go, what to do and how to do it. The energy we exerted usually didn't leave much room for anything else.

I wasn't good at maximizing the minutes in between scheduled activities, usually going to my phone to check in with friends or family. But Laon was infamous for falling asleep anytime he sat down undisturbed for sixty seconds.

I glanced at him across the conference table. His eyelids looked a little droopy now and he'd stopped sipping his smoothie. Even Seojung was spaced-out. Jet lag had gotten to all of us. That was why JNP waited until a few days after we'd arrived to start holding concerts. On me, exhaustion showed the least. I still sat up straight and smiled and laughed at all the right times.

I tried to breathe deeply to manage my stress without anyone noticing me. It helped—a little. It didn't change the tasks hanging over my head. *Just hold on.*

I glanced at Managers Son, Jeon and Yoo. Manager Yoo would be the one who could wrangle around the schedule to give me a free day off. He had the authority.

I resolved to ask him tonight, after I'd been the perfect hardworking JNP idol all day. I straightened my posture a bit, making sure my clothes looked immaculate, and resigned myself to an especially long, taxing day.

☆ ♡ ☆

It was 9:40 at night. The day had been just as long and exhausting as I'd thought, with no breaks, yet it wasn't quite over yet. We were all gathered around in the conference room one more time, while staff gradually left.

"Remember," Assistant Manager Son was saying insistently to us, his eyes bugging wide as he looked at our faces. *"Remember,* tomorrow's the first day of filming. I want you all downstairs here at 4:00 because we have to be starting the actual filming at dawn, and we need time to transport everyone and do your makeup. Don't worry about your clothes. We'll have things for you to change into on site. Okay?"

"Okay, Manager Son," I said, hardly listening, glancing past him to Manager Yoo, who was marking things off on a clipboard, his grave forehead wrinkled up. He was starting to drift towards the door. I hadn't wanted to ask him in front of everyone —especially all my fellow members, who were right next to me and would definitely hear— but this was my last chance.

"Now listen," Manager Son said, looking at each of us in turn—Seojung, me, Laon, Tae-X, Sun Chi-Ho. "I want you all to get some sleep, okay? No phones. You need to have energy and feel good for filming tomorrow. We don't want to use a whole bottle of cream to cover up dark circles and puffy eyes, either. Okay?"

"Okay!" I said with an incline of my head, then hurried away, just catching Manager Yoo before he made it out the door.

"Manager Yoo," I said slightly breathlessly, my posture perfect as I gave a small bow. "I would like to request a favor."

"Yes?" he said, frowning.

"Well, my birthday is coming up... on the thirtieth." He knew that. He coordinated everything, and idol birthdays were important events. I could sense the other Tr3sure members —and Manager Son— listening. My heart was in my throat. "I was wondering whether I could please have my birthday off. Or at least for most of the day, to use freely. I would still do the Birthday Live, of course."

Manager Yoo's frown deepened. "We have much wrap-up filming planned for that day. We're not in L.A. all the time, you know."

"I understand," I said, my desperation increasing. *Just one day. I just need one day to be myself. To not be controlled by someone else. To not have to feel what someone else wants me to feel.* "That's why I would especially like this birthday off. It's my 20th birthday and we're in America. Maybe the other members would have it off too. The fans would love to hear about how we all relaxed and had fun. We've been working so hard."

"I'm sorry, Jongjin, but I'm not changing the schedule," Manager Yoo said, looking at me with one eyebrow raised and tucking his pen into the side of his clipboard. "You should know by now that the other members don't ask for the day off. We have a lot to do. And besides, you're already celebrating. The company is already purchasing special food and decorations for the Birthday Live. Please try to understand this as a more mature person would."

"Right," I said, giving a slow, stiff bow. "I am sorry for stealing your time, sir."

By the time I had straightened up, he had already turned away, striding from the room with the other executives.

Tae-X, Sun Chi-Ho, and Laon had already gone. Only Seojung remained, giving me one lingering, concerned, piercing stare before also turning to go.

I was left alone in the conference room, hot-faced and feeling like I'd just been tossed adrift into a sea of uncertainty. I quickly strode out after Seojung, with my perfect straight-backed posture, with my perfect hair and perfect clothes, looking like the kind of man who should own the world. But I didn't even own myself, quite in the literal sense of the word.

Byun Jongjin. Always behaved. Always did what other people told him to do. Ate what other people told him to eat. Said what other people told him to say.

I walked a little slower behind the others. By the time I got up to the hotel room I would share with Tae-X and Sun Chi-Ho for another whole month, they were already getting ready for bed, brushing their teeth obediently.

I spared them a pained glance before moving on, going to the window, yanking up the blinds, and opening it. I leaned out over the five-story drop, rain falling on my head from the darkened, starless sky. I looked up and took a deep breath, then slammed it closed again.

"What are you doing?" Sun Chi-Ho asked uncertainly. I turned around, my skin still wet with raindrops. He was behind me, looking at me with worry.

"Just wanted to taste fresh air," I said with a harsh, bitter smile. "Or is that not allowed because it's not on the script?"

He stared at me, speechless.

Tae-X had come out of the bathroom and was drinking water in the kitchen, refilling his Styrofoam cup from the jug on the small counter. Gosh, how I hated this place. Everything dim and beige and generic and smelling like hotel.

"Look, Jongjin, about the extra birthday time…" he had begun cautiously, but I interrupted him. "Did you know that you talk in your sleep? Do you know what you say? I've heard you." I put on a fake voice as he stared at me. "'*Hello! We are Tr3sure, and you are GOLD!*'"

Tae-X's mouth dropped open, speechless. Sun Chi-Ho, as well, was staring at me in shock, then at Tae-X.

I'd already gone to my suitcase, which I had yet to unpack, and ripped it open, unfolding my black leather trench coat and whirling it over my shoulders.

Tae-X was frozen with his Styrofoam cup still in his hand. "Where are you going?"

I tied the coat over my white button-up shirt, brushing nonexistent dust off my dress shoes. "I just need to think about things." *I need to get out of here.*

"But we're supposed to be going to be—!" was the last thing I heard before the door snapped shut behind me.

I jogged past the elevator and down the hallway to the stairs, where they probably wouldn't expect me to go and wouldn't find me if they tried to follow. My shoes pressed hard on the metal stairs with satisfying clicks, counting down until I was four flights down, on the main floor.

Each step was another thought in my already overcrowded head.

Please try to understand this as a more mature person would.

Why does being mature mean not asking for anything for myself?

You shouldn't have asked for time, now you look stupid in front of everyone.

I just wanted one day. Not even a full day.

You should be happy that they celebrate your birthday at all.

But it's not for me. I'm always doing it for someone else.

The hallway lights shone brightly to contrast the darkness outside, and I walked past the front desk receptionist, summoning up a brief smile to avoid suspicion.

My smile vanished as I stepped out the door. The cool, humid air smacked me in the face, wind whipping my hair in all directions. Rain was pouring down in harsh showers, even more than when I'd opened the window upstairs. Thoughts spiraled around my head.

What were you thinking?

I'm sick of being a puppet.

You're acting like a child.

I haven't gotten a childhood since the age of eight.

There are years of this ahead of me, and for what?

Shouldn't you be happy? This is exactly what you wanted. What you worked for.

What do I want from my life?

My mind faltered at that last thought and I shivered, stuffing my hands in my pockets. Something was in there—a piece of paper.

I pulled it out and unfolded it, flecks of rain splattering onto my face in the darkness. A choked laugh rose up in my throat. It was the list that I had written down on the plane, my excited scrawl now looking innocent and childish.

What do I want from my life?

I strode over to the trashcan and held the list over the hole, my hand hovering over half-eaten fries, plastic bags, smashed fast-food cups and other miscellaneous pieces of trash, ready to drop it in.

But hesitated.

I slowly pulled my hand back, flipping over the piece of paper to stare at the blank side I hadn't written on.

I wouldn't be able to do the things on my list, but what if I modified it a little bit to something I *could* do?

Something you can do.

If I were just any other random person on the street, if I could just do whatever I felt like doing in the moment without restrictions, without people telling me what to look like, what to do, what to say—

What do I want from my life?

I closed my eyes. I knew exactly what I would be doing.

레일라
LEYLA
5

I raised my head from the kitchen counter, bleary-eyed, a red crease on my cheek. I rubbed it, staring at my phone right in front of me, flipping it around so it was screen-up.

It was 9:40 at night. Still no texts from Amanda. She was supposed to be home by now.

I gave a soft sigh and put it back down again, resting my head back on the counter.

Rude and ugly. It kept slamming against the walls of my consciousness, making my stomach turn. What a day. But I wouldn't cry. I refused. *Just get through it, it'll be over soon.* I wasn't going to think about it.

Amanda still wasn't texting. She hadn't said she was staying this late. What if she'd gotten in a car crash? The roads were wet... it was raining outside, and a full-scale storm was brewing.

What if today, when I'd snapped at her, was the last time I saw her?

"Dad?" I croaked. I could see the light of his office on, slanting through the cracked door.

He answered a second later. "Yes, Leyla? What is it?"

"Amanda hasn't come home yet."

There was a pause, and then I heard his office chair creak and he poked his head through the door. "It's normal, honey. Her boss is really scatterbrained. They work... kind of... off-the-cuff."

I stared down at my noncooperative phone. "Dad?" I said hesitantly. "I was going to, um, take the car and go see Amanda. She hasn't been answering my texts, so I thought I'd... um... keep her company."

"That's so nice of you!" my dad gasped. From the way his face looked, you'd think I'd just told him I was giving Amanda my kidney.

"Right," I mumbled.

"It *is* rainy out there, though, Ley," he said, discomfort creeping into his tone. "Wouldn't it be easier to wait?"

"Please," I said. "I'm so worried. Can I take your car?"

There was a brief silence. "Okay," he finally sighed, pinching the bridge of his nose. "But drive extra-slow. And be careful. And text me when you get there. The roads shouldn't be too wet by now—near us, anyway."

"Yes," I agreed quickly, stuffing my phone into my pocket. "Will do."

I ran upstairs to get my raincoat, then realized I'd left it in Michigan. I ran down the stairs again, grabbed the keys by the front door, and dashed out into the rain. I was in the front seat of Dad's car before I'd gotten too wet, but I still had to wipe raindrops off my glasses.

I called Amanda in the warm silence of the car. The buzzing tones filled the air, and then it went to her voicemail.

I let my phone fall into my lap, looking at the rain sheeting onto the windshield, distorting the lights from streets and houses in the blackness beyond. Except for the dull sounds of raindrops forcefully striking the car, I was enveloped in static silence, in a dry, lonely bubble compared to what was happening outside.

I watched the drops fall, big and harsh, onto the glass, and leaned my damp back against the dry car seat. Then I took a deep breath and pulled up the driving directions to Ginger Bakery, setting it in front of me and turning the key in the ignition.

I had to turn on the windshield wipers almost immediately, but I didn't turn back, white-knuckling the steering wheel as I drove through the dark to the main highway. I had a horrible, gnawing worry in my stomach. I felt so strongly that something might have happened to Amanda. What if she *had* been in a crash? She could be badly hurt. Or... I didn't let myself think about that.

Answer your phone! I thought angrily.

The city was both beautiful and eerie at night, but now the lights shining in the darkness, and the rain speckling the windshield, seemed dangerous. People were getting hurt as I drove. Crashes were happening. Crimes were being committed under the cover of darkness. Lives were being changed forever.

Sirens wailed in the distance as I drove, windshield wipers going furiously. I swallowed hard, taking a deep breath as I kept my eyes on the road.

Just make it to the bakery, I thought to myself, repeating it as there was a loud rumble of thunder. Lightning flashed in the clouds ahead. If Dad could've seen this, instead of the calm drizzling in our neighborhood, he never would've let me leave the house.

It felt like forever before I was pulling into the bakery. I parked in a spot close to the front and got out of the car, looking around, afraid of what I might see. If Amanda's car was gone... that might mean....

There! There it was, her dark red Kia, glinting in the city lights and shining from the rain, in a way so unexpectedly picturesque and beautiful. Tremendous relief crashed over me in a wave, then anger. *Why* hadn't she been answering her phone?

I ran, covering my head from the pouring rain, to the bakery, which was a tiny, narrow place jammed between two other food stores that looked a lot scuzzier, just like the rest of the area around. I hurried to push open the door, a cheerful *tinkle* ringing in my ears as I wiped my glasses on my shirt.

The inside was very warm and smelled like all things sugary, and everything was painted yellow. The bright overhead lights left spots in my vision. There was no one here at the front, though I could hear voices coming from the open door that led to the back. I stepped around the front counter and went towards it, feeling like I was doing something illegal.

"Leyla!" Amanda cried. She'd seen me first. She was at a counter measuring flour into a gigantic bowl on a scale, facing towards me. "What are you doing here?"

"You didn't answer your phone," I said, holding up my own feebly, water dripping from the ends of my ponytail onto the floor. It seemed strange now to have ever been afraid when Amanda had just been busy baking, like Dad said she would be. It seemed stupid now, in the warmth and safety of this yellow sweet-smelling place. Nothing bad could possibly happen here.

A woman looked up from behind a shelf. She had brown hair and was in her middle thirties, with an apron on and her hair tied back—must be the owner. "Is this your sister, Amanda?"

"Yes! Rachel, this is Leyla, Leyla, this is Rachel. I'm really sorry, Leyla," Amanda said, her eyes worried. "It was on silent mode and I left it in the front. We just got a call for three hundred chocolate-strawberry cupcakes for tomorrow and they'll pay extra for speed since it's on such short notice!"

Thunder rumbled outside. I winced slightly. It must be loud and close if we could hear it in here.

"Yeah, that's okay," I said. "I'll just... text Dad to let him know I got here safe. I'll be in the front."

I turned without waiting for her answer.

I spent the next half an hour curled up on the padded bench facing the dark, rain-streaked window. The city lights of the shops and roads beyond were blurred and mixed by the droplets of water. I was used to rain being clean, but somehow it seemed dirty. I guessed big smog-filled polluted cities really weren't as romantic as they sounded.

I didn't know what I was feeling, or why. It was like everything had just shut off and I didn't care about anything. Or couldn't. Yet I could still feel the storm brewing in me, somewhere deep down. It made itself known by a nauseousness in my stomach. I rested my head on my knees, staring out the window, almost falling asleep.

"We need more. Lots of it." It was a worried voice, from behind the counter. The owner, Rachel. I didn't open my eyes.

"I can go get some," Amanda pressed.

There was a brief note of silence. "But then we'll be up even later—I don't know."

Another pause. Then a voice, very loud, right next to me.

"You're Leyla, right?"

I raised my head up, startled. I hadn't heard her approach. "Yeah?"

The owner, Rachel, was standing in front of me, wringing her hands. Up close, she looked haggard and stressed, with worry lines around her eyes. "I just found out we won't have enough butter. I didn't know we'd have such a large emergency order. You drove here, right? Could you drive down to the corner pharmacy and pick some up?"

I stood up and glanced dubiously out the window. It was raining harder than ever, and the thunder was scarily loud.

Rachel caught my obvious glance and wrung her hands even more, voice high and stressed. "I know, the weather's terrible outside, but we really need it!"

I could tell by her voice that *someone* was going out tonight, and it would be either me or Amanda. My gaze flicked to my sister, who was walking up to us, and then back to Rachel. "Sure, I'll do it."

Amanda's eyes were wide as she hurried the last few steps up to us. "Don't do it if you don't want to, Leyla."

There was a large flash of lightning out the window as if to accentuate the point. But I didn't want Amanda driving out there.

"It's okay," I said, purposefully cheerful. "I drove here. I can drive there. Ugh, my hair's all messed up now from the rain though." I ran a hand repeatedly over my rain-frizzed ponytail.

"If looks are what you're worried about, it's not like there's going to be anyone important there," Amanda said with a smile.

"Not at a no-name store late at night in the middle of a storm," Rachel agreed quickly. "I need six pounds! That's six boxes. Unsalted."

"Unsalted," I said. "Six boxes. Got it."

She thrust some money at me—four twenties. "You probably won't need all of this, but just in case, right?"

I nodded.

"It's a pharmacy-grocery," Rachel said. "Pretty big for a no-name mom-and-pop shop. It'll be easy, you'll see. Just turn out onto the main road with a right-turn and turn into the lot once you reach the corner."

I stuffed the money into my pocket and left before Amanda could protest, dashing to my car as cool rain spattered on top of me and sloshed in the gutters.

I got into the car and slammed the door, tossing my phone onto the passenger seat. I put the car into gear and crawled out of the parking lot, following the directions Rachel gave me.

It was so dark. I hated the dark.

Lightning flashed violently, and then, almost simultaneously, thunder split the sky. *BOOM.* I gave a soundless squeak. It had to be really, really close....

I clenched the steering wheel, hands shaking.

Butter. Get butter.

Now that I was out of the bakery, the world didn't seem too safe anymore. It was one of those nights where anything could happen. Where nothing might ever be the same again.

Harsh rain whipped in all directions, and the wind battered the car. It was getting crazy. Maybe I should turn back.

But I was just so close.

BOOM. An earsplitting crack of thunder sounded above me, while a brilliant bolt of white-hot lightning ripped into the graphite sky. The sound of my own scream was muffled in my ears.

My heart pumped wildly as I finally pulled into the pharmacy parking lot. There were just a few other cars here. I got out as fast as I could, running to the safety of the white lights and sliding door below a dingy flickering sign I couldn't read because so many of the letters were unlit. There weren't a lot of other cars or people. What crazy person would be out in this weather?

The air conditioning was still on full-blast inside the pharmacy. People were gathered in clusters, looking toward the black windows, or idly shopping for whatever random things they needed. An old couple had birthday balloons. Another man had a cart full of fresh groceries. I sped towards the refrigerated section, finding the dairy easily.

Just get it and get back.

I pulled out six boxes of unsalted butter, waves of cold air blasting my numb fingers. I winced, balancing them precariously. I could hear the rain hitting the roof in swells, and the rumble of thunder. It was incredibly loud.

BOOM. I was petrified with fear, the sound roaring in my ears. I ducked my head slightly again, then realized I was being ridiculous.

Overhead, the electric lights flickered. In the next aisle, a few customers laughed nervously, saying something to each other.

I let in a gasp of air, hoping to calm my racing heartbeat and the sick feeling in my stomach.

With another flicker, the lights went out completely.

No!

My throat seized up, a hard dash of adrenaline shooting through me. I was frozen for a millisecond, in the darkness, seeing the rapidly fading, dim white glow of the freezer doors ahead. Panicked, I broke into a run without thinking, going toward the last of the light.

It was suddenly pitch-black. I slowed slightly—

WHAM. I crashed into something hard, surprised arms steadying me. I was stunned, pressed against someone's chest almost as if in a hug, hearing their shocked intake of breath as they stumbled backward, one of their arms shooting suddenly away from my back as if to catch themselves on something. My face was against their shirt, enveloped in the smell of cologne on warm skin, sweet and spicy. One arm was still wrapped around me, as if surprisedly and instinctively catching a small bird that had collided with their chest.

I gasped and shoved myself away, panicked, feeling them let go as I practically threw myself backward. I stumbled and fell over, hitting the floor with my butt. I sat there for a second, stunned.

It was pitch-black, and then I saw the briefest, dimmest glow from a phone screen on a trench coat and pale hands before the flashlight came on and shone right in my face.

I instinctively turned away from the bright, piercing white light, narrowing my eyes with a sharply inhaled breath.

It flicked immediately downward, as if the owner had just realized. "Sorry," a man's voice said—neither deep nor high, and young, with a lightness to it. It was a pleasant voice that still sounded startled and alarmed. He had a strong accent. "Are you hurt?"

Though his phone was pointed at the floor, I still couldn't see anything of him at all. My eyes refused to adjust past the bright light, though obviously, because he was on the other end, he could see *me* just fine, even if it was dim. "I'm—so sorry," I gasped, scrambling to get up, my cheeks prickling. A strong hand suddenly grasped mine, lifting me to my feet like I weighed ten pounds. I was too shocked to realize what had happened until those brief two seconds were over. "I'm—so sorry—I didn't—"

"Are you hurt?" he pressed, sounding worried, an urgency to his voice.

"I'm—I'm fine," I managed. Tears had sprung to my eyes. I bit my lip to stop it from trembling, glad my face was no longer illuminated, feeling suddenly overwhelmed. "Are you okay?"

"Yes," he said kindly. "I'm okay."

A hot tear escaped my eye and burned a trail down my cheek, and I wiped it away, trying desperately to not let him see, trying to control myself. But then I let out an involuntary sob.

His voice, very soft, said "Are you... crying?"

He sounded so gently concerned that I just cried harder, standing there in the pitch-black freezer aisle, trembling, my face in my hands. I couldn't muster a response, feeling humiliated and embarrassed, the sound of my pathetic, whimpering, soft crying filling the quiet.

"I'm... sorry," I gulped between tears, my voice a whisper. "I... I just..." I couldn't go on. I was in a place that wasn't my home, surrounded by strangers, still feeling the pain of leaving my friends, after a terrible day, in the dark that I hated, and I'd just crashed into someone because of my stupidity. I could have really hurt him. Yet he was being so nice to me when I didn't deserve it, when hot guilt was bubbling inside me. There was all this and more inside, tangled up in a knot I didn't understand. And now I was crying in front of someone who I'd never even met, who could see me while I couldn't see him, who was now *obligated* to comfort me.

I just stood there and sobbed, shoulders shaking, all of my emotions from the past month spilling out. He let out a soft sigh and bent down, picking up all the boxes I'd dropped. He was keeping his distance, like he was trying not to scare me; I couldn't smell his cologne like earlier.

He said nothing, just keeping quiet, letting me cry, maybe not sure what to say. I was unable to stop myself. Eventually my tears subsided and I took a shaky breath, my hands falling away from my face. I realized just how cold the freezer aisle was.

"I'm sorry," I whispered again. I wanted to run, filled with humiliating guilt, but with no flashlight of my own, I was completely dependent upon his until the lights came back on. "Don't pay attention to me. I just..." I took a wobbly breath, eyes full of tears as I tried to speak.

"It's okay," he said again, in that unbearably kind voice. "It's okay. You don't have to explain."

I looked dully at the ground, too ashamed to face him, my cheeks raw from the salt of my tears, sniffling. In the dim light of his flashlight he held a hand out to me; it had a small folded tissue in it.

"Here," he said. "I'm sorry, I only have one."

I took it, feeling like crying all over again for some reason. I sniffed again. "Thank you," I whispered, my voice wet. I patted my face and wiped my nose, extremely grateful that he was keeping his flashlight pointed all the way down, so he could hardly see me if at all. I wondered numbly whether he was doing it on purpose.

He let out a soft sigh again, carefully setting all my boxes on the ground in a pile. Then he pointed the light towards the freezer doors. "Do you want ice cream?"

"W-what?"

"Would you like some ice cream?"

An employee near the front of the store was shouting, without the aid of overhead speakers. Their voice sounded so far away. "THE BACKUP GENERATOR WILL BE ON SOON! WE'RE SORRY FOR THE DELAY. AS A REMINDER, PLEASE DON'T OPEN THE FREEZER DOORS AND LET OUT THE COLD."

I must've missed the first announcement. I blinked, suddenly aware of what was happening around us. There were zigzagging phone lights in the distance beyond the mysterious man in front of me, and the sounds of customers talking and laughing at this unusual circumstance. Yet everything was still so dark, so disorienting.

"No freezer?" the man repeated. He pointed his phone light at it. "Is *that—* freezer?"

I realized his heavy accent—a soft, almost blunted lilt—was Korean. Not unusual, for this area of California, but he also didn't seem fluent in English. "That's the freezer, yeah," I said quietly.

He let out a sigh. "I was hoping not." There was a pause. "But if I'm quick..." He let the last part dangle meaningfully.

I chanced a glance up at where his face should be, frustrated I couldn't see him at all. Was it strange to care so much?

His flashlight had suddenly switched to the freezer doors full of ice cream. Slowly, theatrically, he stretched out a hand, artistically spreading his fingers across the glass. "Nooo... ice cream. Don't leave me," he said in a fake, small pleading voice, placing his other hand on the handle of the glass door. I let out a tiny smile, leaning forward, distracted from the mess of emotions inside me.

Then he froze. I found myself holding my breath, completely entranced.

He yanked open the door so fast I nearly jumped, reaching in and whipping out a half-pint ice cream carton before shutting the door again. The carton was suspended on his open palm as he slowly pulled away again, letting it fade into the blackness away from his flashlight.

My breath was still hitched. There was something hypnotizing about his dramatic formality. It was odd, but so, so cool.

"You're good at that," I said with a sheepish little laugh. My voice was more steady and normal now, to my extreme relief.

"Oh," he said, and then, very formally, "Thank you."

I didn't know what to say in reply. My cheeks still felt flushed and hot, and I had just realized that he'd done it to distract me, to make me feel better. My cheeks went hotter, embarrassed.

"And yet I *still* can't eat the ice cream," he said, sounding disappointed. "Except with my face."

I laughed at that, taken off guard. I wondered what flavor he'd picked—I'd been too distracted with his theatrics to notice.

"There are..." He made a frustrated noise. "Somewhere around here there are... spoons. I am sorry, my English isn't that good. I know a lot, but I forget."

"Your English *is* good," I said firmly, surprising myself with an actual sentence.

"I am going to find spoons," he said, a bit sheepish, ignoring my compliment. "Would you like to come?"

"I don't have a light," I said quietly. "I left my phone in the car, so...."

"Oh no, that's not good. It's okay, you can stay with me," he said, voice full of kindness. There was a gentle steadiness to the way he was talking that made me know he was still trying to be sensitive, even as he was attempting to cheer me up.

"It's not good," I repeated quietly to myself as we started walking, very slowly, side by side as his phone flashlight illuminated the way ahead. "None of this day has been."

There was a brief beat of silence. "Why not?" he said.

I sighed. "Well, for one, my friends aren't talking to me, and then I had to visit my new school today. Some guy called me rude and ugly."

"That's terrible," he said. "That's his fault, not yours." There was a pause, and then he said in a quieter voice, "Besides, you're not at all ugly or rude."

"Thanks," I said in a voice just as quiet. I looked over at him as we walked, just barely able to make out his broad shoulders against the occasional dim light. He was tall—much taller than me.

I could feel my cheeks warm and wanted to slap myself. *He could be like thirty! Do NOT get a crush on someone you can't even see, Leyla!*

"I had a really bad first day once," he said, coat rustling as he moved the light higher. "My pants ripped. All down the side. I had to sit on the floor the rest of the time."

I gasped. "Why did they split?"

"Too tight."

I let out a small giggle. I couldn't even see this guy but for some reason I had a hard time imagining him wearing too-tight pants.

I could feel him look over in surprise when he heard me, and for a minute I thought I had made a mistake in laughing.

But then he snickered, which turned into a full-out bubbling, hearty, head-back laugh.

I froze, chills shooting down my spine. My eyes widened and my breath suddenly started going very fast for a reason I didn't understand.

He had stopped, realizing I wasn't following. It felt like if I moved, I would never discover what that laugh had done to me. It was like something I should know. Like I should know but wasn't allowing myself to....

"Are you okay?" he asked hesitantly.

It took me a second to find my voice. "Yes," I said, nodding, my heart still pounding in my chest. "I'm okay." But I wasn't, somehow.

There were several moments of silence afterward, neither of us knowing what to say after that. I felt almost dizzy, unable to place the weird feeling in my stomach.

"Why do you want ice cream so badly?" I finally asked. That... laugh....

His steps faltered as he paused to sweep the flashlight across a few aisles, checking for spoons. "Mmm." The noise he made was solid, vibrating. "Well, I am—have been—very involved in... work. It never stops. I'm turning twenty soon, and I feel like I've missed out on life—my childhood. Because of work. So I thought I'd... try to get it back, while I can."

I could feel my eyes widening. He seemed so serious. So vulnerable. Why would he tell me that, such a truthful answer? Was it because it was dark, and that made it easier to confess to complete strangers?

"I just wanted to do something that wasn't my work," he continued, and located a box of plastic spoons on the shelf, pulling it out and ripping open the top. "And I love ice cream."

I didn't know what to say at first. I opened my mouth, searching for something. "What else are you going to do? Besides eat ice cream?" I asked, the question springing from my lips before I realized what I'd just asked. It had been curious, not at all the polite response I'd been trying to summon.

There was a small pause, but with me still unable to see him, he could've been smiling or frowning or neither.

"That... is still undecided, exactly."

"Oh," I said, unsure, but he hadn't sounded unfriendly. "Should we... sit down here?"

"Perfect." he replied, a smile in his voice. "For a snack."

I moved to the side of the aisle, sinking down next to a display and tucking my feet underneath me with a sigh. I glanced up at him in surprise as he moved toward me, aware of how tall he looked from my sitting position. I strained to see his face in the dark, but could only pick out the faint shape of his hair in the wavering phone lights dancing beyond.

He sat down right next to me, sitting cross-legged and picking up the ice cream carton, opening the top and setting the lid down on the floor. The phone light revealed a vanilla and caramel swirl with walnuts on top.

He let out an excited gasp like he hadn't seen ice cream in years, circling the phone light over it like a spotlight and letting out what sounded like "Ohwaaa!"—a phrase I knew from hearing it so many times in Korean as "Wow!"

He turned off the light, plunging us into darkness, tucking his phone into his back pocket.

BOOM.

Another gust of rushing rain pounded against the roof, and I jumped.

I heard a rustling of the spoon box shaking, and he scooted closer to me as if to block out the noise, closing the space between us, the ice cream carton resting in front of me, though I couldn't see it.

"Here."

A spoon was in front of me—he'd turned on his light again so I could see it, the shine of the plastic just barely visible.

I reached out to take it automatically. My fingers grazed against his, feeling his smooth, manly fingers. My whole hand shivered, and I snatched it away.

"Don't worry," he whispered, seeming not to notice my reaction. "I will pay for it."

I could make out him pushing his spoon into the softened ice cream, his phone resting on the ground, the light pointed at the floor. It was nearly pitch-black, but just with the light there, I felt less afraid.

A soft sigh came from in front of me and he paused, intensely savoring the flavor. "Owhaaa. How long I've gone without tasting ice cream. It's *delicious*. Don't you want some?"

"Oh," I said, surprised for some reason. He pushed the carton a little closer to me. I dipped my spoon into what I hoped was the opposite side of what he'd eaten, scooping out a small bite to taste.

It had softened into a creamy, smooth vanilla mass, with a sharp burst of salted caramel in between the topping of crunchy nuts. It was cold, and so was I, but somehow that just made it more satisfying.

"Oh," I said again. "Wow."

He dug some more out of his side; I heard the spoon scrape the carton.

The silence lingered for what felt like several minutes, but I was strangely comforted by it as we both took turns dipping our spoons back into the ice cream.

He finally spoke up. "You asked earlier. About what else I wanted to do."

"Yes?"

"The problem is that I have several ideas but I'm not sure if I'll be able to do them. They're just... *normal,* childlike things anyway. Like eat a slow breakfast or jump on a trampoline."

I quickly sat up a little straighter. "I have a trampoline in my backyard. You could use mine!"

My face reddened as I realized what I'd just blurted out.

"That's very nice of you," he said, laughing a little, but it was quiet, not like the laugh I'd heard before that froze me to the spot. Still, I felt the hairs on my arms stand up.

I stuck my spoon in the ice cream like a flag and leaned back against the shelves. "And what if... after all that, it still feels like your childhood is lost? Like you still didn't get to enjoy it enough?"

There was a small pause. "I'm not sure what I'd do then," he whispered, almost to himself. "Just keep on going with life, I suppose."

His quiet, honest voice had unexpectedly filled my stomach with butterflies. My breath caught in my throat and I looked down, suddenly glad we couldn't see each other.

"And what about you?" he asked. "What brought you here to buy so many boxes of butter? Do you just like it the same way I like ice cream?"

I blushed again, the teasing note in his voice obviously implying that I was going to eat it raw by the stick. "Well, my sister Amanda works at a little bakery near here, and they just received an urgent order. The owner sent me to go get more butter because she was afraid they wouldn't have enough."

"What are they baking?"

"Three hundred chocolate-and-strawberry cupcakes. I guess someone had an unexpected good thing happen to them and they urgently need to celebrate. They need them by tomorrow morning, so my sister's staying the night."

"Oh no," he said.

"No, it's okay. She's used to it. She's been working here for over a year, and I think she knew the owner even before that. It's only new for me, because I just moved here. It's been...." I trailed off, rubbing a worn patch on my jeans.

"Hard." His spoon lay in the container, ice cream melted and forgotten.

"Yeah," I whispered softly.

"Well, I completed one thing on my list today. Eat ice cream. And this is a very small time, and things did not go the way I expected them, but I think I am having fun with you." His voice sounded like he was smiling.

I could feel my cheeks heating up, but a fierceness to say how I appreciated his presence next to me made me desperate to say something. "I-I was scared of the dark before. But not right now. Thank you."

"That's why ice cream is a miracle. I have always said so," he said lightly, but there was something else to his voice that I couldn't decipher.

"I hope you get to accomplish your list," I said in a quiet voice.

There was a pause, and when he spoke, it was warm and full of something else I didn't understand, like before. "I would like that very much," he said. "But... we'll see if I have time. My work, they don't even want me to have my birthday off. That's what—" He paused again, and tapped his fingertips together as if trying to conjure up a word. *"Inspired* me to make the list in the first place."

"What?" I said incredulously. "That's ridiculous." He should be able to use his vacation days if he wanted to.

The circuits up above buzzed and a dim light started to rise. Customers cheered in the next aisle, and someone clapped.

I stared at his hand resting on the spoon, which was becoming clearer with every second. I could not bring myself to look up. It was like my body knew something my brain didn't. After all this wondering, I was suddenly *terrified* for some strange reason to finally see his face.

"It *is* ridiculous! So I said" —he stirred the ice cream that had now melted into liquid— "I said to myself, Jongjin, what would you be doing right now if you didn't have work?"

And the lights came back on.

종진
JONGJIN
6

The girl stood up, practically leaping sideways, looking at me with wide, horrified, shocked brown eyes. She opened her mouth. She took several hard breaths, then turned—and ran.

"Wh—w—" I was taken aback. I couldn't come up with the correct English word for *wait.* I jumped up, furious with myself, stretching my hand out after her.

"No," I gasped in Korean. "Don't—" She had already vanished from my sight.

I sprinted after her, rounding the corner to just see her leave the store. I skidded to a stop, nearly crashing into some bewildered customers and an employee with a vest.

"Are you going to pay for that?" he demanded, blocking my path and pointing at the forlorn half-eaten box of ice cream in the aisle behind me.

"Yes—but—" I was leaning around him, desperately trying to see where the girl had gone. If I waited just two more seconds she would be gone forever—

But the employee was blocking my way, maybe under the impression that I was trying to steal. "Hey, where are you going?"

Panic was battling inside me. I wanted to go after her. I also didn't want to get arrested for theft—I had no idea how things worked here in America. I swallowed hard, feeling a painful lump in my throat as I looked in the direction of the empty door.

But I was too late anyway. I stopped trying to get past him and looked down, taking a deep, slow breath to calm my pounding heart. I couldn't describe the sense of loss and frustration that was ripping at the inside of my chest.

"Right," I said, swallowing again, slowly, nodding. "I understand."

The employee gave me a piercing, dubious, searching look. "Well, at least you're not trying to pretend you don't understand English."

How much Korean had I jabbered out to him in my panic? "I'll pay for that ice cream," I said in English, fumbling open my wallet and slapping some American money into his hands. Then I stepped around him and strode to the front of the store, stopping only when I made it out in the rain.

I scanned the parking lot. Nothing moved. She'd probably taken her car and was long gone. Long, long gone.

I sighed and looked down at the concrete, feeling the sudden urge to kick something. *Idiot.* She'd been a fan, hadn't she? That's why she'd had that reaction. That's why she'd run. She'd been talking to me that whole time and hadn't known....

If only I'd stopped her soon enough. But now she was gone, and I was just as helpless to stop her as I was helpless with everything else about my life.

I was breathing quickly again, rain sheeting down on my head, soaking my clothes, though I didn't move. I didn't even know her *name.* And yet, when I'd shone my flashlight onto her for that brief second after she'd crashed into me, when she'd been on the ground... and later, too, whenever I could see her in the dim light....

She'd been so *beautiful.* Shockingly so. Yet the image of her was already slipping from my mind—her full, oval-shaped face, skin the color of chai tea with milk, black hair pulled back, glasses, her short stature. It went beyond looks, though. There was something... just something *about* her that was *different....*

I felt a connection with her that I shouldn't. We'd only talked for hardly any time at all. It was stupid to be so frustrated I would never see her again, when I hardly even knew her.

If only I had even a picture of her, just to remember.

Get a grip on yourself, Jongjin. I shook my head as if to get the water out of my hair, but I was far too wet for that now. I was dripping. My expensive clothes were soaked as I stood there and the scent I'd put on this morning mixed with the smell of rain. *It was just because she left suddenly. That's all. That's why you're feeling all this.*

It was like I couldn't tell down from up anymore. When she'd run away it was like everything had spun. *You've had a difficult day. Of course your feelings will be mixed up....*

She'd had a difficult day too. I remembered the tears dripping down her beautiful face and clinging to her skin. She'd seemed so lost, so embarrassed and ashamed. There had been nothing to be ashamed about—but I'd still pointed my phone flashlight down deliberately so I couldn't see her.

I'd tried to help the best I could. I'd felt so helpless just standing there, unable to do anything.

When she'd crashed into me it was like it had knocked all my troubles away too. Like I was in an entirely different world. Everything had just kind of... fallen away. I'd been so concerned about her, so frustrated with myself that I could do nothing to help, and then, later, completely distracted. Even... enjoying myself.

"I have a trampoline in my backyard. You could use mine!"

"That's very nice of you."

Whatever I was feeling right now... she had felt it too. Before she even knew what I *looked* like! Before she knew who I was!

There was a warmth spreading in my chest. I shook my head. I was a complete mess right now.

I slowly strolled back to the hotel, totally soaked to the skin but not caring, even the insides of my dress shoes damp. My sopping hair was plastered to my head and I swiped it out of my eyes.

I felt disorientated and lost, but freed. Like the crushing weight of stress on my shoulders belonged to someone else. I didn't want to go back to the hotel, and have it all come crashing down on me again. I just wanted to sit here in the rain, the taste of ice cream still lingering on my tongue.

레일라
LEYLA
7

I pulled into the bakery parking lot, slamming on the brake before I crashed into the parking space curb. Tears cascaded down my face and blurred my vision as I sat there frozen for a moment, my hands stiff on the wheel, and then I threw it into park, yanked out the key and ran into the bakery, slamming the car door hard behind me.

Jongjin. I just saw....

No. This isn't real.

My brain wasn't working. I was overwhelmed, scared, furious, who-knows-what.

Amanda looked up from the front when she saw me enter the bakery. Her eyes gave me a once-over, wide and surprised. I was wet all over, from my clothes, my hair, and my tearful face.

"You said there wouldn't be anyone important there!" I yelled, my voice cracking. Amanda was looking at me in alarm, but I didn't care. "You said...."

I was in almost fits. I hugged my arms to my chest, bending over like I'd been stabbed in the stomach, letting out a sob.

I'd run away. I'd *run away*....

What were the chances? Of me being in the store at the same time he was? Crashing into him? I couldn't understand it, my brain had stopped working the second I'd heard him say his name. *Jongjin. Jongjin. Jongjin. Jongjin.* It kept repeating itself in my spinning mind. I couldn't think straight. I'd eaten ice cream with Jongjin. I'd crashed into Jongjin—touched him. I'd spilled my guts to him. I'd *cried* in front of him. All without knowing.

Rachel had come out of the back. She looked at me, panicked and just as wide-eyed as Amanda. "Hey, are you okay? Where's the butter?"

I couldn't answer. I couldn't put anything into words, not even into thoughts. I didn't understand myself, didn't understand anything at all. I just became aware of myself under the too-bright bakery lights and how I was dripping water on the floor and how they were both looking at me like I was insane and I ran. I ran out of the bakery and back into the rain, back into the dark, back into the rumbling thunder and across the street.

I leaned against the concrete base of a streetlight, the one place with light. Out here again, it felt more real. I shivered in the cool rain pounding down on my head and soaking all of my clothes, tucking my knees tighter to my chest.

Jongjin. No way. Why? How? Jongjin....

Jongjin, the one safe spot in my life. The one thing that would never change. The one person who could never hurt me. *Jongjin....*

There's no way that happened. I had to be hallucinating. It was a dream. I'd just....

What was he *doing* there?

Jongjin. The lights coming back on. *Jongjin.* My face a foot from his, every detail of him in overwhelming, perfect, crystal-clear focus. The kind a camera couldn't capture. *Jongjin.* The slight creases at the corners of his eyes as he smiled, the warmth to his skin, every eyebrow hair. His light hazel-bronze eyes as we stared at each other, and the confusion I saw there. *Jongjin.* The shape of his lips, bare, every tiny line in them visible. *Jongjin.* His smooth, dark brown hair falling across his forehead, a few strands out of place.

It was too much. Too much. I'd panicked and ran. The abruptness of being suddenly a foot away from *Byun Jongjin*—my brain couldn't handle it. I *couldn't handle it.* I was in shock. We had been so close—so close together....

It had felt like I'd been hit in the side of the head with something heavy. I was shocked, disoriented, numb, unaware of what I was doing until I was already gone. Now I was devastated.

Go back, my mind urged me. *Go back. He could still be there....*

But somehow the prospect of that, too, was too much to handle. It terrified me. It terrified me that he would be there and terrified me that he was already gone.

I just cried harder, angry with myself, petrified and trapped and unable to do anything at all.

I rode home in Amanda's car that night. I stayed in the backseat, making the cushions damp from my sodden clothes, feeling completely dead. She kept glancing back at me in the review mirror, worried, at my expressionless face.

I didn't speak at all until we got home. I just went up to my room, changed into dry pajamas, and threw myself on the bed. The glossy, flat Jongjin on the poster above me smiled blankly into nothing, plastic, empty, fake.

My wet, stringy hair was cold against my hot cheek, pressed against the pillow.

"*Idiot,*" I said in between sobs, pounding my fist on the mattress angrily. It was even more real now.

It was the encounter of a lifetime. And I'd thrown it away. Like the most idiotic person on the planet. I hated myself, hated the fact that I'd run away, hated how I'd responded. The overwhelming regret and guilt was almost physically painful. I liked Jongjin so much.

Jongjin. He was someone actually here, now. Someone I'd actually talked to. Someone I'd actually touched. He wasn't just a person on a video, a voice, a poster. He was so much better. He was real. A real person with sadness and imperfections and a *soul.*

How come I'd had to blow it? How come I'd run away?

I understood now—what that laugh had done to me. That bubbling, unique laugh that had frozen me to the spot and made chills run up my body. Had it been blocked from my brain? It was like I was in denial, like a part of me had known it all along. My body had known even if my mind didn't, but I should've.

I argued with myself, random thoughts chasing each other through my head. *His Korean accent.* But I'd barely heard him speak English before. When he did, he suddenly sounded... different. *His laugh.* I would know it anywhere! I'd heard it hundreds, maybe thousands of times, just never in person!

Nothing mattered. Nothing could justify it. I should've *known!* I should've realized! Why hadn't I?

You're so STUPID! I thought, pounding the mattress again, tears and snot on my face.

His gasp when I crashed into him. The way I'd been pressed against his chest, breathing in his heady scent. The way he'd dramatically pulled the ice cream carton from the freezer to distract me. His fingers, brushing mine.

Jongjin, the one thing that would never change... had already changed, just like everything else in my life.

종진
JONGJIN
8

It was a long, hard day of filming—up at 3:30, downstairs at 4:00 to all clamber into the company vans outside the hotel. I drank my same protein smoothie —which I was, by now, sick of— and tried to swallow it as quickly as possible, both to soothe my roaring hunger and not linger on the taste. The staff gave us "on-vacation, American-summer clothes" that we changed into in the high-ceiling van, which was easily tall enough to stand up in, with wide aisles. Laon was so sleepy he nearly tripped over one of the seats with one leg still caught in his new Michael Kors jeans.

We were going to the beach at dawn. As we drove, the General Makeup Artist Ms. Nam expertly smeared us with our regular makeup like concealer and foundation. I looked over at my fellow members—they all looked wide-awake and glowing, the very picture of radiant health and energy. Amazing how much could be faked.

I didn't talk to Tae-X and Sun Chi-Ho about last night. I'd returned late, very late, and gotten only about three or four hours of sleep.

They'd been waiting for me. Even though they were in bed with the lights off. I could tell by their breathing.

Back in the hotel, I'd felt ashamed for the way I'd treated them. And I shouldn't have told Tae-X about what he said in his sleep. It was just something that had burst out of me. I had been out of control and disgustingly selfish. How could I say that to him with his personal/idol identity crisis?

Him talking in his sleep had been a secret I'd been keeping, but it was too late now. I'd said it.

Back in the hotel room, distracted from my own problems, completely cooled down from the state I'd been in before, it was impossible not to see things rationally.

It seemed stupid, what I'd done, how I'd reacted so immaturely, how I'd been so furious. Now that my fury was gone, I'd felt like a hollow, gray shell.

I'd gently run my hand across Sun Chi-Ho's hair as I walked by, and leaned next to Tae-X and whispered: "I'm sorry."

They both pretended to still be asleep.

It had been a relief to climb into bed, exhausted, and fall into oblivion from the shame and embarrassment and regret and whirl of feelings just added on by me meeting the nameless girl. She'd been on my mind almost constantly.

I'd been thinking it over, and deciding. I didn't *want* it to be a one-time meeting, just a good memory. I wanted to know more about her. I wanted to be in her presence again. Not simply because I'd felt unexpectedly free and happy—that could be a fluke, a product of circumstance—but because something in me was drawn to her. I'd *never* had such a reaction to anyone else before.

I couldn't get her out of my head. The things she'd said to me, her voice, her tears, her face. The way she'd looked at me when the lights came back on.

I needed to see her again.

And I'd come up with a plan to find her.

Seojung had been keeping a silent eye on me all morning. The others might've told him how I'd blown up last night, and he obviously hadn't forgotten my plea to Manager Yoo. Seojung was the strict leader and "father" of the group, and obviously took his job very seriously.

Eventually I couldn't stand being looked at and turned my head to look at him, where he was in the seat next to me. "Is there something you'd like to tell me, Seojung?" I said with a groan.

He looked at me with those rich dark eyes and severe eyebrows for a second, then turned to look out the window and said "You've been acting strange lately."

I let out a little scoff. "Me? /?" I let out another scoff, though I privately hoped in a panic that he couldn't read who I'd been thinking about on my face. "You've been the one staring at me all morning."

Seojung actually cracked a smile at that. When he had such a quiet and serious personality, seeing him smile was like a sudden burst of sunlight. I'd known him ever since we debuted two years ago and it still took me off guard.

"Jongjin, Jongjin," he said, shaking his head, still with that brilliant smile. "I haven't been staring, I've been observing."

"Right," I said. "Observe Laon instead."

I had been kidding, but Seojung raised one eyebrow. "*Laon?* He's always asleep! How boring is that?" He turned around in his chair to look in the backseat. Laon actually *was* asleep there, his head lolling every time we went over a bump in the road. Next to him, Sun Chi-Ho was oblivious, his round face focused and smiling ever so slightly as he held his phone up to the window, snapping away at the city lights in the black morning sky.

It'd been two years since we debuted together as Tr3sure. I'd been surprised— I hadn't even met the other members until it was announced we were debuting together. It turned out that we got along well enough, perhaps by necessity, but over the months our politeness had turned to friendship. Now, they were all indispensable to me—Laon, the easygoing, blank-faced middle child who was a piano genius and fell asleep often enough to have us seriously consider whether he was narcoleptic, Seojung, the serious, strict, and stunningly elegant second-oldest who was also the leader and main dancer, Tae-X, the enthusiastic rapper who was the songwriter along with Laon, and Sun Chi-Ho, the photography-loving maknae who called Seojung "Uncle Seojung" for fun and who we all privately agreed, behind his back, to be a soft marshmallow needing protection from the world. He was just seventeen.

I had a fierce love for the friends I now considered my brothers, my coworkers, my partners in crime. I could tell they felt the same—even though in the beginning, it was something we left unsaid. It took months for us to open up to each other, but those months were still speckled with moments where I knew unquestionably the bond between us—Seojung's panicked expression as he scanned the airport crowd for Laon, Sun Chi-Ho watching Tae-X cry into his ramyun with wide-eyed concern, the glowing pride I saw in their eyes as they looked at each other and at me.

After a year, we'd loosened up to the point where it was perfectly acceptable to jump on someone from behind or purposely annoy them. After two years, we were inseparable.

But I still didn't like opening up to people. I liked to keep everything bottled up and hide it with a smile. Happiness was the only feeling I showed willingly. Anger, sadness, everything else—it had to wait until I was alone.

I wasn't ready to tell Seojung, Tae-X, Laon, and Sun Chi-Ho about... her.

Besides, after today, I'd know whether my efforts to find her really were successful. It wouldn't matter if I would never see her again.

"Anyways," Seojung was sighing, *"you're* the one who looks like he needs help, not Laon. I wish Manager Yoo would have given your birthday off. I really do. You need a break like Tae-X needs sleep."

"I know," I said, as the car rumbled to a stop. It only took a minute for the stylist to come around, a cool blast of humid, ocean-scented air coming into the car as she opened the door. The sky outside was still dark. She tugged my white shirt collar open and gave me a leather bracelet to put on my wrist, rolling up the hems of my light blue jeans. It used to be uncomfortable for me—being touched all over—but after all this time it felt kind of nice. Like a mother fussing over me. I hadn't seen my own mother in weeks, though we'd made a point to visit before I went on tour and I'd promised to bring her back a souvenir. "But it's no use whining about not getting my birthday off. I'm over it. I have other plans."

Seojung raised his eyebrow again. "Really?"

"Yes," I said, as the stylist expertly rolled up my shirt sleeves to just-covering-my-elbows to show off my arms and wrist jewelry, including a very summery and expensive sponsored watch. "It involves me making the most of my random free breaks. Expect me to dash off frequently."

He sniffed and smiled. "Fair enough. If you want to make it a mystery, that's fine by me. It's probably better I don't know what you're up to anyway. Makes me innocent."

I could tell he thought that I was going to sneak off and eat American food that wasn't part of our diet. I had already eaten ice cream —which was *very* forbidden— so his guess wasn't too far off.

Diet was one section where Seojung didn't bother trying to keep us in line. He liked to keep his own face razor-sharp, but he privately preferred us to look "healthy"— as he'd mentioned when he'd walked into the dorm one time and caught me, red handed, eating a whole plate of crispy fried chicken covered in sticky, red, sweet-and-spicy sauce. He'd even had a tiny piece to convince my petrified self that he wasn't going to rat me out.

That was *way* back in the early days of our debut. I smiled to myself, remembering.

Well, maybe eating some American food was part of the list I wanted to get done before we left in a month, but it also featured other normal, childlike activities—some of which I had yet to figure out.

And... her.

The stylist had given me a single, crystalline sunset-orange teardrop earring, and then moved on to Seojung while I inserted it. The others' outfits were a little more casual than mine, since I had a reputation to uphold as "best-dressed idol". Sun Chi-Ho was in complete summer-vacation gear, which involved a T-shirt and cargo jeans. His job was to be cute. Mine was to be snazzily dressed.

Seojung, poor soul, had borne the burden of keeping up Tr3sure's metallic color theme. The designers usually liked to toss in at least one or two items to link all our concepts and styles together. He had on a shimmering gold shirt under a beachy jean jacket. Somehow, he pulled it off with casual elegance. If Laon, Sun Chi-Ho, or I had worn it, the stylists would have a much harder time trying to make it not look ridiculous.

Manager Jeon came by and passed out our scripts, the breeze from the open van door ruffling the pages. I took a look. Most of the day we were supposed to just have fun and do the games the staff organized for us, but there were certain things we were supposed to say at certain times. Sometimes it helped the viewers understand what was going on, and other times it was supposed to be adorable, or funny. Above all, we were supposed to be energetic, happy and interesting. Most of it was pre-planned.

And I, as the most popular and adored member of Tr3sure, got the most clever and entertaining lines. Sometimes the other members didn't even get a chance to shine and show the world how amazing their personalities were.

I swallowed as I thought of what I'd said last night. *Or is that not allowed because it's not on the script?*

I glanced in the backseat at Tae-X. I wondered if he was remembering too. He was fanning through the thick mass of script pages over and over with his thumb while staring hollowly at the seat in front of him.

"A piggyback ride?" Laon moaned, making both me and Tae-X snap out of our thoughts to look at him. I scanned down the page until I found a checklist we were supposed to complete "spontaneously". Laon was supposed to give Tae-X a piggyback ride on the beach. "But Tae-X is *so heavy!*"

"Ya, watch your mouth," Tae-X said, but he was smiling. I suspected he liked being carried more than Laon liked carrying him.

"Look on page fifteen!" Sun Chi-Ho whispered excitedly. "A shopping game for American snacks for lunch!" His face fell. "Oh—that's in the whole series outline, not today...."

I memorized my lines with much more difficulty than usual, with thoughts of the girl still taking over my head, and, just as dawn was starting to break, we all headed out to the beach where the camera people already were. Filming was fun, yet draining. The whole day passed until it was three in the afternoon, and then we all headed back to the hotel.

"A one-hour break!" Manager Yoo shouted as we filed out of the vans. "Then, tonight we're going to film the members having dinner in the hotel."

We all let up a cheer. Dinner on camera usually meant it was something *good!*

The five of us took the elevator up to our rooms. I freshened up and drank some much-needed water, then started to head out again still in the clothes the stylist had prepared for me.

"Where are you going, JJ, bro?" Tae-X called incredulously as I put my hand on the doorknob.

"Don't call me JJ."

"Don't stall."

"I'm making the most of my one-hour break," I said, utterly exhausted but determined, and then headed out on my mission.

레일라
LEYLA
9

I'd woken up late with my eyes sore and puffy, and my body feverish. I slowly rolled out of bed and then hunted around the bathroom for a thermometer, finding one after several minutes of opening drawers. With it I took my temperature, staring at my pathetic reflection in the bathroom mirror. I didn't look so good.

It made me wonder how Jongjin saw me, last night. Just the thought made me feel sick with regret again.

The temperature read normal. I put it away and showered mechanically, my head full to the bursting with thoughts of him. It still didn't feel real. Stuff like this didn't happen. It was nearly impossible. It was like meeting him hadn't sunk in. I'd only seen recordings of him, or live streaming. He might as well be on another planet. Even in concerts there was this massive degree of separation between the idols and the fans. The most I could ever daydream about would be to meet him, go back to my home and my normal life, and cherish it forever.

But now....

Well, you got what you wanted, I thought to myself angrily, slamming the bathroom cabinet harder than I intended and hearing something crack. I winced and opened it again, frustrated, seeing that nothing appeared to be broken.

Now it was like I'd had the chance to meet him face to face and I couldn't get over it, couldn't even accept it. How was I supposed to just act normal now?

I'd met him, and everything and nothing had changed all at once.

I morosely ate breakfast, still feeling lost and not knowing what to do with myself. I lay around all morning, thinking about Jongjin. He wasn't just a handsome, charismatic person on a screen anymore, or even just a crush-worthy idol.

He was... a real person.

I'd known that before, logically, but it had never sunk in like it did now. No amount of behind-the-scenes content, no amount of being drawn to his personality, could've done this to me like meeting him last night did.

"I am—have been—very involved in... work. It never stops. I'm turning twenty soon, and I feel like I've missed out on life—my childhood. Because of work. So I thought I'd... try to get it back, while I can."

Why had he just trusted me with that when he didn't even know me? Now, it seemed even stranger. I'd never seen him express anything similar on-screen, and even his fellow members said he only liked to show his neutral or happy face to them and the world. Jongjin usually hid his emotions. It made my own heart feel like he'd taken a key and unlocked it wide open.

I sighed.

Why did they split? - Too tight.

It wasn't hard to imagine him wearing tight pants now. He was an idol. The humorous image that I'd initially thought of was a lot different than the reality, which was probably some sort of thousand-dollar Gucci leather skinny jeans or something. Where had he been when it happened? Did he ever say?

A bittersweet smile curled up my lips at the memory, then dropped.

That was all it was now. A memory.

I threw myself down on the living room sofa, clutching a pillow to my chest. I'd met an idol—met *Jongjin*—and I didn't even have a picture or anything else to prove it. If I had, Jackie would be so excited....

Jackie. What would I tell her? Would she even believe me?

I put on a hand on my phone, and then stopped again, my fingertips against the surface, not quite picking it up. My heart was pounding for some reason.

Jackie would probably be happy for me and it might make the conversation more normal, more like it used to be... but she would also ask what we talked about, and the things that Jongjin had said felt... private.

Maybe Jackie didn't need to know.

I jumped up and walked away, my hand sliding off the phone. I needed to find something to do, before I went mad. There wasn't even Amanda here to keep me busy—she was at work, and wasn't going to come home until seven.

I had decided: I might tell someone I'd met Jongjin, but I wouldn't tell them what we'd said. I would carry that to my grave.

Don't obsess over him, I thought as I started to tidy the already-clean house. *You met him. It's over.*

Dad arrived back home in the afternoon, bringing lunch with him. I'd been so distracted I hadn't really noticed his car was gone on a Sunday. He was covered in sweat and in exercise clothes.

We ate a nice lunch of hot chicken biryani with naan and sparkling drinks. It was delicious, but it made me wonder why he'd gotten takeout. Did he think I didn't know how to cook? It had been years since he'd really known me well....

"I can cook," I announced calmly. "Enough to put together a decent meal, if you want."

He looked embarrassed. "Oh. Okay. Well, there's not enough to work with in the fridge anyway. I need to go grocery shopping. Amanda usually does but the bakery has really picked up speed lately, and she likes the overtime money."

"I'll go," I said almost too quickly.

He looked at me skeptically. "Is that your idea of a good time?"

"Dad, I'm going crazy here. It's summer in California and all I've been doing is laying around inside."

"If you want," he said, sounding amused.

I took his keys from the hall pegs and stepped outside into the surprising blast of hot summer air, the afternoon sun intense and unrelenting. The sky was sprinkled with a few clouds, and the palm trees stood tall and stiff, because no wind moved. Down the street, a few kids were riding their scooters on their tiny driveway, their childish voices lifting my spirits. It was just a normal, hot June day for everyone. Out there, people were living their lives, untroubled, unworried... it was an ice cream kind of summer day.

I stilled mid-thought as I put my hand on the door handle of the car.

Don't think about him, I thought furiously. *Don't think about ice cream.*

I stood there so long, my black shirt was starting to feel uncomfortably warm when I finally opened the door and slid inside. I turned the ignition, trying *very* hard not to think about what happened the last time I got in this car.

The ride to the grocery store was uneventful, just the way I liked it. Instead of turning on the AC I rolled down the windows, letting the wind fly in from all directions and mess with my hair. It was so bright, warm, nice. The grocery store itself seemed cold afterward. I bought a bunch of food as quickly as possible, eager to get back outside, thinking I'd just sit on the driveway and listen to music, or maybe go for a walk. But then I paused in the freezer section, hesitating as I passed by the ice cream.

I think I recognized the flavor we'd eaten together.

"What the heck," I muttered, and threw it in the cart. I was being stupid. There was no way I would ever, *ever* forget meeting Byun Jongjin. Trying not to think about it wouldn't help at all.

I paused afterward, staring at the frosted door and remembering the way he'd stood in front of one just like it, just a dark figure then, when I didn't know who he was—a faceless, mysterious guy who was kind and warm and funny.

My chest ached, and I turned away painfully. *You're being an idiot,* I told myself fiercely.

But a part of my heart—deep down—knew that wasn't entirely true. I was slowly, slowly coming to realize that it wasn't as shallow as just missing the chance to spend some time with a favorite celebrity. We'd talked with each other and connected in a way that I hadn't with hardly anyone else.

It felt like I'd... lost something.

I checked out and headed back to the car, trying to shake off the feeling. The front seat was so warm, it was tempting to curl up there with the door open and close my eyes, but I made myself load the groceries in the back and start driving home.

I'd have to plan dinner; that would be a nice surprise for Dad. He'd like that. Amanda would enjoy it too—I wasn't sure how often she cooked, or if she made anything besides dessert. I would guess she would be burnt-out from so many hours at the bakery.

Since I'd bought some nice bread, I could make some easy chicken club sandwiches for dinner, or banh mi. They both sounded delicious. I was thinking about this as I pulled up to our house—with directions, since they all looked very similar and I wasn't that used to it yet—and parked in the street. I got out and grabbed all the bags of groceries, balancing them in my hands as I walked up the sidewalk.

There was a guy on my driveway. I frowned, slowing hesitantly, and he turned around as he heard my footsteps.

The grocery bag slipped from my hand in shock.

It was Jongjin.

His espresso-brown hair, shining with chestnut highlights in the sun, had a few strands loose from its perfect style. He had on a white shirt tucked into ocean-blue jeans, the sleeves rolled up. For a second we both just stared at each other—and then he broke out in a smile that made my legs weak.

My heart pounded and I felt dizzy, unable to move. I was shocked, rooted to the spot. And he just went on looking at me, looking at me with a kind of unbelieving relief like I was the only person left on the planet and he'd just found me. He took several small, quick steps forward until he was in front of me, where I was still frozen. There was a warmth and softness to his eyes, but he didn't break our gazes. I couldn't breathe. My lungs needed air but I couldn't....

"Leyla Sen," Jongjin said softly.

I just stared at him with huge eyes. I opened my mouth, but only a small croaking sound came out. He knew my name?

Seeing him in full sunlight, *here,* was blowing every circuit in my brain. How did he find me? Had he even been trying to find me? How did he know my name? Jongjin smiled and swiftly strode forward, scooping up the bag I'd dropped on the ground and holding it out to me, straightening up to his full height just a foot away. He was so distractingly tall. His soft brown eyes were close enough for me to see the light glow in them as the sunlight hit his face, caressing his cheekbones.

I didn't even reach out to take the dropped bag. I was still stuck to the spot like someone had glued me, my cheeks scorching. Had I just thought to myself this morning that he was a real person? He looked so gloriously flawless now that I found myself doubting that.

By some miracle, I found my voice. "H-h—H-how—what are you doing here?" I spluttered.

Jongjin just kept silently smiling, giving the bag he was holding a little move forward as if still urging me to take it. The *way* he was *looking* at me....

I looked around left and right desperately, as if hoping someone would save me. Then I looked back at him in disbelief, overwhelmed, and robotically reached out and took the bag from him.

"Th-thanks," I said.

"You do that often?" he said curiously, lips quirking up in a smile.

Whenever he was smiling it was like everything went out of focus and all my thoughts left my head in a rush of pure euphoria.

"Do what?" I said, dazed.

"Drop things."

I opened my mouth in shocked indignation, my scorching hot cheeks feeling even hotter. *"What?"* I spluttered. "No!"

I made a move as if to barge past him, but he, too, stepped to the side, in front of me. I caught just the barest whiff of his cologne on the warm summer air and had to fight to keep my concentration all over again. Especially with the way his hazel-bronze eyes were boring into mine unrelentingly, and the way he let out the smallest sound of a laugh.

"Don't go," he said, voice laced with amusement and something... more sincere. My whole face was burning hot and I looked away from his eyes. "I shouldn't tease you. I am here to use a trampoline. You said I could use yours, *maja?*"

My gaze snapped back to his. I was stunned into a brief silence again, everything we'd said to each other rising up between us. It was like we'd been connected again by a lightning bolt. *His list. The way he wants to be normal for a while.*

"Did I?" I mumbled, feeling suddenly vulnerable, rebalancing the weight of the groceries in my arms. Jongjin reached out to take them, but I stepped back defensively.

"You do not want help?" he asked curiously.

"It's not that," I mumbled again. "I just get overwhelmed when..." *When I see you? When hot guys like you are around? When you bring up that night and it's a lot different now that I can see your face? How are you going to finish that sentence, Leyla?*

"...when, uh, people come demanding to use my trampoline."

"Oh, I see, so *that* happens often?"

His eyes were twinkling with amusement and I could tell he was suppressing a smile.

There was a fabulous retort to that, but it wasn't coming to my mind anytime soon. I turned around and strode briskly to the front door instead, setting down the groceries on the step so I could fumble for my keys.

"You can follow if you want," I said in an embarrassingly lame, fake I-don't-care-one-way-or-the-other voice as I tried desperately to recover my dignity. I might've been mistaken, but I could've *sworn* I heard him laugh.

He startled me as he suddenly appeared next to me, scooping up all the grocery bags on the ground and holding them, waiting for me, as I pushed the door open with my foot.

I couldn't believe this was happening.

"Dad?"

No answer, though there was the muffled sound of dramatic music coming from his office. He was probably watching a movie—good. I hadn't thought about that panicking development of introducing Jongjin to my father.

I hung the car keys on the hallway pegs, hearing the steps of Jongjin's fancy dress shoes echoing off the walls as he followed me. I breathed in deeply, my heart pumping nervously, trying not to hyperventilate. What was he thinking about my house? Byun Jongjin was *in. My. House.*

I went into the kitchen and plopped my grocery bag on the counter, taking out items feverishly so my hands had something to do. I could hear the plastic bags rustling behind me.

Jongjin gave a small gasp. "This is what *we* ate!"

Oh no. I turned around, seeing him holding the carton of ice cream, mortification making my cheeks prickle. But it was my turn to raise my eyebrows. "Well don't go *snooping* in there, Jongjin."

He laughed at my reprimand. "So you know my name?"

I stopped in the middle of taking out the groceries. Did he not *know* that I knew who he was? Why did he think I ran away the first time? I opened my mouth, trying to say something, anything, panic now setting in icy-cold.

"Yes?" I managed to force out.

"So you're a fan of Tr3sure?"

It was surreal hearing "Tr3sure" spoken out loud from Byun Jongjin after seeing it so many times through texts, videos, papers and albums.

I tried to calmly continue taking the rest of the stuff out. "Yes, I am."

"Who's your bias?"

"Why, *you,* of course," I said, my voice dripping with false sarcasm. I took the remaining bags out of his reach by sliding them across the counter towards me, the butterflies in my stomach exploding.

"Who's the hottest?"

Even though my back was to him, I could hear the smile in his voice.

I crossed my arms, turning around again. I hoped the answer wasn't written all over my face. "Okay, now you're pushing it."

Jongjin threw back his head and laughed, that full-out, bubbling, hearty laugh that made my stomach do flips. He put one of his hands down on the counter to hold himself up.

Jongjin is touching my counter. I blinked several times to make sure I wasn't dreaming, feeling lightheaded.

He continued. "Don't worry, I knew you were a fan. The look on your face when you saw me was very... surprised."

We just looked at each other for a moment. There was a warmth to his skin that photos had never quite managed to capture. Especially not the supernaturally pale images in *Iceland*.

He gave me a small, quick smile and leaned against the counter, arms crossed over his strong chest. "You aren't going to say anything, are you? You *are* mysterious."

I could feel my cheeks burning. Was he flirting with me? Of course he was. Jongjin could flirt with a rock. But I still ran a hand over my ponytail, unbearably self-conscious, even as I reminded myself not to take it seriously. I was such a hopeless, naïve fool.

"I didn't mean to run away," I said defensively, not able to look up into his handsome face. "I... wasn't thinking about it."

"It made me curious why."

I stopped. It was strange hearing him speak English—his voice sounded much different than what I was used to. But I was still overwhelmed by it, and how close he was, and the pure solidness of him standing in front of me like a hallucination or dream.

"Well," I said with difficulty, "I don't know. I... just... I wasn't expecting to see you. It was kind of a shock."

"I should've said who I was," he said seriously.

I shook my head, looking up at him. "No, how were you supposed to know? I'm the one who should apologize. I felt really guilty afterwards."

But those words didn't seem like enough—not nearly enough for what I'd experienced during and afterward, and what I might've made *him* feel. Even if I couldn't even begin to guess. They were still the thoughts I would never hear, just like before I'd met him in person.

I felt like I owed him an explanation.

"I don't like change," I added quietly.

Jongjin looked at me for one uncomfortably long moment and then asked "Why?"

I briefly closed my eyes, shaking my head. I didn't know how to answer that, even though I was trying. Instead I said, "We should probably go to the trampoline."

"Right," he said quietly. "Okay."

I walked to the back door and slid it open. Jongjin followed after me.

Jongjin halted in the dead grass next to the trampoline, slipping off his dress shoes and setting them on the ground, which was still a bit muddy from the rains yesterday. He sat down on the edge of the trampoline with his legs dangling, his fancy white socks on display.

I could feel his eyes on me as I set my sandals next to his shoes in the yellow grass, hopping onto the trampoline myself, with a lot more effort since I was shorter.

I sat down in the middle and crossed my legs, looking straight at him even though it made me highly uncomfortable. It would've been so much easier not to look at him.

I tried not to remember what had happened last time we met—me crying and everything. I felt flustered. "How did you know my name? How did you know where I lived?"

"Ah," Jongjin said, swinging his legs over the side and scooting close to me in the middle, crossing his legs too. "Well, you invited me to use your trampoline. I decided to take the offer."

I said nothing. It seemed a little odd to chase someone down just to use their trampoline, but I supposed my house might be the only chance he got. Besides, he had no way of knowing how to find me....

"And you said that your sister worked at a bakery. A bakery that was making so many chocolate-strawberry cupcakes."

I gasped. "You...."

"I searched for close bakeries and walked in. I mentioned the chocolate strawberry cupcakes and the..." he struggled to find the right English word, "...desk person thought I ordered them, so it was the right place. She looked like you. I told her that her sister had mentioned her and I was going to surprise her. She said your name, which was good because I didn't know it. So I asked her for where you lived."

My mouth was open.

There was a pause. Jongjin looked at me sideways, his eyes slightly narrowed. "Who's Milo?"

I blinked. "What?"

His face was still humorless. "Your sister called me Milo."

I burst out laughing. "She must've thought you were this guy who—" I choked. "Who, um, goes to my school."

I suddenly lost the skill of breathing.

-{★ 73 ♥}-

"Hmm," Jongjin said slowly, and then reached into his front pocket without tearing his eyes from me, drawing out a small paper-wrapped package. "Well, she gave me this cookie."

He unwrapped the white paper carefully to reveal a large square of brownie, and a heavenly chocolate smell filled the summer-afternoon air.

Jongjin carefully tore the brownie in half, holding one out to me. I took it automatically.

He didn't let go of it for one second, looking at me, one eyebrow raised. "Don't drop it."

I pressed my lips together and took it, scooting away from him. *If that's the way you wanna play, Jongjin, that's the way we're gonna play.*

I carefully stood up, brownie clutched safely in my hand, taking a defiant bite. But he stood up too, throwing out one arm to catch his balance, and his smile took me off guard. It was glowing, brilliant, sincere. Less like he had decided to smile and more like it had just... happened. And there was laughter in his eyes. He had just been teasing me, and my reaction was amusing to him.

He took a step forward on the trampoline, his weight making me slide a little towards him. I gasped, trying to regain my balance, trying not to drop the brownie in my hand. He didn't try to do anything else, but simply ate his half of the brownie, closing his eyes and savoring. After watching him for a few seconds I took another bite of mine too. It was fudgy, rich, and bitter with cocoa, the sugary sweetness in my mouth offset by the slight pop of salt in an irresistible combination. The edges went from chewy to crispy, and the chocolate was complimented by even more chocolate, the chunks that had been baked into it smooth and velvety and sweet.

"Ohwa," Jongjin said softly, eyes still closed, as we both finished.

He slowly opened his eyes and looked right at me. "You ready?"

"Of course I'm—"

I cut off in a gasp as he took another step toward me, making me slide even closer to him. He smiled playfully at my reaction, giving a little bounce. At this I screamed and lost my balance, choosing to slip onto my butt rather than falling into him, but my feet were now touching his socks.

It was like ten megawatts of electricity had shot through me, but I didn't even have time to catch my breath before he bounced again, sending me into the air. He was laughing and I was stumbling up to a standing position, jumping right in front of him. His eyes widened in surprise as I sent him upwards enough to lose his balance. He landed away from me, nearly falling off the trampoline.

"Falling off a trampoline is not on the list of things you want to do, Jongjin," I called. He shot me a determined look that had enough mischief in it to make me squeak "Oh no," and scramble as far away from him as possible. Jongjin had already gotten up and started jumping near me, trying to send me flying. I wasn't light, but his deceptively lean and tall body was made of dense muscle, and he was more than heavy enough to succeed.

I screamed and tried to escape, but that just landed me back in the dangerous middle, and with one gigantic leap he sent me flying into the air—where I came down right on him.

Jongjin caught me as he fell over, and then we were lying down, me halfway on top of him, definitely close enough to smell his cologne and even the chocolate on his stunned breath. I pushed myself off him, a burn creeping up my neck. He sat up too, speechless, red tinting his face and cheeks.

I looked away from him, embarrassed, my entire face and neck hot. For a few torturous moments, neither of us said anything.

"How many times will you do that?" Jongjin asked teasingly. "It's twice you've crashed into me."

"That was *not me*. That was your fault," I said, crossing my arms. But there was something else in his would-be casual voice I couldn't work out. I just looked at him, thinking what I would never say: *That's twice you've caught me.* Because he had. Both times he could've just let me hit him, but both times his arms had wrapped around me, protecting me, almost instinctively. And both times it'd been me who pushed myself away.

종진
JONGJIN
10

Leyla stared at me, strands of hair fallen loose around her oval face, eyes bright with surprise behind her glasses. There was a slight flush of warmth about her cheeks. She was every bit as beautiful as my first impression of her, but it was the personality, the soul, behind her dark eyes that irresistibly drew me in.

After my teasing comment, I couldn't think of anything else to say. The feeling of hugging her, of her warm softness in my arms, was still distractingly fresh on my mind. Her presence, her closeness, made me feel like I'd been hit across the head. I wasn't my usual smooth, had-all-the-right-responses self.

When there was another second of silence, Leyla mumbled "Sorry. Did I hurt you?"

Hurt me? She felt too soft to hurt anyone. "I'm fine," I said automatically. "Anyway, it was me. My fault. You were right." I smiled at her, wishing I had more English at my command to give some sort of smooth reply.

"So..." She glanced around. "Have you gotten anything else done on your list?"

"Oh! Yes," I said, glad for the subject change to ease the sudden awkwardness of the situation. The list was one of the reasons I was here. It seemed like we were going to ignore what just happened. That worked for me. I didn't know how to handle it either.

I reached into my back pocket and pulled out the small piece of paper with all my ideas written on it. I'd been carrying it around everywhere with me. I smoothed it out gently on the trampoline mat, white against black. Leyla leaned forward to get a better look at it and I scooted closer, watching her face. Her eyebrows went up; it was in Korean, so she couldn't read it at all.

"I'll read it for you in English," I said, my fingers still gingerly smoothing the bent corners of the paper.

1. Eat ice cream.

2. Jump on a trampoline.

3. Go to a party.

4. Have a picnic.

5. Eat candy.

6. Go see a movie in a theater.

When I finished reading it, I looked at her, slightly anxious. "What do you think?"

She looked pensive, still staring down at it. "You'll need help getting some of these done, won't you?"

"Yes," I admitted. "Like a party. I can't do that by myself."

She leaned back, obviously thinking hard. I couldn't help thinking it was just like we were in the dark in that corner store—talking about the list, about our problems.

"Do you really want to do everything on this list?" Leyla said finally.

"I do," I said truthfully.

"What is the point of this bucket list?"

"It's to... steal time?" I waved my hand, struggling to find the right word. "Take it?"

"Take advantage?"

"Yes! Take advantage of the normal things. Childhood things."

"That's what you said last night. Most of the things on here aren't childhood things, though." She laughed. "I see a lot about food."

"I'm turning twenty soon. I guess I need more childhood things on the list."

She traced a finger along the edge of the paper, thinking. After a moment she spoke. "What did you like best about childhood?"

I laughed a little. "That was when I was really young." Before Tr3sure's 2-year existence I'd trained for 9 years. I had been eight and a half when I'd started, just a kid, a kid who'd had no idea what he was truly getting into. What he was giving up.

"I guess I liked just being normal," I said slowly. "And... not saying 'yes, yes, yes,' agreeing to everything. Not be happy and perfect all the time while I'm busy and stressed. And being able to eat whatever I wanted."

Did that sound horribly ungrateful?

"I mean—I'm really happy to be an idol—it's amazing, the opportunities, the experiences—"

"Jongjin." Her voice was quiet. She was still looking down at the paper.

"Yes?"

"I'm not a TV anchor, okay?"

"Okay—yes, of course." I was embarrassed. It wasn't something I felt often. It was very uncomfortable.

I fell back on the trampoline and looked up at the blue sky to disguise my feelings. Heat was creeping up my neck as I realized that I'd just told Leyla a lot of things I hadn't told Seojung, Tae-X, Laon, or Sun Chi-ho. But I knew why. It was because she *wasn't* one of them. I had no duty to be the perfect member, the perfect teammate.

"Maybe it's not the child part you liked about childhood, but the carefree part," Leyla said above me. "The normal, no-insane-idol-pressures part."

"That's it," I whispered. I sat up. "That's exactly it." I smacked my hand down on the list. "I guess I don't need to add any more kid things to this then."

"That's good, because you might not have time to complete everything before you leave." She hesitated. "When *do* you leave?"

"The day after my birthday," I said. "July 1st."

I watched her expressions; relief and dismay in equal measure. I swallowed. Maybe what I'd thought about us yesterday night at the corner store was still true. Maybe she felt a connection to me just as much as I felt to her, and it hadn't gone away when we'd met again under more normal circumstances.

"We're going back to Korea after this," I said lightly, trying not to make it a big deal. "But they are planning to come back for another tour next year. To Atlanta, Phoenix and New York City...."

And just like that, the reminder that I was an idol came crashing down on my brain. Oh no—what time was it? I checked my expensive watch; it was a quarter to five.

I was supposed to be sitting in the conference room in ten minutes.

"My break is over! It's *over* over!" I said, jumping up in a panic.

Leyla jumped up too, with wide eyes, pitching me forward a little bit—we *were* on a trampoline. "Are you late?"

"I'm going to be! Very late!" I was already frantically searching for the taxi on my phone. It might take them longer than ten minutes to *get* here, and then there was the drive to the hotel after that. "Excuse me—I need to call a taxi."

"I can drive you," Leyla said.

I stared at her. "What?"

"I can drive you! It won't take me longer than it would take a taxi, and we can leave right away."

"Thank you," I said, relief flooding my body. "Come on, let's go!"

And then we were both running back through the house—me clumsily grabbing my shoes from the grass and slipping them on, socks now stained from mud—and out the front door again. Leyla grabbed the car keys off the hook in the hallway and then before I knew it I was slamming the passenger door behind me. "That way," I said, pointing down the street.

Leyla did the fastest three-point turn I'd ever seen and then we were on our way. Without taking her eyes off the road, she pulled her own phone from her back pocket and held it out to me. "Can you enter the directions?" she said. "I need to know where I'm going."

I glanced at her as I did so, taking a long time to type on the English keyboard. Her eyes were fixed ahead, and her expression was determined. I couldn't help smiling, even though her phone predicted my arrival time to be twelve minutes late.

She made me feel calm. I liked sitting here with her in the same car like we were old friends instead of near-strangers, the golden afternoon-evening sun bathing us, turning everything a beautiful color.

"Did you tell your parents that you left?" I asked finally.

"I better text my dad after this," Leyla mumbled. Then, after another second, she added "I don't live with both my parents. They divorced a long time ago. That was why I moved to California, to live with my dad and Amanda instead of with my mom in Michigan."

"How do you feel about it?" I asked.

Leyla shrugged.

There was another second of silence. I settled back in my seat, golden sun slanting into my eyes. "How about Saturday? If it's good to complete one more thing on the list?"

She shook her head. "Saturday the 10th? I can't. I'm going out with friends."

I peered at her curiously. "Why do you have a weird voice?"

"What weird voice?!" she said.

"Your face is definitely turning red." I leaned forward and peered at her to get a better look. She set her mouth and her face turned even pinker as she refused to meet my eyes. I studied her, but suddenly realized that my own heartbeat was going fast in my chest. I leaned back, taken off guard by my reaction.

"Remind me never to take K-pop idols driving!" Leyla was huffing.

I laughed heartily, relieved she hadn't noticed any difference in me. "Are you sure? This is nice. I thought about doing it more."

Leyla was smiling and I couldn't hide my grin either, but then I glanced at the clock. I was supposed to be in the hotel *right now.* While I was sitting here in a car with Leyla, having fun, Seojung was probably pacing and checking his watch, wondering when I was going to show up. The camera crew had already set up for our "dinner on film", and maybe the food had even arrived. Manager Yoo was probably frowning over his clipboard, and I could just imagine Assistant Manager Son's nervous face.

It was far too easy to be in an entirely different world with Leyla.

Leyla seemed to sense my heavy silence, because she said quietly, "Are they going to be mad you're late?"

"Yes," I said. "Yes, they will be." I leaned my head on my hand and stared out the window. "I was just thinking they're probably wondering where I am right now."

Leyla's fingers tightened on the steering wheel.

"Don't worry about it. They'll get over it." I hoped. Laon, Tae-X, Seojung, and Sun Chi-Ho would be starving from our day of filming at the beach. *They* hadn't spent their break slacking off and eating fudgy chocolate cookies half the size and shape of a CD case. They would have every right to be angry with me if I made them wait to eat. And the managers... well, I didn't need a lot of imagination to picture that one.

I nervously checked my watch again. Leyla had been pushing the speed limit the entire time, so maybe I wouldn't be too late....

"Leyla?"

"Yes?"

"When did you come to California?"

She was quiet for a second. "Early evening, the first of June. Why?"

I pounded the leg of my ocean-blue jeans. "I *knew* it! That was when we came! When we met last night, you said it was your first real day... and it was mine, too, so I've been wondering."

Leyla actually looked across at me then, eyes wide. "Really? Are you sure?"

"Yes. I think you and I have more in common than we might think."

She let out an incredulous half-sigh, half-laugh.

"Tell me about yourself, Leyla."

"Me? There's nothing interesting about me! There's nothing to tell!"

"Mmm. I don't think so. So mysterious...."

"There's nothing exciting about my life," Leyla said. "I mean, you've already seen where I live."

I couldn't hide my self-satisfied smile as I looked out at the sun setting between the buildings, fiery orange. "Thanks to my detective skills."

"Some people would call that stalking."

I thought for a second. "Well, *you've* basically assaulted me. Twice."

"Let's call it even."

I noticed a package of some kind of candy in the cupholder and picked it up, curious. "What's this?"

"You have a snooping problem," she said.

"You have a crashing on people problem," I replied instantly, setting the candy back where it was and smiling to myself.

"Are you going to hold that against me for the rest of my life?" Leyla cried indignantly.

I started laughing, but was cut off by the sound of my own phone ringing. I was officially one minute late, and the texts and calls started rolling in.

I took and answered them all, apologizing, meek and guilty. First Seojung, texting me incessantly. Then Manager Son, wondering where I was (with a lot of extra words thrown in that made me glad Leyla couldn't understand Korean). At five minutes, I got a call from Tae-X, even though I'd already told both Manager Son and Seojung when I was supposed to arrive.

Before I knew it we were pulling up to the hotel. I jumped out of the car and then bent down next to the open window, looking across at Leyla and then holding my phone out to her. "Oh! Quick, give me your phone number!"

"What?" she said, panicked. "You're already late! Just go!"

"Your phone number!"

Leyla looked helplessly from me to the hotel door, obviously realizing that I wasn't going to leave until I'd gotten it. Then she hastily took the phone and typed it in, handing it back. "Hurry!"

"See you later," I said cheerfully, then sprinted inside.

I ran to the conference room, ten minutes overdue.

I paused before the door. My stomach felt like I'd swallowed lead. I took a deep breath and then opened the door, striding in.

It was like my worst nightmare of being late; there was no one there. I turned my back on the empty room and sprinted to an elevator, punching in the floor number. The ride up to the room was twenty seconds of torture. And then I sprinted down the hallway to our rooms.

I didn't even bother knocking. I flung open the door to Seojung's and Laon's room, being faced with staff members, cameras, Manager Son and the rest of Tr3sure.

There was a table in the room all set with food. Tae-X, Sun Chi-Ho, Seojung and Laon were sitting around it, staring at me with a mix of accusation and worry. Seojung's dark eyes looked like they were burning with fury. Sun Chi-Ho was looking glumly at the untouched food with a hand on his stomach.

"Jongjin," seethed Manager Son, while the camera people suddenly found something to do fiddling with the equipment that they'd already had an extra ten minutes to set up.

I immediately switched to Korean. "I am so sorry, sir. I apologize to everyone here for having to wait for me. It will not happen again and I will be more careful in the future," I said formally, bowing low, though my heart pounded.

The anger in Manager Son's expression melted into worry and stress, the line in his forehead deepening. "OK, OK, apology accepted. Hurry up!"

I quickly sat down, not taking off my shoes. Seojung gave me a pointed glance but I pretended not to see it. I had just remembered how stained my socks were with mud.

"Remember the script, everyone!" Manager Son called, and then they started filming.

My gaze raked across the table in a single second, taking in all the food there that I hadn't fully noticed before; it was Korean takeout.

"This looks amazing!" Seojung cried cheerfully, a rapid change from his expression just moments before.

"I'm so hungry!" groaned Sun Chi-Ho.

"Here!" said Laon, serving him some cold rice while Seojung cut the beef that had been keeping warm on a burner.

We all went through the motions, like we were supposed to. The worst part was watching them all eat politely and happily when I could tell they were starving—or watching them pretend to blow on the food that wasn't hot anymore because it had arrived right on schedule ten minutes ago, unlike me. I didn't even have the chance to thoroughly apologize or explain to the other members because we were so busy acting like nothing had happened. I smiled widely, playing the perfect Jongjin I was supposed to be, saying all my lines, while sipping the lukewarm soup that was my fault.

레일라
LEYLA
11

I fell asleep that night with my phone on the bedside dresser, waiting for Jongjin to text and worrying about him being in trouble. He didn't text at all.

Like the previous mornings, I was woken up by bright, warm sunlight shining in my face. I stretched sleepily, my brain searching for that very-important-thing I was supposed to be thinking about. Then it hit me: Jongjin.

I sat up in bed quickly, throwing off my mint-green comforter and picking up my phone.

No notifications. Jongjin hadn't texted.

I set it back on the bedside dresser and crossed my legs, running a hand through my messy hair and then opening my little window to let the warm breeze in. I couldn't help smiling. It was a perfect summer morning and I was *waiting for a text from Jongjin*. My crush of two years. The person I thought I'd never meet. Jongjin, main vocalist of Tr3sure, had literally shown up on my driveway.

I got out of bed and actually spun around with happiness, smiling until my face hurt. I'd run away, but he'd found me. On such a beautiful day with the sun streaming through my window it seemed like his stated reasons for finding me were a little weak—just to jump on my trampoline? Yesterday I'd shut myself down but now it was like my hope broke through: Did he like me just as much as I liked him? Things we'd said to each other were running through my mind, making me almost giddy.

Who's your favorite?

Why, you are, of course.

I was so energized with happiness that I got dressed and headed outside, going for a run. The air felt moist on my skin and the palm trees rustled high above me as my sneakers pounded the sidewalk. Around me, people were leaving for work or school, and more were walking their dogs or pushing strollers. I waved and grinned at everyone with a kind of inner, inextinguishable glow that I hadn't felt in a long time. Some of them looked surprised, which just made me laugh.

Dad was just coming out the front door in his work outfit when I got back. I slowed, out of breath and still smiling, and he looked a bit taken aback to see my expression.

"Good morning," he said. "I was wondering where you were."

"Oh," I said, panting.

"In the future, you need to tell me where you're going, okay? Even if it's just for a run."

"Ok."

"I have no idea what you're used to doing at your mom's, but here, you can't drive away with random boys."

I was very surprised. Apparently he'd seen Jongjin. "Ok," I said.

Dad nodded and then headed off to work.

Well, that was less eventful than I ever could've suspected. Maybe Amanda had been a complete terror as a teenager. Totally bemused, I headed back upstairs to my room. A text from Carolyn was waiting for me when I got there.

I can't wait to see you on Saturday! It's going to be really fun. 😊 Do you want to come over? We can get ready together.

I couldn't help but like Carolyn, even though I initially hadn't wanted to. Since the first time she'd texted, we'd had a few light conversations about Tr3sure and their songs. It was beyond strange to try and revert back to that pre-first-day-in-California when I'd just been a regular fan. After I'd met Jongjin the first time, it had really hurt to pretend everything was fine, but after yesterday when he'd come over again, it was hard to pretend everything was *normal*. Whatever I'd said, she had been really kind and cheerful, and it was never awkward.

With her, things just went so easily. And she was so excited for Saturday. Making new friends here didn't seem quite as bad if it was Carolyn—it was fun and shallow and distracting and no-commitment. No nasty, tangled feelings and crippling attachments. Nope.

But I still wished I was going back to Michigan before school started. This place wasn't my home and my real friends weren't here. I missed Jackie and Aaron, badly. Lately they were replying to me a bit more frequently, but just when I was feeling like we were back to normal, something would feel wrong and weird again. If I could just go back to Michigan, everything would return to the way it was.

I imagined their shocked, joyous faces if I were to suddenly show up at their houses as a surprise, how tightly I'd hug them both, and the happy image made my eyes fill with tears. I blinked them back.

I replied to Carolyn, trying not to think about Jackie and Aaron right now. **Saturday is going to be fun! I think I'll get ready here though.**

Dad was going to drive me and Amanda had promised she'd find me something from her closet to wear, since I'd brought hardly any clothes with me, so that ruled out the idea of getting ready at Carolyn's house.

I had been lying when I'd said "fun". Actually, the idea of Saturday night made my stomach turn over in anxiety. Not because of Carolyn and the rest of them, but because of Milo. I thought it'd been a bad idea before, but after yesterday it seemed like a *terrible* idea. I didn't like Milo, at all. I'd only said yes because of some stupid need to prove myself after that random jerk had said I was rude and ugly.

That memory seemed so far away now, though. Meeting Jongjin that night had swept everything out of my mind. *Rude and ugly isn't a good combination* didn't bother me anymore, now that I'd gotten some distance from the moment and could rationalize it. Not to mention the fact that Jongjin didn't agree with him.

I wished I was going on a date with Jongjin instead of Milo.

I would just go, and get it over with, and then never go out with Milo again. Simple. Or so my brain kept trying to tell my stomach.

☆ ♡ ☆

I was getting ready on Saturday night and Jongjin still hadn't texted *at all*. I was doing my makeup in the bathroom, the phone screen-up on the counter. I'd already changed into the nicest shorts I'd brought to California and a beautiful white jean jacket I'd borrowed from Amanda. She'd also insisted on giving me a hair clip lined with tiny white crystals to match, so I'd pulled my hair away from my face so that it was half-up half-down.

It wasn't like I particularly needed to look great. Maybe it was better if I didn't, since the only reason I was going was to make Carolyn happy.

I was putting on mascara when my phone pinged with a notification. I glanced at it, then gasped and accidentally dropped the brush, getting mascara on the counter as I snatched up the phone.

My heart rate felt like it'd spiked triple-speed.

It's Jongjin. Sup, Leyla.

'Sup'? After waiting like a lunatic for a text, that's all? I blew out a breath of disappointment, a knot of nerves still in my stomach. I typed back.

Nothing much. I can't talk very long because I'm going out soon.

I bit my lip, trying to think of something interesting and funny to add, but my mind had blanked. He was going to think I was super boring.

My heart rate jumped again as a little typing icon appeared. I stared at it like it was going to explode, almost sick with nervous anticipation.

OK.

There was a pause. Then the typing icon appeared again. It took *forever*. Finally, it appeared.

Do you want to meet next week to complete something on the list? Maybe a picnic?

I re-read it about fifteen times. Of course he had a purpose for texting. It wasn't like he just wanted to chat. We weren't necessarily friends, after all. I just had to help him get things done. Or at least that was what I kept insisting to my noncooperative heart.

I'm not busy, I typed. Then I thought for a minute. Jongjin was so well-groomed and well-tailored he stuck out—in the best possible way, of course, but it would still ruin it if someone recognized him for the celebrity heartthrob he was. I couldn't even imagine him having a picnic in the kind of clothes he normally wore. I added, **We should get you clothes that look more normal though.**

I cringed at my wording. Did that sound rude? **I mean, you look more like a celebrity than a normal teenager.**

If you mean hot, then just say so. 😎

I gaped at the screen. Dang it! Where did he learn phrases like that in English? The rogue.

Whatever. 😑 Meet me at St. Vincent DePaul's at 5:00, I said.

It felt like a very long time before his reply appeared.

😊🍉💟⚙️📏😚

I gasped in horror. Emoji spam? A heart? *A kissing face?!*

What the heck did he mean by that?

Was this even him texting me?

"Leyla?" Dad called from downstairs. "Are you almost ready?"

I stared at my wide-eyed expression in the mirror. Was I already late? I stuffed my phone in my pocket, gave my eyelashes a few more frantic sweeps with the mascara brush and then ran downstairs.

"Ready," I said, meeting him at the bottom. My stomach did a few nervous flips, but they weren't the good kind—not the kind Jongjin gave me when he was around.

"So, is *he* going to be there?" Dad asked, obviously trying to play it cool.

He was asking about Jongjin.

"No, he's not going to be there," I said. I looked back down at Jongjin's emoji-spam, then thought of the perfect response. I punched it and hit *Send,* smirking in satisfaction. That would give him something to think about.

종진

JONGJIN
SIX MINUTES PREVIOUS
12

I sat in the van on the way to back to the hotel, my fingers hovering nervously over my phone.

Should I text her now?

I shoved it back into my pocket. No, it was too soon. It would look weird.

But what if it looks like you're ignoring her? What if she's expecting a text?

I whipped it out again. The number I had entered the night I got back to the hotel room was still on my phone, under the label LEYLA SEN.

But what are you going to say?

I groaned, putting my hand over my eyes. This was a lot harder than it looked.

You need some sort of excuse... some reason for you to text her.

"What are you doing?"

I jumped in my seat, the back of my head whacking into Tae-X's mouth, which had been hovering two centimeters away from my ear.

Rapid-fire swearing started pouring from between his fingers as he clutched his mouth, yelling in the seat behind me like he was dying.

I rubbed the back of my head. *"Sorry.* Are you okay?"

"No..." he wheezed, with both hands still on his face. "Who are you texting?"

I blinked; my mouth opened but no sound came out.

Tae-X froze in the car seat behind me, eyes widening. "It's a girl, isn't it?"

I gulped, looking nervously out the window as all of the heads in the van swiveled around to stare at me.

"It's not- it's not, um..." I broke out in a sweat, pressing my hand to my forehead.

"It's totally a girl." Laon nodded seriously, then went back to composing an insanely complicated cadenza on his portable keyboard piano.

Seojung turned to look at me with his dark eyes. "I didn't know about any girl you liked. Is it Kang Ji-Soo?"

"T-the singer?" I stuttered.

Laon reached across the aisle of the van to smack my shoulder.

"You idiot. We collabed with her, where's your brain?"

Tae-X rolled his eyes. "Give us a break Jongie. Just tell us who it is."

I swallowed. "It's—well—remember when I went out that night?"

A second of silence followed this statement as the words sunk in. Then a collective gasp sounded in the van and Tae-X swore softly again. "You mean... you *just met* her? This girl is *American?*"

I nodded slowly.

Silence lasted for a few beats before Sun Chi-Ho laughed, looking a bit impressed. "You can't even go for a walk without being attacked by girls!"

"She didn't attack me!" I said defensively. "I went after her."

They all exchanged very significant eyebrow raises at my reaction.

Seojung however, regarded me with a sad sort of smile on his face. "You know we're going to leave once this is over, right?"

A muscle in my jaw twitched involuntarily. "Yes."

"I don't want you to get hurt, Jongjin, *or* her."

"It's fine," I said with a big smile on my face. "It's not going to end like that. I don't like her." *Just because I'm attracted to her doesn't mean I have a crush on her. Just because I feel a connection with her I've never felt with anyone.*

Seojung's gaze was pinning me to my seat. "Don't you think it would be cruel to have a relationship with her? You're leaving in a month."

"Relax, Seojung," I said, still smiling, though on the inside it felt like someone had just punched me in the stomach. "It's nothing crazy. We're just friends."

Seojung shifted in his chair and sighed. "I'm just saying this better not be another broken heart you've created by flirting with someone just to play them."

Flirting with someone just to play them?

My mouth stung weirdly at the comment and I swallowed hard.

"I'm *not*. I've only met her twice, and I know we're leaving soon." I fought not to let my annoyance and unhappiness show. "It's just, we have something planned and I need to finish it, after that I won't be seeing her."

The excuses poured out of my mouth like melted butter.

Tae-X leaned forward. "So what's your problem then? You've been looking at that phone like it could explode any minute all day."

"Well... I just don't know what to text her."

I didn't feel very confident speaking English, and saying the same flirtatious lines I'd perfected on other people seemed wrong.

Tae-X flashed a grin and hopped into the seat next to me. "You've come to the right person, dude."

"YA! Stay seated!" the driver yelled, but Tae-X ignored him.

I frowned. "Yeah? What should I start with?"

He leaned forward as if to share a juicy secret with me. "What I hear most on the streets is 'Sup?'. It stands for 'What's up.' It's really cool. You'll sound really smooth."

I nodded slowly, savoring the English words on my tongue. "Sup. Yeah, I like that."

Seojung raised his eyebrows.

I typed it in, hesitating only a second before hitting send, my breath hitching in my throat.

Tae-X watched me closely. "Sheesh. Are you okay? Where's your winning smile?" He pasted a big, roguish grin on his face and did an exaggerated wink.

I laughed and shoved him in the arm before my phone erupted with a *ping!*

"She says she's busy today," I said, typing her back and grumbling. "Dumb English keyboard. It takes me forever to text."

My foot tapped nervously against the seat. She wasn't replying. Americans probably didn't text that much different than Koreans, did they?

Invite her to go somewhere.

Of course. I had gotten her number so I could contact her when we'd do my list, not to actually *talk*. She must be getting confused about why I was texting her.

I quickly tapped out another text, biting my lip. Laon and Seojung both looked at me curiously.

"I'll be meeting her on Monday," I announced. Seojung nodded slowly, a slight frown on his face that I tried to ignore.

Ping!

Laon, Tae-X and I all leaned forward to stare at what had popped up on the screen.

I gulped. "New clothes? She doesn't think mine are good enough?"

"No wait!" Tae-X yelled loudly in my ear. "She's saying something else!"

I gaped at the screen. "A celebrity! That's good then. She probably means I don't want to attract any attention."

I started tapping out an "okay" but Tae-X grabbed my arm.

"No, you have to say something better then just 'okay'. That's boring."

"What do you mean?"

Tae-X slumped back into the chair, closing his eyes dramatically. "You must say... 'If you think I'm hot, just say so'."

I frowned at him. "That sounds rude."

"No, no. You've probably said the Korean equivalent before. It's like, indicating that she thinks you look hot in your clothes, but she's trying to avoid saying that specifically because it might embarrass her. So you're basically calling her out on avoiding that, saying that you *know* she thinks you're hot."

"Ooh. I get it. You're good." I poked him on the shoulder lightly. "I wish I had your English skills."

"And make sure to add a cool emoji. I hear Americans add a *lot* more emojis than we do. Like, Emoji Overload."

Seojung glared at us. "Tch! I thought you said you just had to do that project with her, and then you were done? Why are you trying to be all flirty?"

I guiltily ignored him and read off her next text. "She says 'Whatever, meet me at St. Vincent DePaul's at 5:00.' Is she mad? I think I said the wrong thing."

Tae-X snatched the phone from me. "When in doubt...."

"YA! Give that back!" I yelled in a panic, trying to wrench it back from him. "What are you doing?!"

His fingers flew over the tiny keyboard. "Emoji spam."

"Whatever you are doing, STOP. I will *kill* you if you send anything, do you hear me?" I stretched my arm over the seat, wildly grasping for the phone he was holding just beyond my reach.

"Relaaax. I didn't send it."

I breathed out a relieved sigh. "Good."

"*Now* I sent it!" He gave one last tap and handed the phone back to me smugly. My eyes met the screen in horror.

"A *kissing* emoji?" I wheezed. "I hate you...."

Sun Chi-Ho and Seojung both gasped, whipping around to stare at him. "TAE, you didn't actually send her that, did you?" Seojung said.

I nodded, swallowing hard. "He did. You better get out of reach before I kill you, you idiot."

Tae-X scrambled over the seat into the one behind. There was a long pause of almost a minute where we all stared at my unresponsive phone, and then Tae-X gasped. "Dude, look, she's replying!"

My head snapped down to the phone again where three dots loaded on the text bar. I gulped. Tae-X's eyes bugged out of his head. Laon paused his piano concerto and leaned closer. Seojung's mouth was open in anticipation and Sun Chi-Ho was looking across at everybody, his wide-eyed gaze taking in all our faces.

Ping!

A fractured silence filled the van before Tae-X fell back into his chair, shrieking with laughter. Laon's face contorted as he tried not to smile, badly disguising his guffaws into choking coughs.

"What?" Seojung yelled over the laughter. "What did she say?"

"She just sent... she sent me a gorilla emoji." I let my phone drop into my lap. "What does *that* mean?"

"Huh." Seojung's eyes widened a bit, and then his elegant brows dropped in a frown. "Huh. I don't know."

"What's that supposed to mean?" I cried out again in frustration.

"Well, you did send her a kissing emoji," Tae-X said reasonably. "Maybe it means she thinks there's more chance for a gorilla than for you."

"*I* DIDN'T SEND THAT, *YOU* DID!" I yelled at him.

"Quiet down!" the driver yelled. "If you boys don't shut up, I'm going to complain to your manager!"

We all fell silent. I leaned back, letting out a breath as we pulled into the hotel parking lot. I was going to meet Leyla again on Monday, and that's all that mattered.

In the meantime, I refused to let my break go to waste. I would go out—maybe window-shop like a normal person. It was something I couldn't do back in Korea without fearing people taking pictures or approaching me. Better yet, I could do it without covering my face with a mask, hat, or sunglasses.

Manager Son was there to greet us when we parked and got out. He held up two fingers. "You have two hours, boys. After that we need you all back to film you getting ready for bed."

"Yes, Manager Son!"

I checked back into the hotel along with the others, freshened up a bit after the long day and then headed back out.

레일라
LEYLA
13

Dad dropped me off and I walked up to meet Carolyn, Milo, and another couple I didn't know in front of the restaurant. It was a very nice place with an elevated balcony that overlooked a street full of shops—I could just catch a glimpse of it from the entrance. It was upscale without being pretentious.

"Hi!" Carolyn said, beaming at me as I joined them. Milo smiled at me, and I managed a small smile back before looking away. The other couple didn't look too familiar with each other either. The boy was leaning against the palm tree near the door and the girl had her hands clasped in front of her, though it was obvious there was attraction between them; they kept glancing at each other bashfully. A stark difference from Milo and I.

"Well! This is it!" Carolyn nodded towards the door, and we looked at each other before awkwardly sidling in.

The greeter nodded hello, taking in our group. "Table for five?"

"Aaaactually," Carolyn said, drawing out the word. "I'm expecting Theodore— we're triple-dating—so we'd like three tables please."

Milo shot her a surprised look.

The waiter took over, bringing us out to the balcony that was almost all the way filled up. It really was quite pretty out here, and the street below was milling with people. It was the kind of place you could sit in for hours and just watch the world go by. I tore my gaze from the busy street below to the waiter, who had put the menus on two tables right next to each other. The other couple was already at one of the few empty tables on the opposite side of the balcony, and these were the only two tables left.

Carolyn was looking at the menus too. Milo and I would be right next to her and Theodore the entire night.

"Umm. It's really cold out here, how about I eat inside." Carolyn rubbed her arms.

The waiter nodded, plucking up two of the menus again.

I inwardly groaned. It was June in California and the weather was absolutely perfect, with even a soft, warm breeze gently blowing. At least I had to give her some credit for trying so hard.

"Bye guys," Carolyn said, giving me one happy and slightly mischievous expression before heading inside.

"Alright Carolyn, I guess we'll see you later." Milo smiled and touched her arm before she went.

I looked at the familiar gesture with a slight frown as I settled into my seat. Carolyn was already dating Theodore. Maybe Carolyn and Milo had known each other for a long time?

It was painfully awkward once the door shut behind Carolyn, even though we could see where she was sitting through the huge windows. Though Milo and I were surrounded by the conversation and chatter of all the other diners, not to mention the noise from the busy street below, there was a very stiff silence between us.

I cleared my throat.

"So," Milo said.

"So," I said.

It was a stimulating start.

"What are you getting?" said Milo.

"Oh," I said. I picked up the menu. "I'm not sure. Uh, what about you?"

Milo glanced at where Carolyn was inside, sitting alone. "Not sure," he repeated.

That was about it for the heart-to-heart dialogue. I cleared my throat again and put the menu in front of my face.

Carolyn worked so hard to get us like this, I reminded myself. *I'm doing it for Carolyn. It'll be fine after this.*

I scanned the menu, wondering why the prices were so high for what seemed like simple food. It was hard to focus because I kept turning what Carolyn had said about Milo over and over in my head. *He's pretty popular but hardly asks girls out.* He seemed a bit like a slimy player to me; I recognized his type. Still, it puzzled me why he should want to ask me out for this extremely awkward date that he didn't seem very interested in.

The waiter came to take our orders—Milo a steak sandwich and me an Indian-inspired pasta—and Milo gave another stab at conversation.

"So Leyla, tell me a little bit about yourself." To my surprise, he reached over and entwined my fingers with his; I resisted the urge to jerk away.

Come on, give him a chance. Maybe he's just a touchy-feely sort of guy.

"Well, I, uh, like folding origami. And I'm completely obsessed with K-pop."

Something twinged in my chest as I said the usual introduction me and Jackie would use. It practically defined us. *I'm obsessed with K-pop.*

Now I was more than obsessed. I was literally living it. Jongjin flashed across my mind and for a wild second I was tempted to stand up and leave.

Milo raised his eyebrows and nodded. "Origami. Cool. So you fold papers and stuff?"

"Yeah, I... fold paper." His hand on mine was driving me crazy. It was warm and un-sweaty, but it didn't feel quite right touching mine. I forced a smile onto my face, practically twitching with the urge to jerk my hand away. Was it possible to be allergic to someone else's fingers?

At this point the waiter came back with our food and placed them in front of us. With enormous relief I pulled my hand away, fiddling with my fork and plate, glad for the excuse to escape.

Milo thanked the waiter, gazing at Carolyn's table inside, where she'd been joined by Theodore.

I, on the other hand, looked out across the main plaza with people walking by, the lights coming on, the sky just starting to fade into a soft pink as the sun went down. It was so romantic I could just scream.

"Think we should join them?"

I gritted my teeth. "Who?"

"Carolyn."

"Oh, well, I guess that's up to Carolyn and *Theodore*," I enunciated clearly, sipping my water.

"Alright." He looked down, disappointed.

Really? Couldn't you be a bit more obvious? I thought. Why did he ask me out if he was going to keep focusing his attention on Carolyn?

"So... what about you, Milo?" I said, trying to bring the conversation back—trying to make sure at least Carolyn got to enjoy *some* Milo-free time with her boyfriend. "What are your interests?"

He dragged his gaze away quite quickly. Obviously this was a subject he considered interesting. "Oh, well I play football. Middle linebacker, you know."

"I heard you're good at it." Or at least that's what Carolyn said.

Milo looked pleased. "Yeah, I'm definitely good at it. I love my team though. Great bunch of guys. And Tim, who's over there with his girl, is the Offensive Guard. You should've seen us two weeks ago. Man, it was a sick game."

I nodded and tried to look interested, taking a bite of my Indian-inspired pasta. It wasn't very good. The pasta was soggy and flavorless and the "Indian" part tasted like they'd sprinkled a couple spices onto the otherwise bland food. I couldn't believe I'd just blown money on this.

"Even though we lost, those guys from Decker City were so scared of us afterward." He chuckled, and gave a quick look at the table inside. *Again. This is not a coincidence.*

I was starting to burn with anger, my mind replaying him asking me on this date. Why did he do it? What was the point? He was a popular guy who never asked girls out. He certainly didn't like me, and wasn't even faintly interested.

Then it hit me. Milo had cut off a blonde boy midsentence who looked like he might've been about to ask me the same thing. I was the new girl, and Milo had asked me out just because the other boy wanted to. It was a status move—Milo was asserting he could have whatever girl he wanted and everyone else would have to date his leftovers.

I could feel my cheeks heating up. I'd hit upon the real reason—I just knew it. Right at that moment, Milo reached for my hand again, I looked out at the beautiful street below the balcony, and then—

I saw him.

Jongjin, standing in the street below like he was bolted there, looking up at me, pedestrians passing around him.

I stifled a gasp, my eyes fixing on his own narrowed ones as he took in Milo's hand on mine, and still I did not move. We were locked in each other's gazes, in surprise and disbelief. Jongjin's eyes softened as the breeze ruffled his hair ever so slightly, playing with it. He just stood there, motionless with his hands at his sides, as the pink light from the sunset shone off his caramel-espresso hair and bathed his tall, broad figure. He was like a mirage, yet also the only real person in a faceless crowd. The way he was looking at me with a soft intensity, I could tell he felt the same way.

And then the spell was broken as Milo, finally noticing my face, said "What is it...?" and started turning his head to see what I was looking at.

"Right!" I said desperately in a loud voice, willing Milo to look my way again. "Football! Who's the handsomest on the team?"

It worked. The moment's hesitation as Milo took in my words was enough for him to not bother fully looking behind him, where Jongjin was still standing there like a statue, gazing at me with a softness. My heartbeat thudded erratically as I met his eyes one last time, then shook my head almost imperceptibly, trying to mentally tell him to move on. I didn't want Milo to see him—didn't want to cause any trouble. What was he doing here? And what were the chances of two people running into each other in a city as large as this? Of him being *right here, right now?*

Milo smirked at my question, seeming not to notice as I practically jerked my hand from beneath his under the guise of taking another forkful of bland food. "Well, if you're asking me specifically, Chris has always been the dark-haired brute you'd think the girls would fall for, but y'know how it is. When you're on the football team, girls won't stop pursuing you."

Milo leaned back a little in his chair, and I almost laughed at how easy he'd fallen for that ego trip. I nodded and smiled again, glancing over at Jongjin, who hadn't left.

Jongjin's eyes locked with mine and he stared at me for a few seconds, searching. Butterflies erupted in my stomach. I gave him a small smile to let him know I was doing okay, though I felt a stab of despondency that he was *so close* and I was letting him slip by, stuck between a date who was a jerk and a friend who'd put so much effort into tonight.

People kept sidling around Jongjin as he stood there in the street. Finally he gave a stiff nod and kept walking, sticking his hands into the pockets of his dark jean jacket.

Milo's gaze followed mine over to where Jongjin had just been standing. When he turned back to look at me, I gave an assuring smile.

Everything's fine over here! Except for you!

I breathed out a deep breath, equal parts relief and despair pummeling my emotions, as awkward silence hovered over us. Annoyance welled up in me with each passing second. I was so angry at the feeling of being *stuck* here, trying to brave it out so that Carolyn's feelings wouldn't be hurt. I would endure this and then *never* talk to Milo again.

"Good food, huh?" Milo attempted.

"Mhm." I set my fork down forcefully, feeling like something inside me had snapped. "It's *really* good."

Milo blinked in confusion; I must've looked alarming.

"You know, if you like your food... how do you describe it... *Yeoggyeowo*." I gestured animatedly. "You know?"

Milo stared at me blankly. "Yeah...."

Tr3sure had taught me that Korean word for "disgusting". I could feel my cheeks burning hotter and hotter with each second, especially when the silence grew and Milo's gaze wandered to where Carolyn and Theodore were having a great time chatting and holding hands. I was just about to stand up and push my chair back when I heard a voice next to me.

"This is the table you want, sir?" a waitress said, gesturing to the table that Carolyn would've taken next to us.

"That is it. Thank you."

I inhaled a sharp breath as that distinctly familiar, pleasant, sunny, accented voice reached my ears, relief and tangled emotions overwhelming me in a rush. I was almost afraid to look, but my eyes were drawn to him as if by a magnet.

Jongjin stepped closer to the table, dragging a chair so that it was in a better position to face us and sat down in it, not bothering to even glance at the menu. He kicked his feet up and carelessly leaned his arm over the top of the chair like he owned the world, jean jacket splaying open to reveal a light gray tank top and smooth warm-toned skin.

Jongjin smiled at me, flashing extremely white teeth. My date openly gaped at Jongjin, his steak sandwich *and* ego trip forgotten as a flash of insecurity passed by his expression. Jongjin ran a hand through his shiny espresso hair, glancing around lazily and pointedly ignoring Milo, even though his entire body faced us. He was turning his K-pop allure to max setting.

Milo stared unashamedly at Jongjin, taking in his entire body from up to down with jealousy. Jongjin wore shiny dress shoes that reflected the balcony lights, and a pair of fashionably ripped black jeans. He shifted his position a little bit and that was when we could see the flash of a gold zipper that ran up the side-seam, ending at the pocket. Jongjin ran his tongue gently over his bottom lip as he finally picked up the menu and my inner fangirl screamed, though I was transfixed. Jongjin was so unquestionably, flawlessly *hot.*

Jongjin gave a little indecisive huff as he ran his finger down the menu, head cocked in exaggeration. A silence hovered between us, until finally Jongjin let the menu plop down on the table, turning to face us.

"Oh, excuse me." Jongjin looked directly at Milo, his eyes widening in mock concern. "Is that your girlfriend over there?" He pointed at Carolyn in the window, who was now chatting animatedly with Theodore.

"No." Milo gestured weakly between him and me, very surprised.

Jongjin's eyebrows shot up comically high and the single diamond stud in one ear glinted. "Oh, I'm sorry. I think the way you keep staring at that girl shamelessly that you are here with her. Never mind." He turned away from us, picking up his menu and flipping through it, and even though his English was imperfect it made the message no less sharp.

Milo swiveled around to look at me, as if this was some conspiracy. I had to struggle to keep a straight face.

The waiter came over with our bill, hesitating a few seconds as he looked back and forth from the back of Jongjin's head and Milo's eyes burning a hole in it.

"We'll pay for it at the front," Milo snarled, eyes not leaving Jongjin's casually leaned-back figure. He grabbed my hand in a tight grip and took me with him—it was only with total surprise that I let him as he stalked past Jongjin inside.

I wrenched free of his grasp as soon as we were inside. "I think I'll stay here with Carolyn and Theodore, but you can go ahead."

Milo turned around to face me, angry. "That guy was a jerk. Who is he?"

"I don't know." I tried to keep the glee out of my voice.

"He was a stupid liar."

I gave him my most shining smile. "Thanks for the meal!"

Milo finally turned around. I watched as he paid at the front and then purposely stormed past Carolyn and Theodore and out the door.

Carolyn stretched around to look at the door swinging closed and then whipped back to look at me, her eyes wide.

I waved, unable to keep the smile off of my face. It was with reluctance that she turned her attention back to Theodore. I could tell she was going to make me give a full report later, and honestly, I couldn't blame her after *that* spectacle.

I sucked in a happy breath before practically bouncing back to the patio and sitting down at Jongjin's table, where he was in the exact same position.

Jongjin watched me come, amusement splashed across his face. "I thought he would never leave," he said, shaking his head.

I burst into laughter as I scooted my chair closer to his; he swung his legs off the table and leaned toward me.

"What are you doing here?" I asked with delight.

"Well, I had to come. I hear the food is... let me remember..." he waved his hand in mock concentration. *"Yeoggyeowo."*

I giggled in disbelief and embarrassment. "You heard that? How was my pronunciation?"

Jongjin carefully held up a hand and arranged his fingers in a chef's-kiss position, his eyes sparkling. "On-spot."

"Thank goodness," I laughed. "What are you *really* doing here, though?"

Jongjin turned more serious, playing with the edges of the menu. "I had a break, so I decided to look at stores. Then I saw you. I had no idea you would be here."

I was stunned. "What are the chances of us running into each other in a city this big? It's like...."

His warm, melty eyes met mine. When I didn't finish, he asked, "It's like what?"

I swallowed, wondering what he was thinking. I knew what I was thinking. *Like destiny.* And if it wasn't destiny, then what was? Having the lights go out and crashing into your K-pop idol crush?

Jongjin suddenly smiled one of his small, quick smiles, standing up.

"Where are you going?" I asked, surprised.

There was a sparkle in his eye. "Are you hungry? I'll take you to a place less *yeoggyeowo.*"

I looked up at him, unable to hide the big smile on my face, and he offered me his hand to help me up. I took it, surprised and giddy, but then he didn't let go, still gently holding my hand as if I were a princess and he was going to bring it to his lips.

My stomach was doing backflips as I became aware of every centimeter of his palm, his fingers, his skin, touching my own. Jongjin leaned forward and said in a low voice, "I think I'll be your replacement date for tonight."

I was frozen, butterflies going wild in my stomach. He was flirting—of course. He didn't mean it. It was just what he did. It didn't mean anything.

Jongjin let go of my hand and started out of the restaurant. I followed him, feeling intoxicated by our brief moment of close proximity. My hand still tingled; I rubbed it discreetly, trying to clear my head.

Carolyn was oblivious to us leaving. Before I knew it we were out in front, heading towards the street I'd seen Jongjin on, city lights painting the dusky sky. We were just another pair in the crowd of pedestrians, which had slowed down a little as it got dark, though there were still plenty of people around.

"Where are we going?" I asked.

"While I was out looking at shops, there was this little Korean restaurant. It smelled really good."

I couldn't believe it. My first time eating at a Korean restaurant in California and I was going with Jongjin.

The restaurant was a beautiful place with a red-and-blue neon sign, somewhat small, though there was a concrete table with an umbrella out in front. I could tell immediately what had attracted Jongjin here—the scent of warm, savory food was strong on the air. Rich, smoky chiles and caramelized garlic, and something fried— maybe chicken.

Jongjin ordered a lot of food and we waited outside for it, sitting down at the concrete table. The last of the light had faded from the sky, and now *all* the city lights had come on, winking red and pink and blue along with the distant red-and-green traffic lights. I felt soaked to the skin in the magic of it—of sitting here on such a warm, beautiful summer night with someone I liked.

I'd never felt this before. I didn't feel the need to speak, or do anything. It was just the sheer pleasure of being with him, of having him next to me, that felt so right.

There was a comfortable silence for a few minutes, and then Jongjin looked up at me, slight hesitation crinkling the corners of his eyes. "Leyla?"

"Yes?"

"Who was that you were with?"

"Oh." I felt embarrassed; I traced my finger on the patterns in the smooth concrete tabletop to avoid meeting his eyes. "That was Milo. He asked me out, once. I don't know why I said yes. I really didn't want to go. But my friend had helped set it up and I didn't want to hurt her feelings."

Jongjin nodded.

"I don't like him," I said quickly. "At all. I never did."

Jongjin was still silent, just looking at me and listening. I continued on, my face pink. "I didn't want to talk about it before because I didn't want to go in the first place. And as you can see, he turned out to be just as bad as I thought."

"Mhm."

"Thanks for that," I said quietly. "By the way."

Jongjin smiled, his brown eyes warm. "Anytime," he said. "Though, I hope you don't have to see him again. I might have made it worse, on accident."

My stomach tightened with the reminder. "Well, he's Carolyn's friend... I'll try to avoid him. I don't think he'll want anything to do with me after this." I couldn't help a giggle. "You totally roasted him."

A restaurant employee came out of the door bearing a tray of food. She smiled at us and started unloading dishes on the table; translucent, glassy noodles, a heavy stone bowl filled with all different kinds of toppings, and cubed pickled vegetables. She set an extra plate and silverware in front of Jongjin; he took it with a "Thank you" and she went back inside.

"I hope you don't mind splitting this," he said, eyes sparkling.

"That's fine!" I said. I watched in awe as Jongjin took his spoon and dug into the stone bowl, steam clouding the metal surface. The toppings were arranged in a kind of sun pattern around the middle, where there was a fried egg—but there was also kimchi, strips of fresh cucumber, carrot and white radish; soybean sprouts, steamed spinach, and bright red chiles; red-sauced beef, and more. As Jongjin dug his spoon in and served some onto his plate I realized there was steaming sticky rice underneath. At the very bottom the rice was golden brown, forming what looked like a chewy, crispy crust from the hot stone bowl. It was beautiful—the kind of perfectly presented mix of colors, textures and flavors anyone could ever dream of for dinner. Jongjin even split the fried egg in half, letting the deep marigold yolk drip over the rice.

Jongjin also took half of the cubed pickled vegetable and half of the translucently brown, glossy noodles that were ornamented with julienned carrots, slices of mushroom and sesame seeds.

"What are these called?" I asked in wonder as he pushed the stone bowl and the rest of the food over to me. The smell on the pleasant summer-night air was unbelievable.

"Oh," he said, laughing a little. "I thought you'd know. That's" —he pointed to the stone bowl— "bibimbap, and that's" —he gestured to the noodles and cubed vegetables— "japchae and kkakdugi."

I tried the japchae. The noodles were chewy and springy, with the deep savory taste of soy sauce but also with a slight sweetness. The carrots still had a nice bite to them while the sesame seeds added an extra layer of flavor and texture. The kkakdugi was good too—crunchy, fresh radish in a rich, dangerously red spicy-salty umami-bomb sauce. The bibimbap was also just as good as it looked, and the toasted golden chewy-crispy crust on the bottom of the stone bowl was to die for. I hadn't felt particularly hungry before after a few bites of soggy pasta but now I was ravenous.

Both of us didn't even talk; we just ate. Jongjin seemed even hungrier than I did.

"That was good," he sighed, scraping the last remnant of velvety egg yolk off his plate. He looked down at it, seeming to go still. "I shouldn't have done it though."

The sad comment worried me. "Why not?"

Jongjin shrugged, then smiled at me. "Comeback diets."

I didn't like his smile; it made me uneasy. It was like he was faking being happy for my benefit. It was the quickness with which it came and then disappeared.

But why shouldn't he be practiced at it? Hadn't it been his life for how long he'd been training—nine years? The face of the industry was a cheery smile, even while some artists were driven to suicide.

It was stupid of me to think he'd open up. We weren't even friends, were we? He just needed someone to get the list done. After that we would part ways, forever. What I'd originally thought was true—I *would* never get to hear the thoughts, the soul, behind those bronze-brown eyes. Maybe he'd made a mistake in confessing so much to me in the dark at the corner store. I was a fool for thinking things would stay the same between us as when we'd first met.

"What do you usually eat?" I asked tentatively.

"Smoothies, lean protein, and fruit. Not a lot."

I met his eyes, and then my glance flicked to his chest and shoulders, his tall height. He looked like he needed a lot more than smoothies to survive.

Jongjin's gaze seemed to take in my own, lingering on my face a little longer than necessary. I felt my cheeks heat up and hoped I hadn't been staring.

There was an adult couple going into the restaurant with their young son; his loud, happy voice made both me and Jongjin turn to look. His mom looked back at us and grinned as his dad held the door open for them both. The way she was looking at us I could just tell she was thinking *aw, what cute young people falling in love.* A second later the door swung shut behind them.

Jongjin chuckled, a sound lower and deeper in his chest than I was used to. I distractedly smoothed down the stray strands of hair that the breeze had messed up around my face, shy and embarrassed that he had noticed the woman's look too.

"It's nice not being recognized," he said quietly. "I got so used to being famous back in Korea."

I could almost hear the other half of his thoughts. In Korea, someone thinking we were in love would be a problem. It reminded me again just how worlds away we were from each other, and how temporary this was.

Jongjin stood up. I watched him, dismayed. "Do you have to leave already?" I said.

"I'm sorry," he said. "I don't want to get in trouble." Then he smiled a genuine smile. "You make me curious. Is it okay if I text you tomorrow? When I can?"

"Oh," I said. "Sure. Yes." My heartbeat sped up.

"Thank you for eating with me," he said, inclining his head. "Maybe someday we can do it again, in Korea."

Did that have the implications I thought it did? Why was I such a *sucker* for the flirting I knew meant nothing? "Well, you bought it. Thank *you*," I spluttered eloquently. I paused. "And thanks for rescuing me from that jerk."

Jongjin actually grinned at that, eyes sparkling. "Trust me, it was my pleasure."

I watched him go, melting into the mix of darkness, city lights and other passersby. Within a minute he was gone, and I was left by myself, kicking myself for the way I was hopelessly falling for him. It was impossible. And even if he did end up liking me back, there were only twenty days until he was supposed to leave.

Didn't I have enough pain after moving away from my best friends and everyone I knew? I was just setting myself up for more.

Now I could see I had just two choices: Shut away my feelings for Jongjin—who left in less than a month—or let myself be hurt all over again.

종진
JONGJIN
14

I barely got back to the hotel room that night on time and managed to squeeze in six hours of sleep—really good—before Tae-X's alarm went off and woke me up. It was now Sunday, June 11th, the day before our second concert, though that didn't stop us from filming today. The rehearsal and then the concert would be part of the TV show—the end of our long, successful, and flatteringly edited week.

I skipped breakfast. I'd been really good about keeping the diet, until that fateful night of ice cream with Leyla, which had of course been followed by a brownie and now the hometown food we'd eaten last night. Every single time I'd met her I'd eaten food that wasn't JNP-approved. Maybe it was because being with her felt like freedom.

But it was a fleeting freedom. I couldn't keep eating in secret and not pay the consequences.

So I turned down the smoothie, even though my stomach growled. I smiled and laughed and joked so that even Seojung wasn't suspicious, and he was hard to fool.

We were all out on the beach at dawn. I stood on the sand and looked out at the endless horizon, chilly air playing with my hair and bringing some life to my lungs. I would be glad when the makeup artist finished up with Laon and moved on to me, because I looked more exhausted than ever. When I'd woken up this morning and glanced in the mirror, I'd thought of a vampire. My skin was unusually pale and the shadows under my eyes were worse than ever. Maybe if JNP had given us one day to breathe and recover, I would've been better, but after two years of this I was way beyond burned-out. I wasn't even sure I remembered how it felt to be normal.

Leyla made me feel normal....

I sucked in a breath, looking out at the golden sun just breaking over the horizon.

I turned around when I heard the click of a camera. Sun Chi-Ho was next to me, holding his phone, no doubt taking pictures of everything.

"Sorry, I didn't mean to disturb you," he said, eyes wide.

I smiled. "Oh, you didn't!" I said buoyantly. "How are your pictures turning out?"

Sun Chi-Ho looked down at his screen. "I'm not sure yet. I'm trying to figure out how to tell a story in the photo."

"You want me to look at it?"

"Oh, that's okay," he said, looking embarrassed and uncomfortable. "I'll probably show you later."

I laughed. "Ok, then. I look forward to it."

The makeup artist finally made it around to me, and Sun Chi-Ho ran off—ever the little brother of Tr3sure.

Though more distractions continued to pelt at me throughout the busy hours, my thoughts kept returning to one thing. All day there was an internal battle ripping me apart.

After last night, I had to come to grips with my own feelings. About Leyla.

When I'd first spotted her last night on the balcony I couldn't even breathe. Her presence hit me like a sack of bricks. The thing was, it had since the start, every time. Since she'd crashed into me and I'd laid eyes on her beautiful face. Since I'd spotted her walking towards me on the driveway. She made me feel unsure, awkward, self-conscious, embarrassed, *human.*

And then I realized what had happened to me.

The most popular heartthrob member, the famous flirt, the guy who could make girls melt under his charm, was getting a taste of his own medicine.

This wasn't just mere attraction, like I thought it had been. I was completely, hopelessly head-over-heels crushing on her. Starstruck.

This is a problem, I told myself firmly. *You're leaving.*

I remembered the look of pure happiness on her face. Whatever connection we had, it was temporary. I was leaving. Her home was here; mine was over five thousand miles away across the ocean. And I hadn't forgotten what she'd said— "I don't like change." Moving here had been hard for her, so hard that she'd cried that night when we'd first met. If I pursued this path, there was no future for us. How could I ever ask her to uproot her entire life to move to a country where she couldn't even speak the language? As for me, would I be willing to risk nine years of work—nine years of my life stolen by the industry as I fought hard to rise to the top? If people discovered I was dating or married, it would be the end for me—and maybe for Tr3sure too. The same would be true if I quit. Besides the personal consequences, Seojung, Tae-X, Sun Chi-Ho and Laon would suffer.

You can't do this to her. What were you thinking, flirting like that?

My feelings for Leyla were a path I couldn't walk down. I hated the idea of hurting her. And I'd made a commitment to this dream—to Tr3sure. It was better for both of us that we avoided going any deeper.

The filming of the TV show gave me a distraction from the thoughts crashing inside my head. The others seemed happy; today was the day we went shopping for American snacks. The film crew had secured a little gas station close to the ocean and we loaded up on pre-approved items, plus one extra that could be our choice. Laon fell asleep in a corner clutching a bag of cheese-stuffed pretzel crackers, Seojung carefully selected some honey peanuts and Tae-X fell over himself laughing when he found a bag of Sun-Chips. He chased Sun Chi-Ho around with it yelling *"Sun Chi-ps! Sun Chi-ps!"* Even serious Seojung was having a good time. When Laon woke up again he made sure to grab several bags of Sun Chips, cheddar flavored, so we could share them in the parking lot.

I tried not to eat too much, but the taste of the satisfying, salty cheese powder on crispy, slightly sweet chips was overpowering my self-control. Manager Son raised an eyebrow at me from behind the cameras and I got the hint, passing the bag on.

"You look like you gained some weight," he said suspiciously while we were changing locations.

I smiled at him brightly, like I didn't know what he was talking about, but luckily for me his attention was immediately called away and I didn't have to answer.

While my stomach roared with hunger, I slipped a hand into my pocket, fingers finding the List. The folded corners felt a little softened, a little worn, by now. Somehow it made me feel better.

☆ ♡ ☆

We came offstage laughing and drenched in sweat. Underneath our casualness there was a tension and anticipation for our real concert tomorrow night.

It was magical, being on stage. During our rehearsal it was relatively plain, the seats empty except for a few managers half-watching and half sending emails on their phones. Our footsteps echoed, and the decorations were minimal.

But tomorrow night the seats would be transformed into a sea of waving lights, brightly colored sparks would shoot by the stage, and the music would pound loud in our ears, just loud enough to cover the sound of excited, frenzied screaming that rushed through our veins in the form of pure adrenaline. And we were transformed too—the t-shirts and sneakers being swapped for suits glittering with jewelry, our faces and hair styled to absolute perfection. When covered in show makeup, wearing a signature Tr3sure suit dripping with gold and with a mic near my mouth, I felt unstoppable. Invincible. We would be at our finest, all of us in perfect sync, a team who could almost read each other's minds.

But tonight it was just us, determined to do well, toweling sweat off our necks and cracking jokes.

"I'm exhausted!" Sun Chi-Ho said as we walked through the dark, dimly-lit backstage and into the room where we would wait for the managers. Here, it was bright and clean, decorated with only a large table in the center with chairs lining the walls. We'd tossed our bags, phones and wallets into them or on the floor, with Manager Jeon's jacket draped across the table.

"You won't be exhausted tomorrow," Seojung said as Sun Chi-Ho practically fell into a chair. It was true; after concerts we were so buzzed we couldn't fall asleep for hours, instead opting for a celebratory restaurant meal to wind down and recharge. Except Laon, of course. Laon was asleep instantly and we always had to wake him up when we got to the restaurant.

The sound of a door opening made us all look up towards the exit, with Manager Son coming in with a rustle of his leather jacket. He was beaming and holding a pink box in his hands. "Boys! Good job! And we've just gotten a delivery for Jongjin."

"For me?" I said in surprise. I wasn't expecting anything.

Unless... Leyla had sent me something. But how would she know that I would be here right now, instead of at the hotel?

"Oooh!" the other members chorused as Manager Son handed it to me. I accepted it, still surprised, looking down at the label.

I blinked in confusion as I read it. "It's... from Sugar."

"What?"

Sugar was a soloist who had been on a show with us. No one called her by her real name—Dang Seoyeon—because "Sugar" seemed to fit so well with her sweet voice, cute concepts and youthful face. Like us, she hadn't been in the industry for very long, and was only nineteen years old. We'd had fun bantering and chatting after the show, but I hadn't seen her since then.

Tae-X, Laon, and Sun Chi-Ho clustered behind me, trying to see the note stuck to the top of the pink box. I read it aloud.

"'For Jongjin—maybe we can hang out sometime. Good luck! -Sugar.'" I looked up, surprised.

"Ooh, Jongjin," Tae-X said, jabbing me in the shoulder with one finger. "She *likes* you."

"She knew you were going to be rehearsing the night before the show so she sent it here," Laon said. "She must have been thinking a lot about you. It would've taken way less planning to just send it to our hotel."

"Open it, Jongjin!" said Sun Chi-Ho with bright eyes.

I did. It was filled with a fancy fruit selection—just the kind of healthy food we would actually be able to eat while on tour.

"The perks of dating another idol," Laon said. "They understand you."

"But I don't like her back!" I said uncomfortably. "She wants to hang out... I need to find a way to let her down easy. It's not like she's not nice...."

An image of dark eyes, an oval face and light brown skin swum suddenly to my mind. A short, soft girl with glasses and platform sneakers....

Tae-X was looking at me with eyes squinted in observation. "Why is your face turning red?" he said slowly.

"It's not," I said automatically.

"It definitely is," said Sun Chi-Ho. "Isn't it, Uncle Seojung?"

But Seojung wasn't smiling. I met his black eyes, and our gazes locked.

"Laon, Sun Chi-Ho, Tae-X," he said softly without looking away. "Why don't you go back to the stage and tell Manager Jeon we're ready to go."

The three fell silent. Seojung's authority was absolute, and they all listened.

The door clicked shut behind them.

I set the box of fruit quietly on the table between us. He was looking at me severely. After a moment, he spoke.

"Well, you can't say you didn't see this coming, after the way you acted all heart-winning."

So that was what this was about? "I wasn't trying to lead Sugar on," I said, battling to keep my voice neutral and my expression pleasant.

"It doesn't matter what you were trying to do. You flirted. That's a fact."

"You think I can just *turn it off?*" I said, a smile still on my face. "I can't, Seojung. I'm not doing it on purpose."

It was true. I'd been an idol or idol-in-training for so long, it had become part of me. An easy fallback, a glossy façade.

"You're not the one with an identity crisis," Seojung said. "Even Tae-X knows the difference between behavior around fans and behavior around other people."

"It just happens," I said lightly, shrugging, trying not to get angry. *That's what being an idol is about. That's who I am. Who I've been.*

Seojung was quiet for a second, watching his fingertips drag lightly across the surface of the table. Then he spoke, still in that soft voice. "You know what, Jongjin? You know why you keep accidentally breaking so many hearts? It's because to you, flirting is your job, while to other people it's real. You've never liked anyone enough to mean it."

The smile was frozen on my face.

But Seojung wasn't done. "Now you're playing some American girl too. Is that what she's going to be? Just another broken heart left behind?"

"No."

It burst from me without giving me the chance to censor it first, solid and harsh.

Seojung raised an eyebrow. "No?"

I blinked a few times, trying to get myself back under control. "Seojung... I just... It's not like that. She's going to help me complete a list of activities in America before my 20th birthday. I need to take a break sometimes, act... act...." I made a noise in the back of my throat, frustrated, trying to find the right word.

"Normal," I finally squeezed out, feeling a surprising jolt of disgust that I should even have to try to be normal. *Normal* should come naturally. It wasn't a thing you should schedule like a vacation.

"I know, Jongjin," said Seojung gently. "Just try to make sure that she doesn't get hurt in the process. Even if it's fun—you're leaving."

I swallowed, my mouth suddenly dry.

The door swung open and Tae-X, Laon, and Sun Chi-Ho filed in cautiously. Seojung sighed and turned away, picking up his bag.

I picked up my own phone, avoiding their searching glances, grabbing the box of fruit off the table. I felt like chucking it in a garbage can the first chance I got.

You've never liked anyone enough to mean it.

☆ ♡ ☆

The next day, after hours of filming on the beach, we headed back to the hotel to unwind (still on camera) before the concert tonight.

"Uncle Seojung," Sun Chi-Ho said as he took some more photographs on his phone of the passing scenery, "this is an awesome day."

It was off-script, but something the fans would eat up, so no one minded.

"Good!" Seojung laughed. "I think so too. It's not over yet. I can't wait to get some rest and then perform tonight for GOLD."

I smiled along with them, knowing he didn't mean that exactly the way it sounded. When we were onstage it was amazing, but the quiet hours leading up to the concert were filled with nervous anticipation. It didn't matter how many times we'd done it; we always felt the same way.

I wished I could invite Leyla to the concert—bring her backstage, perhaps. She would like that.

No, I reminded myself. *Stop getting too involved. You know you're leaving.* Besides, it was impossible. Bringing a friend or even a parent backstage was more complicated than it looked. It required all sorts of approval and questions. It was far easier to have them in the audience—if you could buy your own tickets before they all sold out. You'd think idols would get free tickets to their own concerts, but that wasn't always the case.

I'd wanted to text Leyla all day yesterday—and now all day today. But my talk with Seojung had only stopped me more.

Even still, I kept picking up the phone, fingering it, putting it in my pocket and taking it back out again, obsessively checking the screen just in case I missed anything. Every time I opened up our chat I had to stop myself. What I'd done—the way I'd acted—that night when we'd accidentally run into each other was enough damage. Every and any happy moment we spent together would just make it worse when I was gone.

You've never liked anyone enough to mean it. Seojung was right. I never had—until now.

I put my phone down on the hotel bedside dresser and threw a hand over my eyes, sighing. I should just try to get some rest.

Ping!

I shot up like I'd been electrocuted, grabbing the phone and nearly dropping it in my haste.

How are you doing?

It *was* Leyla. My heart raced. Well, if she was texting me first, I didn't want to ignore her. That made it okay, right?

Good. Just resting before the concert. What about you?

It still took me forever to type on the non-Korean keyboard. Was this what having a crush felt like? I was slightly sick to my stomach and short of breath, waiting on pins and needles for her message to appear. What had happened to me?

레일라
LEYLA
15

It was another gorgeous California summer morning, and a lazy Sunday to boot, and I didn't know what to feel. Half of me was completely elated and giddy and smitten, and the other half was already mourning the death of something beautiful that couldn't last. I was deep in thought about this, slouched over a bowl of cereal at the kitchen counter, when Amanda came downstairs.

"How'd it go last night?" she said, rooting through the fridge for bakery rejects she'd brought home.

"Mmh." I swallowed some milk. "Part of it was terrible and part of it was *perfect.*"

"How could it be terrible? I saw Milo. He was a hottie. And he looked kind of like a K-pop star. He was a fancy dresser! I thought you'd love for him to be your boyfriend."

I nearly choked. Amanda thought Jongjin was Milo, because Jongjin had come to the bakery trying to figure out where I lived. I coughed. "First of all—I mean—*he*— It's not that I don't—but not—you know—never mind." I slid off the stool, my cereal bowl still half-full.

"What?" said Amanda, confounded, a pained crease on her forehead.

"Talk later!" I said, walking to bring my breakfast upstairs with me. *Once I can get my thoughts together about this mess.*

"Fine," Amanda said, looking offended.

"I'll tell you later, I promise!" I said as I passed by her to the stairs.

"You know, now that you have a real boyfriend you should take down that poster of that boy band guy, otherwise your boyfriend's going to feel second-best," Aurora tossed over her shoulder.

I was so surprised that my grip slackened on my cereal bowl and it smashed to the floor, breaking into shards and spilling milk and cereal everywhere.

Amanda screamed at the noise. She looked at me standing frozen on the spot, covered in milk and with an expression of shock on my face.

"What's wrong with *you?*" she said.

"Uh," I said, hurrying to get some paper towels.

"Are you insane? What the heck is going on?"

At the same time my phone ringtone went off—Jongjin's best part in *Diamond*, his voice all vanilla butter and sunshine. I was completely overwhelmed. I grabbed the phone and answered it just for an escape from Amanda and an end to the chaos without hardly seeing who was calling me.

"Hello?" I said, out of breath.

"Leyla! Hi!" It was Carolyn.

"Hi, Carolyn," I gulped, glancing over at Amanda, who was giving me a death stare.

"Are you going to explain what happened last night?"

"This *really* isn't a good time," I muttered, bending over and sopping up milk with a paper towel in my free hand.

Amanda had thrown her hands up in exasperation at me and marched out. I was relieved to see her go.

"I'll call you back," I whispered to Carolyn. "Or explain over text."

"Wait! I wanted to ask you whether you'd be up for hanging out."

I was surprised. "Oh! Sure."

"Everyone's invited to my house in two days."

"That's... Tuesday the 13th?" I said, throwing the towels in the trash. It sounded like Milo was going to be there. Not good. Or maybe this was my chance to smooth everything out. Not that I had anything to say to him, but a little politeness never hurt. Hopefully it would make it so me and him could actually be in the same place at the same time without glaring and major awkwardness ensuing.

"Yep, Tuesday. Maybe I could play some Tr3sure albums! I'll make lemonade and everything."

"A bribe. I see."

Carolyn laughed. "See you later, then?"

I agreed and hung up.

Luckily Amanda didn't come back, because I still had no idea how I was supposed to explain this, especially without her freaking out. How was I going to break it to her that "Milo" was actually Jongjin, main singer of Tr3sure, whose poster was on my wall?

She was right, though. I should take it down. It wasn't really Jongjin—the real him, anyway. And now that I knew him in real life it was just weird that I should have a poster of him. It was the same reason I'd replaced my phone wallpaper with a photo of green Michigan trees. I should probably replace my phone ringtone too. From the outside, I'd never appeared *less* Tr3sure-crazy than I did right now.

Tr3sure as a band felt different now that I knew Jongjin. I loved it and the members and it was still his group, but it didn't define his identity. He wasn't "Tr3sure Jongjin". He was just Jongjin and Tr3sure was something he did. He would still be Jongjin long after the band had inevitably broken up, ten, twenty or thirty years from now.

I wasn't sure if he felt the same way, though. Being an idol had been his life, and it was obvious he loved to sing. It was his passion and he was incredibly good at it. Where did he envision himself after Tr3sure?

I had so many questions to ask him. He made me burningly curious about even little things.

Amanda had to leave for the bakery, giving an approving sniff at my bare poster-less wall as she passed, and then it was just me and Dad. He didn't seem in a particularly talkative mood, which suited me just fine.

It was a lazy summer day, and I ate a sandwich and watermelon for lunch, went for a stroll in the sun, and tried some new origami pieces that were more complicated than usual. It was hard to get Jongjin out of my head all day. All day I wanted to text him... but didn't know if I should.

He was busy. I didn't want to bother him. And he hadn't texted me, so he must not have meant what he said about texting me tomorrow....

But near evening time the next day, I finally gave in. From what he'd said before, JNP was running him into the ground, and I was getting worried about him. Even just a quick confirmation that he was okay, whenever he found it convenient to answer, would make me feel better.

How are you doing? I said. It was fine, right? Nice and casual.

To my shock, his typing icon appeared right away, almost like he'd been waiting for me to say something.

That's silly, I thought. *Get real, Leyla. He probably just happened to be on his phone.*

Good. Just resting before the concert. What about you?

The concert! I'd completely forgotten about it!

I'm sorry! I shouldn't bother you then. You should rest.
Wait! he typed.

I waited. It took him a while to send his second message. **I'm happy to have a distraction. I always get nervous before concerts. It's the hardest part.**

That was something I'd never known before. I took a breath, stomach full of butterflies. Before I could type out an answer, another message appeared.

What's your favorite dessert?

The odd suddenness of the question made me laugh. Before I knew it we were going back-and-forth, asking each other questions, ones that got increasingly serious. I learned so much about Jongjin and the things he liked—sparkling drinks, ice cream, the Raccoon Café, saxophones, people with a bit of funny attitude, motorcycles, karaoke parties, dogs, songs with difficult high notes, lazy days. He was relentless in learning things about me, and I answered his questions with a hesitant embarrassment. No one had ever expressed such interest in me before. I also learned about his childhood, and he learned about mine; we talked about our parents, past friendships, important moments. I learned that he was very close to his mom and that both of his parents had always been supportive of his career. That had been one of the hardest things about being such a young trainee—the time away from his mom and dad. I told him about how I'd had Jackie and Aaron as my best friends for years, ever since middle school.

And then suddenly, at the end—

I have to go, he said. **We're leaving for the concert! Thanks for talking... I really enjoyed it.**

You'll do amazing, I said. **Good luck!**

I felt a pang. I wished I was there, cheering for him in the audience, not here... though I wouldn't have traded the conversation we'd just had for anything in the world.

☆ ♡ ☆

The next day, on Tuesday, Tr3sure was so busy with their schedule that Jongjin would respond to me at odd times sporadically, sometimes only able to write one text and other times able to sit for an entire fifteen minutes. Even so, it was bliss, and every time I saw a message from him my heart would jump and I would smile. We hadn't discussed what we should do next on the List, but I knew that as soon as he got a decent break, he would tell me.

But something else had also been brewing in the back of my mind, ever since Jongjin and I had run into each other that night:

Jackie and Aaron.

Hey guys! Do you want to video call?

For some reason I had been scared to ask before. Maybe it was their obligatory and lackluster responses to my texts. Maybe it was the fact that they hadn't brought it up either even though I'd been gone for over ten days. But being with Jongjin two nights ago had boosted my courage. I was still riding on the giddy, disbelieving high of him crashing my date and how often we'd texted since then.

I'd enjoyed Jongjin's company so much that night. He'd treated me like we were the best of friends, maybe even more than friends, and we'd talked and laughed together and he *cared.* I could see it in his expression, in his warm eyes. His kindness had reminded me what friendship was. And Jackie and Aaron were my friends. Why shouldn't they want to video call? It could be an entire summer... or more... until I was able to get back to Michigan.

The thought of being stuck here for an entire school year made my stomach twist. I loved Amanda and Dad. Even Carolyn and her friends (minus Milo) were okay, but I just couldn't be content here. I needed to go back.

Jackie and Aaron weren't replying to my text. I turned my phone off and on again to make sure I didn't miss anything, imagining how I would feel when I finally got to see their faces over video.

Ping!

Even though I was expecting the message, it startled me. It was Aaron.

A: a video call would be awesome. not today though. Dad's going on a yard work spree and wants to employ our slavery

My face fell as I read it. It was a perfectly good excuse. *I guess.*

Next was Jackie.

J: Same! I can't do it today! Some other time though!

I breathed hard through my nose as I stared down at it. They were both busy?

~{★ 120 ♥}~

How about tomorrow? I asked.

J: Not sure. Miss you so much and think about you all the time! 🖤

Aaron didn't respond at all.

I threw my phone down upon the couch cushions. Hurt was turning to anger. Did they even *want* to call? It was like they were conspiring not to talk to me. What happened to my "best friends"?

"That's fine," I shouted to the air. "I get the message. Loud and clear."

It didn't seem like they were angry—but they were definitely avoiding me. Something had changed.

I jumped up, channeling all my hurt into fury as I jammed on my sneakers and stalked out the front door, jogging and then starting to run.

So it had changed and no one knew why and that was it, then? They'd just *let go?*

I'd spent almost my entire time here wishing to be back with them, missing them like crazy. Going back to Michigan—going *home*—meant Jackie and Aaron waiting for me at the same comforting school in the same comforting place that we always sat, with their same smiles on their faces. And then everything would go back to being what it was before—maybe better.

But it looked like they'd spent the time hardly thinking about me at all. Did they even miss me? Did they even care?

My shoes pounded the concrete, hard, each strike a satisfying blow that released my pent-up energy, fueling the fury I refused to let leave me. If I stopped being angry, I would break. I couldn't stop being angry—couldn't let myself stop and think and spiral down, down, down.

My thoughts kept spinning around—Jackie and Aaron, Carolyn and Milo, Dad and Amanda. I hadn't told any of them about Jongjin or who he really was. And then there was Jongjin himself. He was going to leave after June was over. Two choices for me: shut my heart away or let it get smashed to a thousand pieces. Each day the consequences mounted—because each day I learned a little bit more about him, liked him a little more, and our unforeseen friendship went a little deeper.

Jongjin had been there for me when I needed him. I could do the same for him.

I pulled out my phone and called Carolyn; she answered almost instantly.

"Carolyn, I *need* you to do something for me. You won't regret it. I promise."

Carolyn's reply was serious; she could tell by my voice just how important this was to me. "What do you want me to do?"

"Throw a party," I said. "I have a friend who *needs* to go to a party."

☆ ♡ ☆

Later that day I went to Carolyn's house for her casual Tuesday hangout where everyone was invited, with the promised lemonade. I thought being around people would make me feel better, not worse. At first it was okay; Carolyn made me explain what had happened that night with Milo, and I just told her that he seemed more interested in hanging out as a group than he was with me, and that I'd run into a "friend" of mine, which made Milo mad.

"Oh!" she said. "And who's the friend I need to throw a party for? Is it the same person?"

Luckily, at that moment, Milo showed up with a few girls and the conversation was thrown off track. I recognized the girls from that first day in the high school parking lot; they were the ones who had looked snotty. I was glad at the excuse not to tell Carolyn about Jongjin yet, but Milo's presence made me nervous.

At first Milo acted normally, like nothing was wrong, so I was relieved, thinking he'd just shaken it off. Still, we didn't directly interact much. Carolyn had carried most of the conversation while we all lounged on the driveway in front of her open garage... but then she went to fetch the lemonade she'd promised.

We were left in awkward silence; the girls didn't seem very interested in conversing with me, but instead trying to catch Milo's attention and show each other things on their phones that they'd laugh at in a quiet, condescending way. I put in my earbuds and fiddled to find a song just for something to do.

"So who was that guy last week?" Milo asked suddenly, almost casually.

I was taken off guard. "Um, he's just..." Panic set in. How was I supposed to answer that?

"I thought you said you didn't know. You lied," he said with a harsh laugh. "You're a double-timer."

"No," I said, taken aback by his rapid-fire switch from friendly to hostile.

Milo crossed his arms over his chest, seeming even taller than usual. I took an automatic step back. "Guess we'll know soon, huh?" he said, his voice abrasive and fake. "You know, if I ever see you and him together again. Then I'll have proof you're lying."

I didn't know what to say to that, but my panic increased. What if he did see us together again? What would he do to Jongjin?

The other girls had stopped showing each other things on their phones. They were listening, but either glaring at me or refusing to look at me at all. For a second I was confused, but then I realized by the way they were casting glances at Milo, they were hating me for taking up Milo's attention. The reason didn't make it feel any better. He was a brute.

"Why do you care, Milo?" I said in exasperation, trying to escape, but his hulking frame was too close in front of me, blocking my path when I tried to step aside. "I told you, he's not—"

"Yeah?" he said. "Then explain why he showed up and took you somewhere? You humiliated me. People don't dump me. I dump them."

"I went on *one date* with you. I don't owe you anything." I ducked my head, adrenaline making me tremble as I tried not to show my fear. I tried again to step past him, but Milo reached out a quick hand and grabbed the string of my earbuds, yanking them out of my ears.

I was unmoving for a second in shock, unbelieving that this scene was even happening, part of my ears now stinging faintly from the force of the plastic being jerked out. I held out my hand, feeling my cheeks burn in humiliation and alarm. "Give them back, Milo," I said calmly.

One of the girls let out a haughty, false laugh.

"Tell you what," he said with a smile that made me want to punch him in the mouth. "You go on another date with me and we pretend that you didn't run off with that sleaze."

"I'm not interested, Milo," I said firmly, my hand still out. "Now please, give me back my earbuds."

The garage door opened loudly behind him, and I saw Carolyn appear. Milo heard the sound without even having to see her and lowered his arm, dropping my earbuds back into my hand.

"You spend too much time in those anyway," he said in a voice low enough so that Carolyn wouldn't hear. "It makes you weird."

My fist closed protectively around my earbuds, my face burning in anger.

Carolyn had just made her way out to the driveway with lemonade. The smile dropped off her face when she took in everyone's expressions with one quick glance. I adjusted my expression to one of calm. I refused to leave now and give Milo the satisfaction of thinking he'd succeeded in bullying me, or these girls either. I was going to stick it out and act like everything was just great.

The next hour passed excruciatingly slowly, even though Milo behaved himself fabulously in front of Carolyn, reverting back to an entirely different person. His warm cheeriness was authentic enough to almost make me doubt whether I'd imagined some of our earlier interaction, but I *knew* what had happened. Milo was just a superb actor. I swallowed my anger and pasted on my own fake smiles, not really present. By the time I collapsed in my bed that night, I was completely exhausted.

종진
JONGJIN
16

Hey, can I call you?

The message sat there while I waited for Leyla's response with my heart in my throat. We'd never called before. It was nine at night, and I was exhausted, but I needed to hear her voice.

My heart pounded like someone was hammering my chest. I leaned against the bathroom counter of the hotel, the door closed to the room for some privacy. Sun Chi-Ho was out visiting "Uncle Seojung" in the next room and Tae-X was trying to get some sleep. He had a pillow over his head when I'd quietly stepped into the bathroom for lack of a better place.

Leyla's message popped up on my screen, simple and brief.

Yes

I took a deep breath and then called her.

It took a second for her to pick up; she sounded breathless. "Hey."

"Hey," I said, and my voice betrayed how tired and weary I was even though I was smiling. *"Geuraeseo...* did you meet Carolyn and her friends yesterday?"

"Oh," she said quietly. "Yeah, that."

I waited. Milo had been there, as she'd told me over text. She sounded okay, but I needed to know.

"I went. Milo was terrible. He kept asking about you and demanded to know who you were. I kept telling him I wasn't interested in him, because that was the thing. He wanted to go on another date—probably trying to prove to himself that *he* dumped *me* and not the other way around. When I tried to ignore him he even yanked my earbuds out."

Cold, hard fury replaced the nervousness in my stomach as my brain slowly caught up to the meaning of all those English sentences. I was stiff, every muscle tensed, though worry for Leyla won out. "Are you okay?"

"It did hurt," she said. "But I'm fine."

"I should go tell him—tell him—"

"You don't have to do anything," she said. "I don't need protecting."

I disagreed, but I didn't say so.

"The most frustrating part for me was that he kept doing all that stuff only when Carolyn was gone—he acted like an angel when she was there. There were a few other girls there, but they glared at me like they were jealous. I can't imagine anyone wanting the attention of that brute."

The words poured out of her like they never would if we were texting. I was so grateful we were calling and I was able to hear her voice.

"Just wait," Leyla muttered when my anger rendered me temporarily mute. "They're only interested in me because I'm new. They'll get bored of me soon."

"That hasn't seemed to have happened yet," I said, cocking my head.

Her voice faltered on the other end. "Well... I just... it's not like a lot of people think I'm good-looking or anything...."

I started pacing in the tiny bathroom, frustrated. She didn't realize how beautiful she was. Every fiber of my body was yearning to tell her, to let it all spill out, every way I'd described her in my head since I'd first laid eyes on her. But I didn't. It would be akin to a love confession. We were supposed to be friends and I was supposed to be leaving. But who was I fooling, really?

"I wouldn't be so sure about that," I said quietly.

It was Leyla's turn to be speechless. I swallowed hard at the sudden silence on the line.

"Hey," I said quietly. "Is there something else bothering you?"

There was a pause.

"Where are you?" she asked, her voice soft.

I looked around me at the generic soap-scented hotel bathroom, not really wanting to answer that.

"Hold on," I said, turning the door handle and stepping outside. "I'll find someplace quiet."

I glanced back at the huddled form of Tae-X sleeping on the bed, then very gently pushed open the hotel door so as not to wake him. Then I was striding down the hallway. Even though I didn't have a plan as to where to go, it was like my brain already knew where it was taking me. Before I knew it I was on an outdoor balcony, several stories up, the lights from the city and the streets stretching before me in the darkness of night. The air was cool, making me glad for my leather jacket. I took a seat in the corner, looking out at the starless sky.

"Here," I mumbled as I zipped up my jacket against the chilly breeze. "I'm somewhere quiet. There's nobody around."

"Oh." Leyla's voice still sounded soft. "Where are you now, then?"

"Outside. Hotel balcony. I can see the city." When she didn't say anything, I continued. "It's beautiful. And it's dark, but full of lights. I wonder if I can see the store where we first met from here."

She made a little "mmh" noise. "I'm in my room. It's also dark. I didn't feel like turning on the light."

I wondered if she was thinking the same thing as I was—it was like the night we first met. Both of us talking when we couldn't see each other, or much around us, for that matter.

"So what is it?" I asked. "What's bothering you?"

Leyla went silent again. But then she spoke, hesitantly. "Did you ever feel like you'd be happy if you just got something, and then discovered that you wouldn't be?"

I closed my eyes as her voice washed over me.

"Yes," I murmured. I thought I would be happy if I could just achieve my dream—if I could just be a K-pop star, and sing for the world, no matter what it cost. But two years into my debut I was finding out that the happiness never came. Each day I reached out a little farther, pushed a little harder, told myself to hold on just one more day, week, month, year. And then I'd finally get it. I'd finally be happy. Or so I repeated over and over.

Leyla was waiting for me to say something. When I first spoke, my voice came out a little hoarse. "I keep telling myself—and everyone else—'what more could I want'? I achieved my dream. I made it. I'm even the most popular in Tr3sure. We're on our first US tour." I smiled sardonically. "But I never feel how I think I'm going to feel. And I'm afraid..." I closed my eyes, struggling with the words. I wanted to admit it to her, but it was so hard.

"Afraid of what?" she asked quietly.

"I'm afraid that I'm doing it again. With the list. If I just complete the list, I'll be happy. But I don't think that's true." The frustration came through my voice; I ran a hand over my hair. "I am. I *am* doing it all over again."

"I envy you," she said, and I could just picture her splayed out over her bed in the dark, beautiful hair across her pillow, looking up at the ceiling as she said the words. "I've spent my life hating change and hiding from it. Sticking to a routine. But you've always run towards it. You want more. You want better. You want different. You audition and appear on shows and make lists."

"But I'm still not happy," I whispered. "I made the list for my escape. I thought if I could just do everything on it before I turned twenty, I could continue with the rest of my life content. I don't think I'm going to be."

It was the hardest thing I'd ever admitted out loud. I ran a hand through my hair again, anxiety tight in my chest as I breathed in a lungful of cool night air.

"I wanted to go back to Michigan," Leyla said. "And back to my friends. I thought that would make me happy. But it's different now. It's... *changed.*" She made a disgusted noise in her throat.

"What happened?"

When she finally answered, she sounded like she was about to cry. "You know my friends. Jackie and Aaron. They said they'd text me when I left and we'd stay friends." Her voice dropped to a whisper, so quiet it was almost inaudible and I had to stay completely still, straining to listen. "They haven't really talked to me. It's like they're avoiding me and I don't know why. Even if I went back to Michigan I don't think it would be the same. And now I feel lost. I don't know what to do."

My chest hurt for her. I wanted to reach out and comfort her, but I couldn't. We were both alone in our own versions of the dark.

"I spent the whole time here telling myself that if I could just leave, I'd be happy again. But I don't think that's true anymore." She was definitely almost crying. I felt so frustrated, so powerless, just like I'd been that night in the corner store.

"I wish I could do something to help," I said in a low voice. "Tell me. Tell me what I can do. Please."

"You already are," she whispered. "You don't have to *do* anything. I know we're so different. But it's like... we understand each other, anyway."

The silence that followed was so vulnerable, so intimate, that I closed my eyes again, overcome.

We did understand each other. Better than anyone else I'd ever met. Once again I knew that I hadn't imagined our connection that night, hadn't made a mistake in finding her again.

Nor had it been a mistake when we'd run into each other by accident. It was like we were meant to be together.

My voice came out hoarse. "Leyla...."

The door to the balcony swung open and I jumped. It was Sun Chi-Ho, the ends of his hair dripping wet from a shower. "Hey!" he chirped. "What are you doing out here? Oh, *wow,* this needs to be in a photograph. It's magical."

Regret lanced through me, almost physically painful.

"I guess someone's here for you," Leyla said quietly in my ear, hearing the disturbance.

I swallowed. "Yeah," I said faintly. "I'm sorry."

"Don't be." She sounded sad. "I guess I'll see you later."

I had barely said goodbye before she hung up. I let my hand holding the phone drop limply to my side, utterly frustrated and filled with emotion.

Sun Chi-Ho was looking at me, noticing my expression. "What is it?" he said.

I forced a smile. "It's nothing."

Sun Chi-Ho didn't quite seem like he believed me, but he glanced down anyway, uncomfortably fiddling with the settings on his phone as he prepared to snap a picture.

"I didn't know you were on a call," he said, avoiding my eyes.

I almost laughed, though in sadness or exasperation I didn't know. He was so young, so innocent.

"Don't worry about it," I said gently. "What kind of pictures are you going to take?"

The excitement lit up in his eyes as he gave me a tentative smile. "I was thinking ones that zoomed in so that the city seemed close up. When the lights blur together it will look really pretty."

"Mmh." I smiled, a real one this time.

There was another moment of silence as Sun Chi-Ho tilted the phone this way and that, trying to find the perfect angle to capture the shot.

"Were you talking to that girl?"

The question took me off guard. It took me a second of deciding whether to tell the truth, but Sun Chi-Ho just cared about me. He deserved to know.

"Yes. Leyla."

"You like her a lot." It was a statement.

I sighed, gripping the balcony railing in my hands and staring out at the starlike horizon, full of spatterings of lights, of movement, everything so small and distant from this far away.

"Yes," I said in a quiet voice. "I do."

"But we're going to leave in two weeks!"

I ruffled his hair. "I know," I said, swallowing the lump in my throat. "I know."

I went inside. Sun Chi-Ho didn't try to call after me, and I appreciated it. I sucked in a huge breath, needing to be alone.

The hotel was almost too warm and stale after the fresh coolness of out there, and the yellow lights overhead artificial and stifling. As soon as I had taken just a few steps, Seojung was right there down the hall, leaning sideways to see me.

"Bed," he called. "We've got a concert tomorrow."

"You want me to tell Sun Chi-Ho?"

Seojung looked around, to the side and behind him, as if he'd lost something. "Isn't he already in your room? Where'd he go?"

"I'll get him," I said, and headed back towards the balcony. I opened the door, but Sun Chi-Ho was already coming inside, bringing a gust of cool, chilly air with him.

As the door swung shut, I savored that last taste of freedom. I needed more than just a list for the rest of my life.

레일라
LEYLA
17

Jongjin's next break was on June 17th, one that lasted two hours before he had to go back to film games for the reality show. We arranged to meet at the St. Vincent DePaul thrift store to get him some clothes that weren't designer and didn't have a price in the triple-digits—hopefully he could blend in a little better when we went out.

He also needed something he could swim in. When I'd asked Carolyn to throw a party, she'd responded admirably, inviting practically everyone she knew to a pool party in her backyard (best of all, Milo couldn't make it). It was just the kind of party Jongjin needed—and Carolyn didn't even know who my "friend" was yet. Considering that we'd met because of the Tr3sure stickers on my water bottle, I should probably tell her the truth of who he was before he showed up on her doorstep and gave her a massive heart attack.

I waited for him outside the thrift store on the cracked sidewalk at two in the afternoon, glancing up at the too-bright pale blue sky and palm trees as the sun beat down on the concrete. Since he was using a cab, almost any car could be his. Every time one passed by I felt my heart flutter, and every time one slowed down in the parking lot I felt almost sick with the anticipation. I tried to appear nonchalant as I waited, strolling a bit back and forth, checking my phone (but not too much in case he happened to see me and I looked desperate) and glancing around at the scenery and cloudless sky.

Since our phone call, I'd realized a lot of things, and they were running through my mind now on endless repeat. *We understand each other.* I thought Jackie and Aaron had understood me. I thought that was what friendship was.

But somehow with Jongjin it had gone far deeper. I'd told him things I'd never told anyone—maybe even myself. I'd seen the same insecurities, the same fears, reflected in him, even though we were different.

And I was only more attracted to him, yet not in the light, surface-level way I had been initially. The "Jongjin" I'd had a crush on since Tr3sure's debut was almost a different person altogether than the one I knew now. I'd gone so much deeper and better with the real Jongjin that they were almost like separate personalities in my mind. But even with the "real" Jongjin... I was more than just attracted to his handsome face, quick smiles, buoyant laughs and sparkling eyes, more than just his soothing vanilla-butter voice and jokes and kindness.

I was attracted to his frustration and anger, to his fears and vulnerabilities, to the tears I had never yet seen fall. It was like my soul cried out for his. I longed to hear everything about him, the good and the bad, wanted to see him happy and tired, hungry and sad, hopeful and touched, annoyed and embarrassed.

I was falling in love with him.

As I stood there on the sidewalk under the burning blue sky waiting for him, my thoughts made me feel exposed and vulnerable. My heart had been cracked wide open, just waiting for it to be crushed.

Because, inevitably, it would be crushed.

He was leaving. The truth made me want to scream at the sky, to collapse into a ball. Even if he felt the same way, we were destined for two different continents, across thousands of miles of ocean. His days were my nights, and while he was on stage, bowing to a sea of waving lights and screaming fans, I would be curled up alone by the window with a cup of coffee. Where he would be smiling on interviews, I would be looking up at the stars knowing we were never seeing them at the same time.

I might watch the interview later. Look at his smile. Know that it was fake, a façade, and underneath it lay the most beautiful sadness and search for happiness.

We were both the same in that way. But how did you tell someone that you think you've found what you've been looking for, and it's him?

I could already feel myself shutting my heart away.

The depth, the vulnerability, the falling for him—it had to stop. I'd brush off his flirting comments, I wouldn't confide in him no matter *how* desperate or lonely I was, and I'd put myself behind a wall where he couldn't reach me. I'd already been separated from people I cared about once, and they'd already let me go. I never wanted to feel that kind of hurt again.

I *would* never feel that kind of hurt again.

That's what I kept repeating to myself as I walked up and down the sidewalk. I cared about Jongjin in a way that was already shattering me. It had to stop. There was no future for us.

That was when his car pulled up.

Even the way he got out of the car was hot. Elegantly, smoothly. My mouth felt dry and my heart pounded uncomfortably in the long moment before our gazes connected, even though it lasted only a second. Jongjin's face broke out in a delighted smile that lit up his expression as he approached me.

And then all of a sudden, like the first time he'd come to my driveway, he was right in front of me. His tall, towering form was dressed in black jeans and a fitted black dress shirt with the sleeves rolled up, the highlights in his caramel-espresso hair were glinting in the sun, and there was a sparkle in his eye just as bright as the single earring he wore. All of it was fairly casual, yet on him somehow business-sharp; maybe it was his favorite dress shoes that tipped him over the edge.

"Hi, Leyla," he said with a smile, but there was something different in the way he said my name. A warmth—a quiet intimacy—that wasn't there before.

It was like a shot of pure adrenaline and butterflies. With two words he managed to totally melt all the walls I wanted up.

"Hi," I muttered, struggling to emotionally close myself off again, my smile vanishing.

There was a ripe pause, and in the brief moment where I glanced at his bronze eyes, everything we'd said to each other that night on the phone passed between us. I was the first to look away as my heart felt like it had just been bruised, deliberately ending the closeness.

I looked back down at the sidewalk, at the crack separating our shoes. It was a line drawn between us.

I was just trying to reinforce that line mentally when Jongjin literally stepped over it. He didn't seem to notice it. Or care.

"Are you okay? Come on, let's go inside, you look hot," he said, sounding concerned.

This was going to be hard.

"So, since Carolyn is throwing a pool party, you obviously need something to swim in," I said as we stepped into the blast of air conditioning and smell of old furniture. It was back to business. We were just friends on a mission, nothing more.

I looked around for the right clothing section; the store was relatively small. There were glass cases full of watches and jewelry, racks of women's clothes, and furniture scattered throughout the big room. At the very back there were shelves full of books and movies, and racks of men's clothes.

I turned my head back to Jongjin, suddenly distracted by the fact that I could smell his cologne. Spicy, just like when I'd crashed into him in the freezer aisle. It made me want to wrap my arms around him in a hug and breathe in his irresistible scent, and just hold him—and have him hold me.

But I resisted the impulse, looking him up and down. He raised his eyebrows at me.

"Are those the most *normal* clothes you own?" I asked accusingly.

Jongjin seemed disappointed. He paused and looked down at himself, then said in an injured voice, "Well...."

"You really did try to be casual, didn't you?" I shook my head and couldn't help a laugh. "Do you even *own* sneakers?"

It took him a second too late to respond, even though his answer was "Of course."

"Just for practicing dancing, then?"

"Yes," he admitted. "They won't allow dress shoes in the practice rooms."

"They're the first things that should go," I said as I strode towards the men's clothes.

"No—don't take away my dress shoes! Not the dress shoes!" Jongjin ran after me.

"They make you look too fancy," I insisted as we arrived at the men's shoe section.

"Not the dress shoes," he begged, as we stopped.

"But they're too—"

"Here," he said, taking off his beautiful silver ring and dropping it in my palm. "Hos—" it took him a second to find the right English words "—hostage exchange."

I laughed out loud, unable to help myself, his ring heavy and burning warm in my hands. "I don't know, I might want the earring now too."

Jongjin looked at me sideways. "Anything but the dress shoes."

"Fine," I groaned, still laughing, offering his ring back to him. "Keep the dress shoes, and the ring, if they mean that much to you."

Jongjin took the silver ring from my fingers with great deliberation. "Wow, proposing already." He shook his head.

"What?!" I spluttered. "It's—you—"

"I accept," he said, sliding it onto his finger.

"Stop!" I said, punching him in the shoulder, my face red. How come every time I felt like I had the upper hand he pulled the rug out from under me?

There was a long and tense pause where Jongjin rubbed his shoulder.

"That makes *three* times you've assaulted me, I think," he said.

His teasing was relentless. "Fine," I moaned. "I won't ever try to touch your precious dress shoes again. Can we move on to buying some clothes?"

Jongjin threw back his head and laughed, the sound like a shot of electricity through me. "Okay," he said, still chuckling to himself as we moved to the racks of men's clothes. "So what are we looking for?"

"I'll try to find a t-shirt and jeans while you can look at swimwear."

I bit my lip as he departed to the other side of the aisle while I sorted through some discounted jeans. *Just friends. Nothing more. Don't let your walls be lowered.* So far, it had been going disastrously.

I'd barely had time to gather even one pair of jeans that would fit Jongjin when he came back with a pair of swim trunks and a long-sleeved, light blue water shirt. He held the shirt up to him. "What do you think?"

The light sky-blue brought out the gorgeous brown shades of his eyes and hair wonderfully. I blinked a few times and nodded. "Yes," I said, trying to sound businesslike.

Jongjin whisked the swim trunks off the rack and lifted them up for me to see; they were still brand new with the original tags. "And these. It says they're *fifty dollars* but here they're only four."

"That's the joy of thrift stores," I said. I held a pair of blue jeans up to him; he became very still, but instead of looking down at the jeans he was looking into my face, much longer than necessary. There was a soft intensity in his bronze-brown eyes that melted me.

"What?" I mumbled, dropping my arm holding the jeans.

The corners of Jongjin's mouth curved up slightly, but he didn't look away.

"What is it?" I said again. Suddenly I was intensely frustrated. I needed to push him away, kept trying to, but he wouldn't let me.

I turned away, swallowing hard, and the moment thankfully broke. Relief and disappointment in equal measure rushed through me as Jongjin said cheerfully "Why don't we go look at shirts instead? I have a pair of jeans at the hotel already."

"*Expensive* jeans," I muttered in protest.

Jongjin laughed. "To me they were free."

I groaned and rolled my eyes, following him to the t-shirt section. "Of course."

A lot of the shirts were worn, but others looked new, and a lot of them had logos or events on them that I didn't recognize. We both looked on different sides of the aisle, and every minute or so I would pause and hold a shirt up next to his broad back, trying to imagine him in it.

I tapped him on the shoulder when I found a particularly good one—a basic, soft shirt in a dark green. "How about this one?"

Jongjin stopped looking through the racks and turned around. "It's... very plain," he said with a consternated expression.

I smiled. "That's the point. You're trying to blend in here and not *look* like you're wearing a thousand dollars."

"OK, you win," he said, and then checked his expensive watch. "Oh look, I've got lots of time left. Now let's go look for you."

Alarm shot through me. "What?" I protested. "No way. We're not here for that."

Jongjin shot me a smile that was all mischief as he strode away towards a different section. I raced after him. "Wait—wait!"

There was nothing I could do to stop him besides physically grab his hand and dig in my heels, and I almost did—but I knew I couldn't handle that. Frustrated, I just left to go look at the books, abandoning him as he settled in the women's shirts aisle. As I looked over my shoulder, I saw him watching me with a slight smile on his face.

I went behind a tall bookshelf, out of sight, and stomped my foot in aggravation. "Fine," I muttered quietly to myself. "Go ahead. See how long you last picking out women's clothing by yourself." He was bound to get embarrassed sometime. Probably soon.

I picked up an old Asian cookbook and started flipping through the pages, my eyes skimming over images of soups, dumplings and pickled vegetables without really seeing them. A few minutes passed. I set the book down and peeked around the corner of the bookshelf.

Jongjin was still there, across the room, flicking through all the different shirts with an expression of concentration.

I let out a noise of frustration and looked up at the ceiling for ten long seconds. Obviously he wasn't going to give it up.

종진
JONGJIN
18

Leyla trudged across the store towards me, rolling her eyes and putting up a great show of exasperation and annoyance. I couldn't help a grin. She knew she'd been defeated and was going to moan and groan to cover it up.

"How about this one?" I called as soon as she approached, holding up a mint-green blouse that was silky and light.

"I hate mint-green."

I shook my head. "Tch. I believe you told me it was your favorite color."

Leyla was clearly caught. She started looking through the racks. "You know Carolyn?"

"Changing the subject," I commented.

She ignored me. "Carolyn's a Tr3sure fan."

"I didn't know that."

"So, I've got a problem. How do I break it to her that you're going to attend her party?"

I thought for a second. "Why not call her right now?"

She gaped at me. *"Now?"*

"We can't avoid telling her sometime. Besides, it might be good I'm here."

Leyla bit her lip, thinking. "Okay," she said slowly. "Want to go sit down?"

I agreed, and we quickly found and fell into a pair of overstuffed armchairs huddled up next to each other. It felt good to sit down and rest, especially in a place so soft.

Leyla pulled out her phone and called her friend. I watched her; her whole face was nervous.

"Hi Carolyn," she said. "I, uh, have something to tell you about the friend I'm bringing to the party."

I couldn't hear what Carolyn said, but Leyla nodded. "Yes, um... you already know *of* him. Don't overreact, but... it's Jongjin."

There was a pause, and then Leyla looked over at me. "She doesn't believe me!"

"Give the phone to me," I said, and she handed it over.

"Come on, Carolyn, you have to believe Leyla," I said in Korean, in the exaggerated tone I often used on TV shows.

Dead silence on the other end of the line.

"Yeobosseo?" I said. *"Yeobosseo? Yeo*—did you hang up?" I pulled the phone away from my ear to check.

Leyla took it back from me. "No, it's not a prank!" she said, in response to whatever Carolyn said. "But it's top-secret! He just wants to experience what it's like to go to a normal party, and you can't tell *anyone!"*

I leaned over so my voice could be heard, trying to clearly enunciate my English words; it made me realize how comfortable I was talking to Leyla, how my sentences tumbled out with a very thick accent.

"Carolyn, I thank you very much for your party," I said.

Carolyn sounded like she was in shock. "This isn't a prank?"

"It's not," I said.

"You're not a recording?"

I laughed. "No. It's the real me. Byun Jongjin. You knew we were visiting California, right?"

The rest of the conversation was brief but energetic. When Carolyn hung up, Leyla looked across at me with a glowing smile on her face.

"That went great," she said.

I might've been mistaken, but there seemed to be something... *more* behind her eyes. She seemed happy, but it was also mixed with something else—longing, maybe, or regret.

She looked down at her shoes, breaking our eye contact. She'd been doing that a lot today. Avoiding connection. Not wanting to go deeper—or maybe not wanting to have to reject me. I liked her, but did she like me? Before, I'd thought maybe she had, but now... something had changed.

I hid my hurt behind a smile, just like always, but Leyla wasn't even looking at me to see it.

It was just how much it hurt that made me finally realize, finally put into words in my own head what I'd already been feeling:

I loved her.

I *loved* Leyla.

I didn't just like her. I was far, far beyond that point.

"Leyla?" I said.

Her wide-eyed gaze swept up to mine, sensing something different in my voice. "What?" she said, slightly out of breath, but something... tense in her tone.

I just had a feeling that I shouldn't say anything. I swallowed, feeling like there was a lump in my throat, suddenly left with nothing to follow up. I licked my lips nervously.

Instead I said "What does a gorilla emoji mean?"

For a second, she froze—and then she burst out laughing. "That's exactly what I wanted you to wonder."

"So it doesn't mean anything?" I persisted.

Leyla took in my pained expression and laughed even harder. "No, it doesn't. I just wanted to drive you crazy. Did it work?"

"Yes, it worked," I admitted grudgingly.

"I drove you crazy?"

I nodded.

"Hooray! We completed an item!"

"That's not on my list," I said.

"It's on *mine*," she said in an innocent tone.

"Not as enjoyable as going to a party."

She laughed. "How many items have we crossed out so far?"

I pulled it out of my pocket. "Two—eat ice cream and jump on a trampoline. After the party, we'll be halfway done. But eating candy, a picnic, and a movie should not be hard."

종진
JONGJIN
19

I pulled up in a cab to the address that Leyla had given me; the street was cluttered with cars so I assumed it was the right place. It was a nice house, with a green front yard. As I walked up to the door I couldn't help feeling a bit self-conscious. I had already dressed in the shorts and swimshirt that we'd bought, and it clung to my chest and shoulders tighter than I'd predicted. My face, in preparation for swimming, was almost bare—I'd only tried to cover up the shadows underneath my eyes. I didn't have any earrings, any jewelry, or even a watch. It made me feel undressed and vulnerable.

Carolyn answered the door when I rung, instantly recognizable because of her blue-and-blonde hair. She looked like she was holding back a scream, entire face pink.

"Hi!" she whispered, then burst into a fit of giggles.

"Hi," I said. "Nice to meet you."

I extended my hand when she didn't move to let me in. Carolyn took it like it was going to bite her, almost afraid to touch me. We shook hands.

She stared at me some more, then apparently realized that she shouldn't keep me on the doorstep. She gave a start and jumped aside. "Please! Come in!"

"Thank you for having this party," I said as I stepped inside.

"Oh, don't thank me. It was all Leyla's idea."

I was speechless; it took me a second to find my voice. "Leyla did this?"

Carolyn nodded. "Well, I took care of all the details, since it's my house. I wasn't even throwing a party until she brought it up!"

"Oh," I said softly.

"Come on!" Carolyn said, waving me forward.

I took off my shoes and walked to the kitchen, where I could hear many voices and laughter. As I stepped through the doorway the sheer volume and energy of it all hit me, several different conversations, about thirty people. My eyes ignored the details and immediately raked the room, searching for one person.

Leyla was already here. Her brown eyes had met mine in the same moment I'd spotted her, because she'd been looking towards the doorway—looking for me. Even though we were in a crowd of other people, we were connected by our gazes, by the sheer fact that we were waiting for the other person. Electricity shot through me and I suddenly *knew* that she felt the same way about me that I did about her.

It didn't matter what had happened yesterday, or how she seemed to be backing off... protecting herself, almost. At that moment I saw the truth.

I headed straight toward her. Her hair was half-up and half-down and she had sandals with extra-tall soles and a t-shirt that she looked adorable in. She was the glowing embodiment of a real, *normal* summer, all untamed beauty and soul.

"Hi," I said, the adrenaline of her presence rushing through me as I smoothed down the back of my gelled hair self-consciously. I became very aware of my bare, vulnerable state, the imperfection of my more human, less-K-pop-star self.

"Hi," Leyla said shyly, gaze quickly taking in my torso and face. We were both a bit embarrassed. I didn't know what to say.

"Do you like the shirt?" I asked, somewhat jokingly, gesturing down at the light blue, long-sleeved swimshirt we'd bought yesterday.

Leyla nodded, but seemed like she didn't know what to say either, looking away.

Did she think I was less attractive now that I didn't look like the perfectly styled, flawless Byun Jongjin of Tr3sure? I couldn't help worrying. Laon was right—I'd forgotten how to be normal, how to not be an idol.

Everyone headed outside to the pool. I got dragged into conversation with some of Carolyn's male friends; it was nice having no one know who I was and being able to talk to people my age who had chosen all different paths of life like continuing school or college. There was even a Korean-American guy who knew how to speak the language, much to my delight, and we talked and joked around a lot while other people looked on completely bamboozled. Somebody brought an ice chest full of Popsicles, and me and Leyla sat by the pool with our legs dangling. The air smelled like warm grass, chlorine, and sunblock, and I tilted my face up to the sun and heat and closed my eyes. I was savoring this moment, wanted to remember it forever—Leyla next to me, her leg touching mine; the taste of sour-sweet Popsicle on my lips.

Leyla and I sat and talked about anything and everything we hadn't already covered over texting and calling, and I learned even more about her. She seemed to relax, and it was like her distance of yesterday had never happened. While we chatted she took a napkin and folded it into a perfect origami crane.

She held it up to the golden sunlight, inspecting her work. I watched her, enchanted. Her fingers curled around it, ready to crush it.

I caught her hand. "Don't!"

Leyla tossed a glance my way, lips parted. There was such a softness to her bare face that it made me want to take it in my hands and kiss her. I settled for the feeling of my hand on hers, pale and darker skin, my large fingers and her smaller ones.

"I want to keep it," I explained.

Leyla snorted. She uncurled her fingers and I let go of her hand while she gently smoothed out the crane again. "I can make hundreds of these."

"But this one's from today," I said.

For a second her expression was sad. We had both just been reminded that this—that we—couldn't last forever. "Okay," Leyla said quietly, placing the crane into my palms; I received it with both hands, swallowing hard.

I gazed intensely at her eyes, her beautiful face. She was unlike anyone I'd ever met. How many hundreds and thousands of girls had passed me by, a million blurred faces, without me ever feeling for any of them? Because the one I was destined for was in a grocery store during a storm, holding six boxes of butter and running because she was afraid of the dark.

And we were separated by five thousand miles of ocean.

I didn't care. I had to tell her how I felt, give us a chance. As she looked into my eyes I saw the person that I couldn't imagine life without.

I swallowed, already feeling the sorrow of leaving, and reached up a trembling hand. Leyla went completely still, eyes wide, as I slowly grazed her cheek with my fingers. She was so warm, so soft. My hand slid into place until I was cupping the side of her face in my palm tenderly, oh so gently, little finger along her jaw and thumb against her cheek. She sucked in a breath.

When I spoke, my voice came out quiet and clumsy. "Leyla...."

Just then someone jumped in the pool with a loud yell, showering us with water, and the moment was shattered. I pulled my hand away from her face as I was startled and the crane tumbled from my lap into the pool.

I gave a little cry and snatched it up again, but it was ruined. I looked at it with pain.

"Hey," Leyla urged, nudging my shoulder. "Hey. I'll make you another one."

I was being stupid. Like usual. I deliberately turned to face her and smiled, a smile that covered up my real feelings.

"Yes, sure." *It's not just a crane. I love you. I'm already missing you.* But I laughed, as if it were no big deal.

Leyla wouldn't let me go that easily. She looked into my face, a crease between her eyebrows, searching. "Tell me what's wrong," she said.

I shrugged and turned my sparkling smile upon her. "Nothing's wrong. It's an amazing day."

The happy enthusiasm in my voice was almost enough to fool me, but not her. She didn't say anything else, but she stood up and wiped the water that had been splashed onto her face, pushing back sodden strands of hair, and got us two more Popsicles—hers orange again, mine a rainbow. We sat together in contented silence and ate them, the sun beating down hot on us, our legs cooled by the water as we were splashed in droplets and mist by people in the pool. I wanted to tell her the truth about how I felt, but I didn't try again. Leyla of all people deserved a smile.

Carolyn came and summoned Leyla to the house to help with something; they brought out watermelon and nachos. When Leyla got caught up in conversation with the other girls and didn't come back, I dove into the pool.

The water washed over me, shockingly cool and refreshing on my skin, and the sorrow I felt at the moment that had been interrupted between us seemed to sweep away. I would get another chance to declare how I felt. Sometime. I didn't know when it might happen, but it would.

I couldn't remember the last time I'd swam, and it was amazing. I came up for air, throwing my head back so water droplets flicked from the ends of my gel-styled hair, not caring that chlorine was probably off-limits because it was dyed. The rich caramel-espresso brown could do with a little fading.

In one stroke I glided to the edge where Leyla was sitting. She was talking with Carolyn; the sun shone on her tousled, messy hair and she'd knotted her t-shirt over her swimsuit and black shorts. Her legs were crossed and I admired the fact that she looked so comfortable. Where did someone get that kind of peace? The lack of self-consciousness?

For me it haunted my every move. My entire life was carefully crafting how I appeared to others, whether in dance moves or the smiles I didn't always mean. Even when I'd first met Leyla, and she'd started crying in the dark—what had I done to comfort her? I'd performed. Pulling the ice cream out of the freezer dramatically, distracting her, trying to cheer her up.

Leyla never performed. She just lived and felt, spontaneous, true to her feelings. She was everything I wasn't.

I swam right up to her and the other girls chatting on the edge. Leyla looked down at me, raising her eyebrows when I didn't stop looking at her.

"Do you want something?" she asked, aloof.

I laughed buoyantly, reaching up to her. "Take my hand."

There was a brief flash of confusion across her face, but she took it before she could think twice—and I pulled her in.

Leyla screamed as she fell into the water with a huge splash, colliding with my chest. She came up quickly like a furious, spluttering wet cat, skin and hair glossy with water, and I laughed so hard I had a difficult time keeping us both afloat. Leyla wiped water from her eyes and looked at me with such trouble that I quickly let go of her hand and dove towards the edge, hoisting myself out of the water and onto the grass. She was not far behind.

"Byun Jongjin!" she shrieked. She had jumped out of the pool into just the right position to corner me in the yard—the gate was behind her. "If it's normal you want, that's what you're going to get!"

Leyla ran for me but I was too quick, even while I was laughing so hard my stomach hurt. I dodged her, wet bare feet slipping on the grass, while everyone around us yelled and cheered and egged her on. I just barely managed to escape towards the gate, tears of mirth clouding my vision, and she shot after me. I was a fast runner, but fiddling with the latch on the gate had cost me one precious second, and as soon as I'd flung it open and taken a few steps out, she'd wrapped her arms around me from behind.

I was knocked off-balance and tripped; we tumbled in a heap to the grass in the front yard and rolled. The two of us ended up in a dazed sitting position, except Leyla's arms were around my neck and our faces were inches away.

We both froze. I was stunned by her sudden proximity; I could see every eyelash, droplets of water still clinging to them, smell the scent of the popsicle on her orange-stained lips. I couldn't breathe, aware of the weight of her arms still around my neck.

"Hi," she whispered after a second.

Neither of us pulled away.

"Hi," I repeated in a low voice, like her, every nerve electrified. Our breaths came uneven yet in unison as my heart pounded.

I tilted my head, bending forward, savoring our closeness, a mere inch away from her face—her breaths and mine, mingling. I looked into her eyes, lost in those dark pools, and then she was closing them and my lips were pressing against hers, hard and passionate, aching with sweetness. I was kissing her and she was kissing me back, fireworks exploding in my head as my hands instinctively went to her face, clutching it close as her fingers slid through my wet hair.

It felt like forever, yet not long enough. Leyla was kissing me with as much enthusiasm as I was kissing her, but suddenly the gate banged open and we broke apart. Her cheeks were hot and flushed but she smiled at me with giddy bliss.

"Oh, *sorry*," said one of the guys that had opened the gate, and he closed it again. Neither of us looked up, looked away from each other's eyes.

"You won't let me go, will you," Leyla said in a quiet voice.

I shook my head, temporarily unable to find my voice. "No," I agreed softly.

We sat there, breathless and smiling, for another moment.

The gate opened again, and someone called, "Come on, guys—we're going to start poker."

A faint smile was still on both of our faces as we went inside. The rest of the night it was like we were friends, playing games with everyone else and laughing until we cried, having the most fun I'd had since as long as I could remember. People told stories and jokes and ate salty chips and salsa, and I sat across from Leyla, occasionally catching her eye as we both found something funny.

But eventually the glow faded from her eyes and she became more reserved, quiet. She avoided my gaze. I watched her, frustrated and confused. Had I done something wrong? What happened?

I was second-guessing myself as I looked at her across the table. I could tell she could feel the intensity of my gaze burning into her by the way she refused to look up from the table, focusing much more intently than necessary on her cards. Was she upset because I'd kissed her? But she'd kissed me back... hadn't she? Or maybe I'd been too rough. Maybe I'd accidentally hurt her somehow. Yet she'd been happy at first, so that couldn't be it either. What had changed?

레일라
LEYLA
20

We were walking quietly down the dark street, occasionally peppered by streetlamps, the night sky black.

"Thanks for coming today," I said quietly. My house was only a few blocks away, but we were walking slowly, like both of us didn't want this to end.

Jongjin gave a small laugh next to me. "I should thank you. *Gomawo.*" Our arms occasionally brushed as we walked, our clothes still ever-so-slightly damp from the pool. I felt a fuzzy warmth in my stomach.

It was dark—I should be scared, should be jumpy. But all I felt was safety, Jongjin's presence wrapping around me like a cozy blanket. I was completely relaxed, because nothing bad could happen while he was here.

"You didn't have to walk me home, though," I continued quietly. "But I really appreciate it. I'm really glad."

He sounded like he was going to answer, but he suddenly slowed down a bit, squinting into the darkness ahead of us.

For the first time I heard voices, saw shadows move. People were laughing and talking. Three young men passed under the yellow glow of the streetlamp, on the same sidewalk we were, heading towards us.

I stopped.

"Don't be afraid," Jongjin said in a low voice. He started to walk forward again, and I followed, hanging back slightly behind him.

The three young men were going to pass us on the left. Jongjin suddenly gripped my hand and pulled me to his right side, putting himself between me and them. His fingers were strong and tense around mine. I was shocked, but followed his lead instinctively. It was powerful, possessive.

The young men passed us by, hardly paying attention to us, laughing at something.

Jongjin didn't relax his grip on my hand until we were almost half a block away.

"You can let go now," I whispered, my stomach fluttering, every nerve in my hand electrified.

He suddenly stopped, making me stop with him as he turned towards me and looked into my face. Though it was dark, I could still make out his features, the shine in his eyes and on his hair. "Do you want me to?"

"I—" I searched for words. I didn't want him to. But I also couldn't bear the way it was making me feel.

Jongjin took a tiny step towards me, so the tips of our shoes were touching. He tipped his head sideways, a strand of hair sliding in front of his eye. Our faces were suddenly very close.

I wasn't breathing.

"I swore that as long as I'm here, you should never have to be alone in the dark again," he murmured, looking into my eyes.

I swallowed, still no air coming to my lungs.

"I swore you'd never have to cry while I was here. I swore I'd always catch you when you fell."

My eyes had suddenly filled with tears, my volume rising. "But you can't do that all the time, Jongjin! You're not going to be here all the time!" I said, unbearably frustrated.

"That's why I want you to be as good to you as I can," he whispered. "Before I leave."

It was like an invisible wall had been thrown up between us.

"Let go of my hand!" I snapped, tugging, but he didn't let go, his eyes sad. I was lashing out in hurt and he knew it.

"Leyla," he whispered.

"Let go," I said again, without any conviction, and I started to cry.

Jongjin let go of my hand, but it was only to wrap his arms around me in a hug, pulling me to his chest. I clung to him, my face buried in his shoulder, my body shaking as I sobbed. A pathetic sound—but he just held me tighter, rocking me gently as we both stood there, the side of his face resting against my hair.

I didn't want to get hurt again... I didn't want to miss him when he was gone.

But it was already too late for that.

"I don't want you to go," I said. I sniffed so I didn't leave my snot on him, but he didn't seem to care. He didn't pull away.

"I don't want to go either," he said softly. "I love you, Leyla."

I went stiff, the words sounding like they were underwater from the rushing noise in my ears. Had Jongjin really just said that? That he *loved* me?

"No," I said, my fist clutching his shirt, my sobs shocked out of me. I was stunned. "You don't mean that."

"I don't?" Jongjin said, and then suddenly he was bending down, one arm under my knees as he swept me up in a princess carry.

I gasped, hitting his chest with my fist. *"Jongjin!"*

Jongjin wouldn't look down at me as he started to walk again, his face resolute, carrying me home. His hands were burning warm. "I like you so much I'd carry you miles if I had to. I like you so much that when I go back to being an idol in Korea, I won't be able to flirt with anyone else. I've played that part for years, but this is the first time I experienced meaning it. I meant everything I said to you."

I was looking up at his face in shock, my cheeks suddenly prickling.

Jongjin was still looking forward as he carried me, and it seemed like he'd be able to do it the whole way home. It was falling into place for the first time how strong he really *was*. I gave a half-hearted thrash, without really pushing him away, but his muscular arms just tightened around me so he wouldn't drop me.

Jongjin was refusing to look down at me and I realized, stunned, that his eyes were glossy. But his steady voice betrayed nothing as he spoke again.

"And now when a fan asks me to marry them I'm not sure I can bring myself to say yes, even as a joke."

He met my eyes then—his gaze lingered, completely serious. "Because love isn't a casual word to me anymore, and I'm in love with someone else."

I stared back into his bronze-brown eyes, vulnerability threatening to tear my heart apart in that moment. *I love you too,* I wanted to say. But I didn't—I couldn't.

"Most of all, I want you to be happy," Jongjin whispered. "Even when I'm gone."

"That's what I'm afraid of," I said. "I'm afraid you won't be there!"

Jongjin kept walking, not letting me down, not looking into my face. He seemed lost for words.

Always hiding his negative emotions, always pretending he's happy!

"Look at me!" I said, punching him in the chest again, my words cracking. "Stop hiding and look at me!"

Jongjin did look at me, stopping in his tracks. His breath caught as he looked down at me, his eyes still glossy with unshed tears, looked at me with such intense emotion that I forgot how to breathe.

I was the one who broke eye contact now, flushing, my voice thick as I said, "You're always pretending you're okay, you never allow people to see that you're tired or angry or sad. It's okay to not be happy all the time. No one's going to be disappointed in you."

I self-consciously added in a mumble, "Are you going to carry me all the way home, anyway?"

Jongjin gently, carefully, set me down with a tenderness that made me almost sick with butterflies. But I didn't step away from him. We were standing so close together.

"What else do you know about me?" Jongjin said in a quiet voice.

I was so amazed I didn't have an answer. He hadn't shut down—he hadn't shut me out and pasted on a smile.

"I..." It suddenly became hard to focus under his intense gaze, as he looked into my eyes. Slowly, his gaze strayed down to my mouth, then—after an agonizingly long time—back up to my eyes.

Jongjin lifted up a hand, his fingers sliding through my hair and to the nape of my neck. I was breathless, my whole body feeling light and fluttery, skin on fire.

His other hand found mine, coaxing my fingers to entwine with his. The feeling was gentle and sweet and electric, different than when he'd protectively gripped my hand before. My fingers responded, interlocking with his.

Jongjin's gaze drifted down to my lips again, his eyes soft.

I stood on tiptoes and closed the last inches, kissing him. He sucked in a surprised breath against my lips, and then his hand on the back of my neck grew firmer, pulling me closer. My soul ached in the bittersweetness of it. We kissed like it was the last time we would ever do so, and maybe it was.

종진
JONGJIN
21

You idiot.

I slammed my fist against the table again, the sound echoing off the smooth wooden floor and generic walls. Pain shot up my wrist, which I gladly welcomed, taking another swig of lemonade.

Yes, lemonade. Even this stupid hotel couldn't let a guy properly lose his mind. I had escaped our room where Tae-X and Sun Chi-Ho were sleeping and went down to one of the conference rooms, where there was a small coke fridge huddled in the corner. I had reached into it and all that was left was a piece of lint and a lonely lemonade bottle shoved in the very back.

I sat at the head of the empty conference table, fingering the plastic cover on the lemonade bottle and staring dully ahead of me like a drunken man.

Seojung is right. How could you act like that to her? How could you be like that when you KNOW you're going to leave? Of course she was trying to push you away.

I massaged my sore knuckles, wiping the weariness from my eyes. It was 11:45 p.m. now, and although I should've been sleeping, reliving everything that had happened tonight was keeping me awake.

Guilty pleasure of how happy Leyla had looked on the front lawn shot through my veins like the sugar in the lemonade. I gritted my teeth.

Don't you dare feel happy about that, you don't have the right. Of course she had been so distant after our first kiss.

I fumbled in my pocket for the List—it was *always* in my pocket, and I carried it around everywhere, waking or sleeping—and smacked it down on the table. I unfolded it and smoothed it out with a gentleness that was at odds with the rest of my rough, angry conduct tonight.

It was more than just a list of things to complete for me now, to scrabble for some chance of happiness before my twentieth birthday. Every item meant I got to see Leyla.

For a second I had the wild urge to add more items, but it would do nothing. I still only had a number of days left until it was back to Korea.

~~1. Eat ice cream.~~

~~2. Jump on a trampoline.~~

3. Go to a party.

4. Have a picnic.

5. Eat candy.

6. Go see a movie in a theater.

I found a pen from a jar next to the conference room door and crossed out *Go to a party* with slow, deliberate care. Just three items left now—4, 5, and 6. And ten days until I had to leave.

I took another swig of lemonade, the acid burning my throat. Why did she have to be so far away?

The door of the studio creaked open, and I whipped around so fast my neck cricked.

Tae-X entered the room in his fuzzy blue pajama bottoms and ragged white t-shirt, hollow eyes laden with sleep. Silence lingered as he looked from my face to the lemonade bottle.

"What are you doing up, man?" he said in a raspy whisper.

I scrubbed my fist over my eye, not answering.

"You can't drink that stuff," he continued. "We're on that special diet."

"Way to state the obvious..." I mumbled.

He shuffled over to where I sat, pulling up a chair and sinking into it. "Something happened, didn't it?"

I surveyed him gravely.

"I haven't been in this group two years for nothing," he said, grabbing the bottle out of my reach. "Just tell me what's going on."

I clenched my teeth so hard my jaw twinged painfully. "It's that girl. Leyla."

It seemed like everyone in Tr3sure was learning about her one way or another. He nodded for me to keep going, eyes wide.

"She... I... I kissed her."

I could practically feel myself going pale just speaking the words aloud. I ran my fingers through my hair, messing it up, as Tae-X let out a low whistle.

"Are you serious?" he said.

"Twice."

Tae-X shook his head, wild neon-orange hair flopping around as he slouched in his chair. He didn't seem to know what to say as he took in how affected I looked.

Silent seconds passed.

I moaned, putting my head in my hands. "I'm just as bad as Seojung said," I whispered. "I don't want to go back to her, but at the same time I do."

Tae-X let out a breath. "I wasn't there for your and Seojung's conversation."

"He said I was a big flirt who never liked anyone enough to mean it, I was abusing my position as an idol by leading her on, and that even if I actually liked her, we were leaving."

"Ouch," he said, wincing. "He's only half right, though. We're leaving, but I've never seen you act this way around a girl. I mean, it's your job to flirt. Your literal job. But... behind the scenes... I've never seen you act this crazy. Like when you were trying to text her."

"It's like she brings something out in me," I mumbled.

"Have you ever stopped to think this may not be a bad thing?" he grunted. "What do you like about her?"

I stayed silent for a few beats. "What don't I like about her?" I asked hollowly. "She's amazing, Tae. Ever since I saw her that night I left the hotel, I've been utterly starstruck. I've never felt so connected to anyone." I swallowed. "We understand each other. It's like we're meant to be together. But we're *leaving.*"

I made a failed grab for the lemonade in Tae-X's hands, which he held just out of my reach.

"She's gorgeous," I continued glumly. "And she always brushes me off when I try to flirt with her... which honestly makes me want to fight harder to get her attention."

Tae-X smiled. "Ya, that doesn't sound like you are abusing your position. It sounds like you have a major crush on her."

It's more than that. I love her. I sighed and made another grab at the lemonade, but he evaded me again. "She just... I feel like she sees right down to the core of who I am and she likes me anyway."

Tae-X gave a nod and smiled sadly. "I don't think you're wrong, JJ. And I would love to meet the girl that captured this heart." He reached out and tapped a finger lightly on my chest.

"You know I hate it when you call me JJ."

"All I have to say now is, you should still take care of yourself, and don't just throw everything you have worked for away at your own guilt. We all need you here."

I smiled at him. "You idiot. Don't get mushy on me."

He grabbed me in a hug, simultaneously pouring the rest of my lemonade in the trash with his free arm.

"YA! I was going to drink that!" I struggled free.

"No, you were going to bed," he said sternly. "And waking up in the morning to go along with your normal routine. The situation may seem impossible now, but look on it with fresh eyes tomorrow."

We walked back to our hotel room and entered quietly so as not to wake Sun Chi-Ho. As I lay in my bed in the darkness, I slipped a hand into my pocket and rubbed the folded paper creases of the List absentmindedly with my thumb.

I had hardly any time with Leyla left. But I wasn't going to abandon it. Backing out now, suddenly cutting it off to save us both from the pain, was pointless. Now or in a couple days—what was the difference? We were already in way too deep.

When I closed my eyes I could almost imagine her beautiful, oval face inches from mine, standing up on tiptoes the last distance to kiss me. It made my heart feel like it was going to burst with happiness and regret.

And yet... she hadn't claimed she loved me back. The unspoken words seemed to hang in front of me, haunting me, flying around my head.

I let out a stream of breath. It was better for her if she didn't feel the same way I did about her. I'd already done enough damage by kissing her—she was right if she wanted us to stay more like friends. Or maybe she didn't. Maybe everything had just been moving so fast and she just needed more time.

No matter what happened, I would try to make sure she never had to cry, never had to be alone in the dark, just like I'd said. I would be here for her and drink in every single moment.

☆ ♡ ☆

I got a bag of candy, her text read late afternoon a few days later. **Heath bars and a bunch of other delicious ones.** 😊

As usual, my heart jumped to see the message, but I couldn't answer it right away. We were in the rehearsal studio for an American television station whose logo was plastered all over the walls. After doing so many television interviews and appearances in Korea, everything blurred together and I didn't even notice or care what the name was. Manager Son was sitting right next to me, frowning and scrolling through his phone, and Manager Jeon was racing around doing who knew what. Even Manager Yoo, with his clipboard, was here, directing the staff and being the sour-faced authority on the schedule.

The other Tr3sure members were doing a variety of things to entertain themselves while we waited. Tae-X was thrown across a sofa next to the wall, asleep; I myself had nearly been asleep when the buzz of the phone in my pocket had woken me up. Our late night had drained us of stamina, but I was even more exhausted than he was. Every break I raced out to be with Leyla instead of getting some quiet time to relax and breathe, and it was dragging on my energy (and frustrating the makeup artists who had to hide the dark shadows under my eyes). Every second with Leyla was worth it, though.

I discreetly pulled out my phone again and re-read the message, smiling to myself. Kissing hadn't made it awkward to communicate. Clearly she also wanted to enjoy every second we were together, according to what she'd said last night. *I'm afraid you're not going to be there.*

Sweet sorrow welled up in me and I closed my eyes for a moment, then stood up. Manager Son looked up at me in surprise. "Where are you going? We're on in half an hour."

"Just outside for a moment," I said. "Bathroom. Stretch my legs."

He nodded, looking back down at his phone.

I headed out—past the rest of the Tr3sure members, past the hallway full of crew members and makeup artists and guards. I finally arrived at a quiet sitting room with a few modern armchairs, and gratefully collapsed into one. Each step had gotten heavier and heavier.

Now that I was alone, I could respond to Leyla; I wouldn't have to hide my smile.

That sounds great, I said. **The only free time I have is tonight, when our work ends at 9. I can probably be anywhere at 9:30. Can we meet then?**

She agreed, and we named a public place somewhere between her house and my hotel. I couldn't believe I got to see her again tonight. I clutched the phone to my chest and leaned back in bliss, closing my eyes with a content smile on my lips.

And then the next thing I knew, someone was shaking me awake and shouting expletives in my ear. *"Jongjin! Where have you been?"*

I was so, so exhausted. My eyes didn't want to open, but they did, unwillingly, because someone was yanking me out of the armchair. I more fully woke up when my knee hit the hard floor. I gasped as whoever was manhandling me also hauled me to my feet, his voice harsh in my ear. "Come on!" he yelled. "We're supposed to be on in one minute!"

It was Manager Son. I followed along as he dragged me down the hallway, dazed and alarmed.

"What's going on?" I mumbled. "How long have I been there?" My free hand, the one Manager Son wasn't gripping onto, clumsily and frantically patted my pockets.

"Where's my phone?" I shouted, digging my heels into the floor and forcing us to stop. "I think I left it!"

"*I* have it," said Manager Son, yanking me down the hallway further. We had both started to run now as I looked sideways at him in confusion. There was something in his voice I couldn't make out, but he refused to meet my eyes in an almost guilty way.

"Manager Son," I said searchingly as he pushed me towards the closed door of the filming room, stopping in front of it and staring intensely at his face and worry lines.

"Go on," he said, not meeting my eyes for more than a moment. "You're on in ten seconds."

I didn't have a choice. I whirled around in frustration and went through the door.

레일라
LEYLA
22

See you at 9:30, the last message read. I couldn't help a huge grin as I looked at it, giddiness shooting through me. I was sitting on the front step of the house, soaking up the glowing sun. I rubbed my arms, nervous excitement tight in my stomach. Even just seeing his name on the screen brought a rush of euphoria. I was falling in love with Jongjin, and he loved me back. The thought filled me with so much energy that I wanted to jump up, laugh, dance. Every time I closed my eyes I was back on Carolyn's front lawn, sitting in the grass and kissing him, my hands in his wet hair.

I slipped my phone in my pocket with an uncontainable smile and stood up to go inside, passing through the narrow hallway with Amanda's neon pink bag hung on the pegs. It'd been one of the first things I'd seen when I'd first set foot in the house. I would be lying if I claimed that I was comfortable here—especially with what a wild time I'd had since I'd arrived—but my feet readily tread the path through the kitchen, past the bar counter and to the tiny living room couch, where I jumped on it, curling myself into a ball.

I breathed out a sigh, wrapping my arms tightly around myself. Everything with Jongjin was so exciting, but so uncertain. It was a good change, but one that had happened so fast. How was it possible to feel so much happiness and so much anxiety at the same time?

I couldn't handle any more change right now. Everything had been a whirling, nonstop blur since I'd arrived here.

Light footsteps padded down the stairs and into the kitchen. I listened as they paused, and then walked over to behind my couch.

"Boy trouble?" said Amanda.

I quickly sat up, smoothing down my hair as she came to join me, flopping down next to me. Since she'd gone to work early this morning, she still smelled like sugar.

"I spotted you from across the room," she said, wagging her finger. "I recognize that body language. It's the fetal position of uncertainty, coupled with a bittersweet smile of infatuation, bliss and worry."

The way she said it, it was like she was advertising cupcake ingredients to a customer. "With just a touch of vanilla," I said.

Amanda picked up a pillow and halfheartedly hit me with it. "I've been in that position myself. So, what's up with your boyfriend Milo?"

It was like a little jolt to my brain. Amanda still didn't know.

"Yeah, um, about that," I said, feeling my cheeks flush hot at the word *boyfriend.* Was Jongjin my boyfriend now? For some reason it hadn't occurred to me.

She swiveled her head to look at me closer, eyes wide. "Are you dating someone else?"

It was time to come clean. I took a deep breath and told her part of the story—in a fragmented way. I started with "the guy" coming to the bakery and her assuming it was Milo, about me and the actual Milo's disastrous date where he'd come swooping to the rescue, about how I thought I loved him and he'd already confessed to me—without mentioning who he really was. Amanda listened patiently, nodding.

I took the biggest breath of all. "And," I said slowly, "this guy... is... Byun Jongjin."

She looked at me blankly. It appeared to take a second to sink in, and then she leapt up like something bit her. "WHAT?!" she shrieked. "WHAT? ARE YOU—you're kidding me, right? What do you mean? It's—he's—"

"The lead singer of Tr3sure. The guy on my poster."

Amanda didn't even have the capacity to breathe. She just stood there gaping at me with an open mouth. Then she cracked up. "NO WAY!" she yelled. "YOU'RE KIDDING ME!"

"Calm down," I urged her, grabbing her hand and dragging her back down onto the sofa, forcing her to sit down. I couldn't help laughing. I tried to say something, but Amanda interrupted me. "DID YOU KISS HIM?!"

I actually put my hand over her mouth, temporarily muffling her. "Shut up!" I whispered frantically. "Did you want Dad to hear?"

"YOU DID! OH, GOSH!" she yelled, bouncing up off the couch again. "WHY DIDN'T YOU TELL ME?"

"Maybe because *this,*" I said in a half-amused, half-exasperated way, but Amanda didn't hear me; she was too busy repeating swear words over and over.

Eventually I got her to calm down enough to explain more, like that night at the bakery when I'd gone to get butter. Amanda kept a hand clapped to her mouth like she was restraining herself, but her eyes were huge and at the part where I crashed into him without knowing who he was, she started jumping up and down.

"NO WAY!" she shouted again, staring at me. "NO—WAY! Well, that explains why you were acting like a lunatic," she added a second later in a very calm, reasonable, matter-of-fact tone.

I cast her a deeply incredulous look. "*I'm* the one who acted like a lunatic?"

Amanda flopped back down onto the sofa again. "Wow," she said, shaking her head. *"Wow."*

"I'm going to see him again tonight," I said. "Late, when he gets off work. He didn't have a break today." I jumped off the couch and went to the bar counter, where I held up a plastic grocery bag full of candy—mostly chocolate—for her to see. "We're going to eat this. It's on his bucket list."

"That's my kind of date."

I smiled. "I'm glad I got to tell you. I'm sorry I didn't before—it felt kind of hard to explain."

Amanda waved a hand. "That's okay. I'm here to support you anyway. That's what sisters are for."

Dad came in the room, looking wary. "What's going on over here? Amanda, why are you yelling?"

"I'm done now," she said brightly. "Leyla likes *a boy.*"

Dad raised his eyebrows. My face went hot.

"He only came to California for a month. He's leaving soon." I took a few short breaths. "I'm really overwhelmed. I don't think I can handle anything else right now."

The conversation seemed to grind to a halt. Dad and Amanda exchanged a look in the silence.

Dread curled in my stomach. I didn't like that look. "What is it?" I said, trying hard to keep the fear out of my voice.

Dad was the one who spoke. "Well... one of Amanda's friends she wants to go to university with this fall found a nice place right by the campus, and they snatched the opportunity."

The room seemed to spin.

"Amanda's moving out next week."

종진
JONGJIN
23

Manager Yoo was waiting for us when the interview was over. My phone, no longer with Manager Son, was in his hands.

He saw me looking at it and glanced down at it himself, turning it over in his fingers like it was an interesting object. I felt my blood pressure rise.

Seojung, Tae-X, Laon and Sun Chi-Ho kept their heads down as they passed by, everyone making their way out of the building and to the vans. I stayed behind, standing in front of Manager Yoo as people moved around us.

"This isn't the first time you've been late," Manager Yoo said in his slightly gravelly voice, when we were the only ones there.

I didn't say anything.

He continued, gaze penetrating me, eyebrow flicking up. "Ever since you asked for time off, you've been... acting out."

I still didn't say anything. Even though my contract didn't forbid me from dating anymore, I thought my relationship with Leyla would be better off as something JNP didn't know. But Manager Yoo had my phone. How much did he know already?

"WELL?"

His shout made me flinch. I watched him as he angrily threw his arm out. "Do you even take this seriously? You're in America. This is one of the biggest opportunities of your career and you're taking it for granted."

"I apologize, sir," I said with composure, bowing my head.

"You've been late or almost late countless times since then! Are you trying to push us?"

"No, sir."

"And then returning to the hotel at hours so early in the morning that no one else is awake! Messing around on your phone and sneaking off before a big interview!"

"I apologize, sir," I said again.

Manager Son appeared hesitantly in the doorway. Manager Yoo looked up at him. "Well?" he snapped.

"The vans are ready, sir," Manager Son said in a subservient, timid voice.

Manager Yoo gestured in my direction. "Take him to the hotel, then. Make sure he doesn't leave. He's going nowhere tonight."

Heat burned my neck. I opened my mouth to protest, but Manager Yoo whipped around, holding up my phone.

"And I'll be keeping this for the time being," he said.

"Manager Yoo," I said, my respectful tone barely restraining the anger and panic in my voice, "I was supposed to be somewhere tonight. At least allow me my phone briefly so I can cancel."

Manager Yoo shook his head, slipping my phone into his pocket. *"You've* done this, not us. Maybe I'll give it back tomorrow, after you've learned your lesson." He shot Manager Son one last look before leaving the room. "Confiscate the other members' phones so he can't use theirs either. Keep him on a tight leash."

Manager Son bobbed his confirmation, shooting a worried glance at me.

I was grinding my jaw so tightly that pain shot through my molars.

"Come on, Jongjin," Manager Son said nervously.

What choice did I have? I didn't have control over my own destiny. I was a pawn in their game, a possession that made money. I was powerless.

I was still wearing a shiny silver Tr3sure dress jacket from the interview. I looked down at it, seized with a sudden rage. I ripped it off and threw it across the room, where it hit the wall. Manager Son watched in wide-eyed alarm.

I was breathing hard; my show of fury only seemed to make it course through my veins even hotter. I was *trapped.* Trapped in a glittering golden cage.

"Jongjin," Manager Son said, swallowing hard, in the kind of cautious, soothing tone used to calm a wild bull. "Jongjin...."

I spun around and gave him a sharp smile. "Of course. I apologize, Manager Son. Let's go."

What I wanted to do was scream. What about Leyla? What would happen to Leyla?

레일라
LEYLA
24

I waited on the curb under the streetlight, watching the darkness beyond. I was clutching the bag of candy I'd brought, alone.

Jongjin was supposed to be here. He said he'd meet me here....

I set the bag of candy aside, then pulled my phone from my pocket. I pressed my lips together and took a deep, shaky breath before I hit *Call.*

The mechanical voice was always the same. *"The number you are trying to reach is either turned off...."*

I waited until the entire message was done, like he would suddenly pick up, even though I knew he wouldn't. I lowered the phone from my ear, dazed.

A car drove by, casting me in its too-bright headlights and slowing down as it went by me. I stood up, adrenaline making my heart pound. It was probably just someone slowing down for courtesy. But I was also alone at night....

It vanished at the end of the street, around the corner of the road. I sunk back to the ground again, the concrete uncomfortably warm on my skin.

My eyes felt sore and puffy from earlier today. The news of Amanda moving out had completely crushed me—was *still* crushing me. It felt like the world was just a spinning, out-of-control car crash and I was a helpless rag doll in the passenger seat. Almost everyone important in my life had either left or was going to leave.

I was so alone.

"I need you," I whispered, the words barely discernable. "I need you, Jongjin."

Where was he? I needed him to hug me, to tell me it was going to be okay. I needed his strong hand in mine that made me feel safe and made my fear of the dark go away.

I needed to know he was okay, too. What had happened? Why wasn't his phone working? Where was he?

It had been half an hour already. I gripped my arms and looked down at the empty road, half-expecting him to come running toward me out of the dark, relieved and out of breath and with his eyes sparkling.

There was no one there. I continued sitting alone, my chest tight with anxiety and loneliness. The bag of candy we should've been sharing was sitting forlorn and out of place on the concrete sidewalk. I reached my hand in and pulled out a candy bar, ripping open the wrapper and stuffing the chocolate in my mouth. It flooded my tongue with sweetness, but it tasted sad. I sat there and ate it until it was gone, wishing more than anything else that Jongjin would come, and then reached in the bag and pulled out another one.

I sat there on the sidewalk for what felt like hours. Waiting. Not knowing what else to do. Not having the energy to do anything else. I hugged my arms around myself and rocked back and forth, the only person around, in a patch of light from the streetlamp but surrounded by darkness.

I picked up my phone and called his number again, the same thing happening. *"The number you are trying to reach...."*

He never came.

레일라
LEYLA
25

At dawn the next morning I gradually drifted into consciousness. My eyes were still closed, and I was snuggled in my warm comforter against the chilly dawn air.

For a second I wondered, vaguely in a half-sleeping state, what had woken me up.

Then I heard a slight scuff of shoes on concrete. My dreamy brain wondered, confused, what or who it could be that was making noise outside.

The only person that ever tended to show up on the driveway was....

The realization hit me and I jerked upright in bed. Just as I strained my ears to test whether I was actually dreaming, the scuffing noises stopped. I looked towards my tiny window, cracked to let in the cool morning air, quizzically—half hoping, half not daring to hope, hardly able to believe it was possible.

And then there was another small noise. I jolted out of the covers and to my window, opening it the rest of the way and scattering all the origami lined up on the windowsill in my haste.

Jongjin, walking back and forth on the driveway, went still as soon as our eyes met. There he was, one story below, in a thick jacket against the cold and his hair messy and tousled, looking up at me.

I didn't even give him the chance to say anything. "I'll be right down," I said, words mumbling and hard to understand through my sleepiness, and I shut the window.

I staggered out of bed and to my closet, grabbing a jean jacket that I clumsily pulled on over my thin t-shirt and shorts, and then went to do a quick check in the bathroom mirror. My eyes were puffy and my hair appropriately looked like I'd just rolled out of bed. I quickly tied it up in a ponytail and then was rushing down the stairs, unlocking the front door.

The concrete was cold on my bare feet as I padded out to meet him. Jongjin looked relieved to see me; I felt the same way as I stopped right in front of him, studying his face.

He'd just waken up to come here too. Though he had on regular clothes and his dress shoes, he didn't have any makeup on. The shadows under his eyes were dark, almost bruised, making him look a little haunted as he smiled. I could see every beautiful human imperfection in his face, every little freckle that was usually hidden beneath. It just made him more real, more handsome, more vulnerable. His hair was still tousled from sleep.

"Hi," he said in a voice that sounded a little scratchier than usual. "I didn't know how to wake you... or if I should...."

"What happened?" I said, clutching the arms of my jean jacket against the cold and crossing my bare legs; I wish I'd thought to throw something warmer on over my shorts. "Why didn't you show up last night?"

"They took away my phone," Jongjin said, pushing a hand up through his hair and making it even messier. His eyes took in my face with an intensity that was almost devouring.

I felt self-conscious and feverish; my gaze drifted out towards the empty and silent street to avoid meeting his eyes. We were the only ones out at dawn.

"I thought it was something like that," I finally managed quietly.

"Leyla."

It forced me to look at him. He was continuing, voice slightly ragged. "I'm so sorry. I didn't know what to do. The thought of you out there, alone, in the dark, waiting for me—"

"It's okay, Jongjin. You couldn't help it."

He gave a small, short laugh that didn't hold a lot of humor. "I feel like I should've... but I didn't know what to do. I don't have your phone number in my memory, but it wouldn't have helped anyway. They took away the other members' phones too so I couldn't use theirs. They even set a guard in front of the door last night."

I stared up at him; he really was so much taller. "What? Are you serious?"

Jongjin nodded. "Otherwise I would've come. I'm so sorry. It was my fault the phone got taken away. I was late one too many times..." He ran his hand through his hair again. I wondered if it was a motion of his that his too-perfect idol persona never did. I'd never seen him do it before.

"When are they going to give your phone back?"

"I don't know. Maybe today. Maybe months from now."

"How are we going to complete the list?" I exclaimed. "How many items do we have left?"

Jongjin stuck a hand in his jacket pocket and pulled out the familiar, worn square of paper that he unfolded. "Three," he said. "A picnic, eating candy, and a movie."

"It's June 25th!" I cried. "We only have five days until you leave! What are we going to do? How are we going to complete them all, especially with you on lockdown?"

"We can't," Jongjin said gently.

"No!" I said, throwing my hands down in frustration. We'd failed at the one thing that was so important to him, the one thing holding him together until his birthday. "We *have* to! You need to get this done before you turn twenty! You need—"

"The list doesn't matter anymore," he whispered, grabbing my hands. "You do."

His smooth, manly fingers were burning warm on mine. I gazed up at his handsome face, surprised, lost for words.

Jongjin's serious eyes met mine, and they were full of a sad softness. "I want to thank you. For everything."

I could feel a lump in my throat, and my eyes stung. "No," I said, trying to control my emotions. "This is too much like goodbye. We're not saying goodbye yet."

Jongjin reached up a hand and gently brushed my cheek with his thumb. I looked up at him with blurry eyes.

He closed the distance between us and wrapped his arms around me in a hug, my face in his shoulder. My fingers clung to his back, and he held me, swaying gently back and forth.

I closed my eyes, smelling his clothes, remembering the feel of his hug and his strong arms holding me tightly to him. He was perfect hugging height. I knew he had to leave, that this hug couldn't last, this moment couldn't last.

"We're not saying goodbye," Jongjin whispered, his breath against my neck. "Today, we'll still be happy."

I nodded, taking calming breaths. We both stood there for a long time, still and motionless, holding each other tightly like we were the only ones left in the world.

Finally he pulled away, gently. "I'm sorry," he said softly. "I have to go."

"It's okay," I murmured. "Thanks for coming to see me, Jongjin."

"We *will* see each other again," he said. "I'll find a way. We'll work something out." He gave a small, quick smile. "Maybe even complete something else on the list after all."

"Whatever you want," I murmured, still feeling warm from his hug.

He gave me one last sad yet happy beautiful smile before turning to go. I watched him walk down the street and to a car he'd called, holding that image in my mind forever—his tallness, messy hair, big jacket, the only person in the scene. It was a familiar figure I realized I wanted to see every day for the rest of my life, no matter what circumstances they were under.

"I love you," I said to his distant figure, the words so quiet they barely moved my lips.

It was only after it had come out of me that I knew. I wasn't just *falling in love* with Jongjin. It was past tense. I had *fallen in love* with him.

I loved Jongjin.

He had just reached the car, looked over his shoulder one last time, and my heart skyrocketed to my throat.

"I LOVE YOU!" I shouted.

Jongjin paused—I was too far away to see his expression—and then I heard a faint laugh as he shouted back the same.

I was flushed with adrenaline, my heartbeat going fast. I watched as he got in the car and was gone, vanishing around a bend.

I clutched my hands to my heart and stood there beneath the orange dawn sky. *Today, we'll still be happy.*

종진
JONGJIN
26

The five of us sat together in the empty van, still with our seat belts on, looking out the windows. We had just parked in front of a garden as the staff set up to film us on one of the last days of the reality show.

The driver had left somewhere several minutes ago, and the five of us had sat there quiet since then—Sun Chi-Ho, Laon and Seojung in the back, me and Tae-X in the front.

"I'm sorry they took away your phones," I sighed.

"Don't mention it," Seojung said crisply.

"I just wish I could take pictures," Sun Chi-Ho said sadly. Tae-X patted his arm, mouth quirking downwards in sympathy.

"They're going to have to give them back sometime, because my latest piano concerto is recorded on mine," Laon said, looking out the window in his characteristic blank-faced way.

The four of them had taken everything so well. I felt a rush of gratitude. They could easily hate me for being the most popular, or causing trouble lately, but they didn't blame me at all.

"It's not fair they took away your phones too, though," I said in a quiet voice. "The only reason they did it is so that I couldn't contact Leyla."

My feelings toward Leyla had already affected their lives. They needed to know.

My chest felt tight and my pulse raced. "Guys... I have something to tell you... about that."

The atmosphere of the van seemed to tense up.

I tried to speak again, but something seemed lodged in my throat. Tae-X nudged me, murmuring in English, "Go ahead, man."

They were nodding. It bolstered my courage.

I took a deep breath. "I'm in love with Leyla."

There was a stunned silence. They all glanced around at each other—and then Tae-X gave a start.

"I don't believe it. He's fallen asleep!" he said, looking at Laon, whose head was lolling gently onto his chest.

"Slap him," said Seojung.

"Yes, Uncle." Sun Chi-Ho leaned forward and slapped Laon in the face with a loud and hard smacking sound.

Laon jerked awake instantly. "Ow! What did I miss?"

Seojung gave a longsuffering sigh and closed his eyes. "Jongjin here has dramatically declared his love for Leyla."

"Oh."

Laon still looked a little dazed; he rubbed his red face where he'd been slapped. "Congratulations."

"Thank you," I said.

Seojung was looking at me. "Don't say it lightly. Do you really—"

"I love her," I said, gazing at him steadily. "I would do anything for her. I want to marry her someday."

"But... Jongie, how...?" Tae-X licked his lips.

"I don't know how it's going to work in the future," I said. I took a deep breath. "Us being so far apart, and with my career. We'll just have to find a way. We mean that much to each other."

"What about the fans?" Sun Chi-Ho said, sounding stunned.

I closed my eyes briefly, struggling. *What about the fans* was the same thing JNP said every time they forced me to do something. It was easy to direct my frustration towards the undefined "fans" because every drop of sweat, every sleepless day, every moment without a break, JNP told me was "for the fans". *What about the fans, Jongjin? It's for the fans, Jongjin.* JNP was the one who was truly trapping me.

"I'm not sure the world is ready for idols to have their cake and eat it too," I said carefully. "Obviously I'll keep my relationship with Leyla a secret. She understands. But JNP is the one that's really standing in the way now...."

How was I supposed to see her if they'd taken away my phone? How was I supposed to ever see her again if I never got even a one-day break?

"There's only three days left," Seojung said. "What are you going to do?"

I clenched my hand into a fist on my lap. "I don't know. But I need to see her at least one last time."

"You have to find a way," Tae-X said. "We'll help you."

I turned and looked at him, surprised, but to my even greater surprise, *everyone* was nodding—even Seojung.

The van door slid open. Manager Son was there; he stuck his head in. "Hey guys. Manager Yoo has decided to give you all back your phones. You're going to need them tomorrow to do a self-filmed run."

We all looked at each other.

레일라
LEYLA
27

Jongjin had told me to meet him at the park. But when my eyes fell upon him, it *wasn't* just him. It was the entirety of Tr3sure.

I froze.

They hadn't seen me yet, at this distance. They were all standing around in the grass in a circle, Jongjin the most comfortably familiar and distinguishable with his tall height and sharp clothes—but then there was Sun Chi-Ho with his dark pink hair lifting in the breeze, Seojung with his strikingly dark, elegant eyebrows, Tae-X with neon red pants, and Laon, standing as he always did when he was quietly taking everything in, blank-faced. Even from a distance they were perfectly recognizable—their features, their body language, the way they interacted as a team. They stood out, with their brightly dyed hair and designer clothes; everything about them screamed "famous".

Adrenaline was all of a sudden rushing through me. I stared at them like I was dreaming, feeling like it was unreal. I knew they were real people just like Jongjin, but to have them all assembled here made me realize that collectively, they were Tr3sure.

Jongjin looked up from saying something to Laon, and that was when he saw me. He waved, and then started striding over. I met him halfway, my heart beating fast at the smile of pure happiness on his face as he looked at me, eyes shining.

"C'mon," he said. "You have to meet them."

"I didn't know they'd be here!" I hissed, ducking self-consciously. "I thought it was going to be just us!"

"Well... it is." He grinned. "You'll see."

"I'm nervous," I said under my breath as we started walking towards them. The four of them were all watching now and it occurred to me I had no idea what they thought of Jongjin and I together—of us. "Is this like the equivalent of meeting your family?"

Jongjin threw back his head and laughed. "They'll like you. So will my parents." He reached out and took my hand. His touch was warm and safe and comforting.

We were walking up to Tr3sure *holding hands*. I was too nervous and shy to do anything but give a meek little wave when we finally stopped in front of them. Seojung, Tae-X, Sun Chi-Ho, Laon—they looked amazing in real life, and yet somehow just like I'd expected them to from the photos and videos. They were staring at me—Laon, with his very familiar blank-faced, almost bored kind of way; Sun Chi-Ho, with bright interest and a smile; Seojung, black eyes studying and intense; and Tae-X, friendly and calm and relaxed.

Jongjin said something in Korean to them that included the word "Leyla". They smiled and bowed; I tried to do the same, blushing. Sun Chi-Ho waved with all the film equipment he was holding. It looked like several fancy selfie sticks and an actual camera.

"So," Tae-X said in English, looking right at me. His voice was deep and friendly and wonderful to listen to in person. "Jongjin doesn't actually have a break today. We're all supposed to be self-filming an episode of the TV show—together."

"Okay," I said, surprised.

"And that's why," he said, clapping his hands, "we're going to cover for him—try to pretend like he's here while he's off having fun with you."

My mouth dropped open. I turned towards Jongjin. "What if everyone gets in trouble?"

Jongjin smiled as he looked at his team, and there was genuine gratitude in his eyes. "They're going to try not to, but they're willing to face the punishment."

"They'd do that for you?" I said, feeling the corners of my eyes sting. I looked at the four of them standing there, some starting to look a bit awkward or self-conscious, Seojung gazing at me steadily, and I was seized with the desire to hug them.

"Thank you," I whispered. "So much."

"Ije shijakabnida," Seojung said, piercing eyes turning upon Jongjin. He tapped his watch.

"Right! We can only give you so much time, dudes," Tae-X said.

"We've got one hour," Jongjin said to me, squeezing my hand. "Let's go!"

"It was nice to meet you!" said Sun Chi-Ho with an adorable grin. Laon gave another little bow and Tae-X winked at me.

And then we rushed to split ways, the clock counting down. While the rest of Tr3sure headed away from the park, Jongjin and I went deeper into it. Jongjin explained that the members were going to split up for their TV mission; Laon and Jongjin were supposed to be going shopping for certain items, but Laon was going to do all the shopping for the both of them and only film himself, getting hardly any footage on the premise that Jongjin was on a "secret" shopping mission for secret, surprise items. After an hour, Jongjin would return and grab the shopping bags and Laon would film him running up as if he'd been shopping all along.

"So," Jongjin said, eyes sparkling, "you want to cross *Picnic* off the List?"

"In an hour?" I said. "Let's do it."

"I looked on the map," Jongjin said, pointing to somewhere in the distance. "There's a hamburger place. It's across from a playground."

"Let's go!"

But then my gaze caught sight of a person about fifty feet away, near the parking lot beyond the trees, someone with dark hair in a group of other guys. It was Milo. I could hear his laugh as he guffawed about something with his dumb friends.

I temporarily went still as he faced in our direction, but his gaze slid past us, moving on.

"What's wrong?" Jongjin said, sounding worried.

I hesitated. Milo and his group of friends were already moving out of sight behind some cars, leaving. "It's... nothing," I said, forcing myself to look back at Jongjin. Why point out Milo and upset anyone? I couldn't even see him anymore, and he hadn't noticed us.

As we approached the hamburger place, we ran into a group of people in bright yellow T-shirts who'd set up a promotional table on the grass at the park. Their sign said *Ocean Pollution Awareness*. One of the people waved to us and flagged us down, calling, "Would you like a free bracelet?"

Jongjin and I looked at each other, and then he laughed. "Sure," he said.

The person fetched two cheap yellow rubber bracelets that had their logo and *Ocean Pollution Awareness* printed in white across the band. We each slipped ours on and kept walking, after thanking the people running the table.

"It will be a... a... something to remember this day by." Jongjin searched for the right word.

"A memento?"

"Exactly," he said. His voice went a little quieter, his eyes full of warmth as he looked at me. "A memento."

"I'll wear it forever," I teased.

Jongjin looked back at the table with a grin. "Do you think I should get another one as a souvenir for my mom?"

I gasped. "Jongjin! Are you telling me you haven't bought a souvenir for her yet?"

"I'll get one at the airport when we leave," he said.

We were both quiet for a second at the mention of him leaving. Then I looked down at our entwined hands, with matching bracelets.

Maybe this was the last time I would see Jongjin before he left for Korea. I didn't know. But it didn't matter now. He was real and right here, and that's what I focused on—the sound of his voice, the sight of his handsome face, the feel of his fingers wrapped around mine. I didn't know what the scary future held, but I loved him, and he loved me—and that was enough for now. We had a really long time to figure things out.

We'd approached the edge of the park—we could see more grass, trees, the playground, and buildings across the street, which included the hamburger place.

There was nobody else inside. It was a very quiet day, since we'd missed rush hour. Jongjin ordered two classic hamburgers for us, and while we waited for it to be ready, we went back outside to look for a good place to have a picnic.

"Is this American enough for you?" I teased, leaning on one of the metal folding chairs that were scattered outside next to the tables.

He surveyed the scene seriously. "Looks just like the movies."

"Really?" I said, a little bit incredulous.

He tapped me lightly on the nose. "Well, you're more beautiful, but other than that—"

I cut him off with a very loud scoff of disbelief, but I couldn't contain my smile. Jongjin laughed at my expression, that overflowing, bubbling laugh that had frozen me to the spot the first night we'd met.

"I think our food's ready," said Jongjin, peering through the window.

"I'll go reserve our picnic spot."

Jongjin stepped inside the building and I turned back towards the park—and then stopped.

Because Milo had just rounded the corner.

He stalked towards me and I took a few steps back, afraid.

"What are you doing here?" I said.

He gave a harsh laugh. "So you *are* sneaking around with him. I knew it, you liar."

"I don't owe you anything!"

"You think you're fooling anyone?" Milo said, voice rising to yelling volume.

"Milo, leave me alone," I said, heart pounding. I took some more steps back and he took more steps toward me. I looked frantically at the door that Jongjin had vanished into.

Milo didn't miss that look. "He's not here. I thought we should have this conversation alone, first, and *then* I can have a chat with him." The threat towards Jongjin was clear.

I could feel the blood drain from my face. "Leave us alone," I said, voice shaking.

"You know, other girls would feel lucky that I wanted to go out with them."

"Milo—"

Behind him, Jongjin had come out of the shop, holding the bags of food in his hands. A flicker of confusion passed over his face as his gaze traveled back and forth between us.

"You don't need him. Come on." Milo lunged, reaching out to grab my wrist, but before I could even gasp Jongjin had cut right in front of him, his body a wall between us. In one powerful, muscular movement that I would've missed if I blinked, he snatched the arm Milo was reaching out and twisted it, making him yell as his knees buckled and Jongjin slammed him into the ground. One polished dress shoe dug into Milo's back, keeping him down flat on the concrete as he kept holding his arm at an angle it wasn't supposed to be bent.

Milo yelled and tried to struggle, cheek pressed against the concrete, but quickly froze as Jongjin applied pressure to his bent arm.

"*Mwo hae?! Neol pagoehagesseo* if you dare move," Jongjin hissed, his face a mask of fury as he kept pinning Milo down, not seeming to realize in his anger that he was firing off a mix of both Korean and English.

"Don't—don't—ah—" Milo begged, trying to move his torso in a way that would untwist his arm. Jongjin dug his dress shoe a little harder into his back and he gasped.

"If you try to touch her again," Jongjin snarled, "I will break your arms. Do you understand?"

Milo nodded, still gasping. "Yes—yes—don't—"

Jongjin released him and stepped back, directly in front of me, still shielding me with his body, broad shoulders thrown back.

Milo dragged himself upright, face flushed, a bead of sweat near his hairline. He was the same height as Jongjin, but all beef, whereas Jongjin was slender and much lighter. He stared wildly at Jongjin, with me forgotten.

Then he threw a punch at Jongjin's face. I screamed, but it was his mistake. Faster than I could process, Jongjin ducked sideways and somehow used Milo's momentum, with his own body as leverage, to throw him into the metal chairs on the ground with a crash.

Milo staggered up, obviously trying not to let Jongjin know how much it had hurt. For a second I thought he was going to try and attack again, but he seemed to think better of it. Instead he sneered, flicking hair out of his face. "You're not even worth the fight." And then he walked away.

Jongjin stayed in front of me, in the same shielding position, until Milo was well out of sight. Then he turned around to face me.

He was still breathing hard, but his shirt wasn't even askew. A single strand of hair had fallen out of place and I reached up and brushed it back; at my touch, the tension in his tight shoulders seemed to melt away.

"Are you okay?" he asked, warm brown eyes studying mine intensely.

"Never been better," I whispered. My face was tilted upwards towards his as I looked into his eyes. "You beat him up in your dress shoes," I added afterward, as an observation.

"Yeah, they're more useful than they seem," he murmured.

The bell over the door of the shop rang loudly, and a woman yelled, "If you're going to keep beating people up, take it somewhere else! I saw the whole thing, and I'm glad you protected your girlfriend, but I don't want trouble on my property!"

Jongjin and I stepped apart, the moment interrupted. We apologized, Jongjin picked up the plastic bag full of food he'd dropped on the ground, and we made a quick exit.

Without having to say anything to each other, we made our way over to the grass near the playground.

"How did you *do* that?" I asked in awe.

"Don't sound so surprised," he muttered. "JNP made us take self-defense classes. Because we were becoming popular, they worried one day someone might attack us..." He shrugged.

"Wow... and have you ever...?"

Jongjin shook his head. "This is the first time I've ever had to use it."

"And where'd you come from?" I said. "You appeared out of nowhere."

Jongjin smirked as he unwrapped a hamburger, raising one eyebrow. "I used the door."

I made a noise of indignation. "Byun Jongjin...."

Then I went still, remembering the last time I'd threatened him using his full name. Obviously he remembered too, because he looked up, his eyes sparkling just as brightly as the diamond stud in his ear.

"Are you going to finish that sentence?" he asked.

"...if it's normal you want...."

"....That's what you're going to get," he said in a mock-high voice to imitate mine. "You, Leyla Sen, are a handful!"

We ate our food. I thought it was the best hamburger I'd ever tasted, but I think that might've been because Jongjin was here. Sitting with him on the grass, laughing, on such a perfect summer afternoon was the best day I ever could've wished for.

종진
JONGJIN
28

"It's funny," Leyla murmured, holding her arm out in front of her and observing the bracelet on her wrist. "When you're gone, these will be the only proof that this month ever happened, and that it wasn't a dream."

We were sitting on the swings, slowly kicking our legs.

I reached out and placed my hand over hers. "We'll see each other again."

"Yeah... you can always come and visit. Or I can visit you."

We lapsed into a comfortable silence.

I looked down at our fingers entwined together, yellow bracelets crossed. Such a small token from today, from such a small moment. But it was times like these that I would later close my eyes and try to relive.

"Jongjin, as an idol... aren't you not allowed to date?"

I nodded. "Not in public. But I have lots of friends from other groups who are dating. One's even married. I'm not worried about it."

"And JNP?"

"Tr3sure never had a no-dating clause in the contract. I think they thought if they kept us busy enough, it wouldn't happen. But as long as we're careful, it's fine." We both looked out at all the people in the park, playing, happy, minding their own business.

I continued on. "It's amazing being here in America, where nobody knows who we are. If you were to visit me in Korea, it would be different."

I felt her hand slip from mine. "I have something for you," she said, pulling a little square of paper out of her pocket and passing it to me.

I took it. It was full of carefully printed English handwriting in black pen—all of Leyla's contact information. Her address, phone number, email, and multiple social media accounts.

"Just in case they take away your phone again," she said, kicking some mulch.

"It will be impossible not to reach you now," I said with a smile, tucking the paper into my wallet and making sure it was tight. "No matter what JNP does, I always have access to the internet."

"Now there's no way we won't be able to talk," she said, satisfied but resigned. The breeze ruffled her hair ever so slightly, gently, playing with it. I suddenly longed to run my fingers through that dark hair, feel the lightness of a few soft strands against my hands as they danced in the wind, kissing my skin.

My gaze roved over her face, drinking it in. I adored her. Would this be the last time I saw her?

Maybe I would get a break tomorrow on my last day. Maybe I wouldn't.

We were both resigned to our fates. Our separation was inevitable.

"Aren't you worried about having a long-distance relationship?" I asked, genuinely curious. "You don't know when we're going to see each other again."

Leyla swung a little on the swings. "I was," she said. "A few weeks ago. I didn't think our friendship was strong enough to last." Her brown eyes had a glow in them. "But I'm not worried anymore."

"I'm not either," I said quietly.

A few moments passed in silence.

"I just wish... I could stay here," I said. "Especially to protect you from Milo." My voice took on an intense, protective edge.

"You already have protected me, and you'll continue to."

"But I'm going back to Korea," I said, confused.

Leyla raised her eyebrows. "But *Milo* doesn't have to know that."

I laughed, but when I glanced over at her, her eyes were misty.

"What is it?" I said, tenderly grasping her hands in mine, taken aback and full of concern. "Are you scared?"

She shook her head, laughing a little. "I'm happy."

"Happy?" I said, again confused. "Why are you happy?"

Her eyes shone with tears that refused to fall. "Because you're the most amazing person I've ever met and you're treating me like I'm special."

I leaned forward and kissed her gently on the forehead, lost for words.

Just then, my phone alarm went off. I closed my eyes, regret washing over me.

"It's time to go, isn't it," Leyla whispered.

"Yes," I said. "Time's up."

We slowly headed back to the place where we were supposed to meet up with the others, holding hands the whole way. Seojung, Tae-X, Laon, and Sun Chi-Ho were already there. Leyla stuck around as they filmed me running up with Laon's shopping bags, supposedly back from my mystery shopping trip.

And then there was nothing else left to do, and Tr3sure had to go.

I stood and faced Leyla.

"So... I suppose... see you later," she whispered.

I took her hands in mine, looking into her eyes. "See you later," I repeated quietly, with a sad smile.

We stood there for one long breath. For a second, it seemed like she wanted to kiss me, but instead her glance went to the Tr3sure members waiting behind me, watching, and then back up to my eyes with a regretful, bittersweet look.

"We need to go, Jongjin," Seojung said gently.

I let her hands slip gently out of mine and took a few steps backward, savoring my last few glimpses of her with that same sad, now almost wry smile as it felt like a knife was being slowly twisted into my heart.

I turned to follow after my Tr3sure brothers. *Maybe you'll see her tomorrow,* I thought. *Maybe this isn't the end.*

But I looked back, somehow knowing that it was. She was still standing there in the grass, watching me with the same kind of lonely desperation that I felt towards her. As the cab started to drive away, I tried to wave one last time.

But I was a second too late. We rounded the corner and she passed out of sight.

종진

JONGJIN

29

"What *is* this?" Manager Jeon shouted, flicking through the scene edits on our camera. The five of us stood nervously in front of him where he sat at the table. "There's barely any footage of Jongjin! Where....."

He trailed off, then turned to face me, eyes blazing. "Empty out your pockets. NOW!"

I could feel myself go pale. But I knew I had no choice, and any sort of protest would only make it worse.

From my pants pockets I pulled out my phone, my wallet, and the List. I laid them out on the table, thankful I'd thrown the hamburger receipt away at the park—but I was still filled with fear. My most precious possessions were in front of Manager Jeon for him to do as he pleased.

Manager Son walked through the door, then froze as he saw the scene, taking in the charged atmosphere; my tension, Manager Jeon's anger, the way Seojung, Tae-X, Laon, and Sun Chi-Ho were keeping their eyes downcast, quiet. He made a movement for a second as if he meekly wanted to backpedal and go the other way, but of course Manager Jeon and I had already seen him.

"Son!" Manager Jeon yelled.

"Yes?" said Manager Son, cringing.

Manager Son was our General Manager and Manager Jeon was our Production Manager that handled the TV show and public appearances, so technically they were on the same level; not like Manager Yoo, their boss. But Manager Son's avoidance of any conflict made him easy to steamroll.

"Guess what Jongjin has been doing *under your nose.*"

Manager Son looked like he didn't want to know the answer to that. "What?"

"That's what we're going to find out."

Manager Jeon made me pull out my pockets entirely to prove that they were empty, then picked up the List.

"'Eat ice cream'?" he repeated in a mocking voice.

Anger burned in my throat. I could almost hear Seojung praying desperately behind me that I would not fight back.

With a little sneer, Manager Jeon threw the List back down on the table, looking at the ones that had been crossed off. "I see you've been *busy*."

Manager Son looked at me, concern in his eyes. "Jongjin, why didn't you tell me?"

"How could I?" I said with a disbelieving laugh. "I asked for a break. All I've done for two years is say yes to anything JNP asks me to do. No matter how tired, burnt out, or—"

"You ungrateful wretch!" Jeon bellowed. He stared at me for a second in shock, stunned that I'd done something besides hang my head, apologize, and put on the signature everything-is-just-great Jongjin smile. He dropped his voice lower. "What is wrong with you? Do you know how many other trainees got the opportunity you did?"

I closed my eyes. Nine years of training, nine years of sacrificing everything else in my life, including my own happiness—for this.

I was right. The opportunities I'd gotten *were* a debt to repay. That's how Jeon saw it. No matter how hard I worked, it was never enough to deserve it, to be a reason I'd lasted when others hadn't, to have a break.

My silence was something Manager Jeon was more used to. He sniffed, confident that he'd put me in my place, and grabbed my wallet off the table. He thumbed through it, then pulled out the piece of paper where Leyla had written down her contact information.

His eyes widened and his voice dropped down to a deadly whisper. "What is this?"

I couldn't breathe.

"Jongjin," he said, voice low.

"It's the contact information of a friend—"

"No. It's a *distraction.*"

"I need a distraction," I said desperately. "Please, Manager Jeon, I need a break. I'm run-down. I love to sing, I love Tr3sure, but we've been working so hard we don't even have time to breathe. Maybe after we get back to Korea, since the TV show is over, I could have just a few days, a week maybe—*what are you doing?"*

My last words were panicked. Manager Jeon had pulled a lighter out of his pocket. Stony-faced, holding it underneath the paper with Leyla's contact information, he clicked the sparker.

"NO!" I yelled. I sprang forward, trying to grab it, but it was already burning up in soft, devouring flames. I gasped as my fingers touched the fire, and both me and Manager Jeon dropped it as it wrinkled into black char, falling onto the table.

"Jongjin!" Sun Chi-Ho cried out in fear as I clutched my wrist in pain, looking down at my burned fingertips. The sound cracked my heart into pieces.

I stared in disbelief down at the destroyed paper on the table, and the ashes on my pale skin. Then I slowly lowered my burned hand.

"Okay," I said, deadly calm. Manager Jeon's eyes, just as deadly calm, stared into mine. Then he threw my wallet at Manager Son, who caught it against his chest, and thrust my phone into his own pocket, standing up.

He swept from the room.

"Come on, Jongjin," Manager Son said worriedly, shaking my arm. "Let's go get something for your burned fingers."

They throbbed painfully, but I didn't move, gritting my teeth, staring at the door where Jeon had vanished. I didn't care about the pain. I wanted to chase after him, to take my phone back by force, now my only link to Leyla.

Suddenly Seojung was behind me, grabbing my other arm, his eyes—dark, inky black pools—intensely taking in all the trembling, furious wildness of my own.

"Let's go," Seojung said, tugging me towards the door. "We can't do anything now."

I let myself be tugged. My gaze roved over at the other members; Sun Chi-Ho looked like he was in shock, Laon and Tae-X comforting him. Tae-X was shaking slightly.

Back in Seojung's hotel room, he found some ice and gently pushed me into a chair. "Hold this."

I took the ice, feeling the shocking coldness numb my burn while I looked without really seeing anything at the floor.

"It's gone," I whispered. "Jeon took it. Those were the only ways I had... to contact Leyla...."

I slammed my fist on the coffee table. Everything on it jumped and there was a cracking sound.

"Careful," Seojung said nervously. "You're stronger than you know."

I didn't answer, still staring down at the floor.

Manager Son came in without knocking, huffing and puffing; he had apparently run to go get some burn medicine.

"Here," he said worriedly, struggling to open it.

"It's not that bad," I snapped. "Everyone needs to stop freaking out."

Seojung took the medicine from Manager Son and ignored me as he dried off my hands—the ice had melted by now, dripping onto the carpet—and smeared the white gel on the burns.

The other Tr3sure members came quietly into the room, shutting the door behind them. I straightened up and put on a smile, a smile that hurt a thousand times more than my scorched fingertips.

"I'm okay," I said in response to their worried glances. "It doesn't hurt anymore." That was definitely a lie.

"That's good," Tae-X said quietly. He seemed a little relieved, though still worried and not entirely believing.

"I was stupid to try and grab it," I said, still trying to smile, trying to make the situation lighter. "I'm sorry for scaring you guys." I was sorry they had to watch the entire interaction. I didn't want to be someone who was desperate or tired or needed a break. I wanted to be the perfect member for them, the teammate who was always ready to cheer or try again and never needed anything. They'd already given enough today by trying to cover for me.

"Is there... anything I can do?" Manager Son asked with worried creases in his forehead. He gestured awkwardly towards the door. "You all have to be downstairs in fifteen minutes; tonight you'll all be modeling for an LA-based luxury brand."

Seojung looked up in surprise, from where he'd been trying to open a bandage on the table. I stood up, sweeping it away. You couldn't wear bandages while you modeled, as Manager Son knew perfectly well. "Let's go then," I said.

Laon leapt up, normally blank eyes blazing. "You can't make him go without—"

"Let's go," I repeated, biting off his words, brushing past Manager Son on my way out.

It was extremely late by the time we got back to the hotel. I washed my face, brushed my teeth, and finally put some cream and a bandage on my burned fingers with a sigh of relief. They'd hurt the whole time I was modeling, and I'd had to be careful not to show the pain on my face, as well as angle my hand so the burn mark wasn't visible. I stumbled into bed fatigued, still with my clothes and that bright yellow rubber bracelet on, which I'd forgotten because the sleeve of my shirt had hidden it. If only I could somehow warn Leyla what had happened, that I wasn't ignoring her, and she shouldn't be worried if I couldn't answer the phone... but Jeon made sure there was a bodyguard outside our hotel door.

I fell asleep with Leyla being the last thing on my mind.

The next day—our last day in America, June 30th, my birthday—was extremely busy, full of final interviews, a featured radio appearance, and of course my strained birthday live video, where Manager Jeon and Yoo breathed down my neck. Even still, I found time to ask Laon for his phone, which he graciously let me borrow. I thought I might have remembered Leyla's phone number—and tried all the ones I thought of, but with no luck. They were all wrong.

We were supposed to leave early the next morning—but due to a tight schedule, even that plan was changed, the last few hours in America cut short.

We left for the airport at ten at night.

Happy 20th birthday to me. "I'm so sorry," I whispered to the black sky before I stepped into the van.

레일라
LEYLA
30

I stepped out of the shower, dripping with water, my hair slicked back. The drops that ran down my face mixed with my tears.

I didn't even know why I was bothering trying to hide the fact that I was crying. The only person left in the house now was Dad. Amanda was gone, long gone, her bright pink bag missing from the pegs next to the front door, her room empty. It was too quiet.

I stared at my red-eyed reflection in the fogged mirror. It reminded me of that night—dripping wet from when Jongjin had pulled me into the pool with his strong arms, looking into his face, noticing the droplets of water clinging to his cheekbones.

The sky outside the window was pitch-black; it was late at night. As if in a dream, I picked up my toothbrush, then let my hand fall limply back down. I couldn't muster up even an ounce of willpower to do anything.

Jongjin hadn't contacted me at all ever since that day we'd said goodbye, five days ago. Nothing. Not a text, not an email, not a message on any social media. It was like he'd dropped off the face of the earth.

And yet I'd seen his picture, smiling for the fans as he arrived back in South Korea, in a polished airport surrounded by screaming girls throwing flowers. Most of them were prettier than I was. Perfect, delicate, tiny, and cute, with new clothes that fit just right and glossy hair that never frizzed.

A part of me knew this was stupid, irrational thinking. But staring hollowly at myself in the bathroom mirror, it was too easy to think.

I'd run out of excuses for him. I'd made *sure* he'd had ways to contact me, regardless of whether they took away his phone or not. It had been days. Hadn't he had a chance, one single second, in *days* to respond to my increasingly worried messages?

For how often we'd been talking before, even on his busiest schedule, this sudden cutoff was disconcerting. I kept picking up my phone, checking everything, making sure I hadn't missed anything.

But one glaring answer, the most obvious explanation, remained. He just didn't want to respond.

He'd forgotten me. Like Jackie and Aaron had. Entertainment for the moment, until it wasn't fun anymore.

I dully pulled out the toothpaste, putting some on my toothbrush much slower than normal and then putting it back in its place. Not that I needed to bother with organization. The cabinets were unfilled and bare, the counter uncluttered, without Amanda's things in here. Gone. It was just me standing in a stark and empty bathroom.

Vacant. Hollow. Void.

Jongjin had seemed so sincere. But then, so had Jackie and Aaron.

Maybe he really was just the chronic flirt. In love with falling in love. Excited by the chase, until he'd finally caught me. Feeling everything he claimed to feel, except that those feelings changed with the snap of a finger; until someone new came along, or I just stopped being exciting.

How could I guard against that? I couldn't. I was helpless to whatever change happened. There was nothing I could do.

Maybe if I had just been a little wittier... a little more kind... a little more *something,* I would have been able to keep his interest. Or maybe I'd been too much of something. Too bold. Too open with my feelings. Too clingy.

But how was I supposed to have known that we were playing a game? I didn't know there was a game. I thought it was as simple as the fact that I loved him, and he... said he loved me.

Forgotten. Just like before.

I brushed my teeth and fell into bed without even bothering to comb my wet, tangled hair. The sky outside my window was black and starless, as usual. I fell asleep on top of the sheets, to the hum of the air conditioning, drifting off into somewhere blank and free of thought, if not restful. I didn't dream.

Waking up was worse than falling asleep lonely. Because after the several seconds where I slowly came to consciousness, everything I'd lost hit me full in the chest, like an anvil slamming into me and staying, weighing me down. It made me lose every motivation to get out of bed.

But I did. I had to. There was no other choice.

I tried to keep contacting him. I called, called, called, no answer. Days stretched into weeks of silence—smothering, suffocating.

After a while I just stopped.

Jackie and Aaron were just as silent as ever—more so, even. Between their silence and Jongjin's, I felt increasingly isolated. Frustration was building up inside me until it threatened to burst.

I paced my room, growing angrier and angrier until I felt like screaming. The summer day outside my window, past the origami and little plant Amanda had put there just for me on my first day, was bright and scorching. The July sun and heat had me trapped inside, with nothing to do but get lost in my own head. The house, as usual, was deathly silent and empty.

I finally felt like I was on the verge of snapping, and grabbed my metallic Tr3sure album to distract myself—just like the old days—but stopped.

I couldn't handle this right now.

I chucked it back down on the shelf, way rougher than I ever would've dared before Jongjin. What was it but just paper and cardboard? I remembered how gingerly I'd handled it, like it was precious gold, when Jackie had first given it to me.

Thinking of Jackie again just made rage surge through me. How dare she ignore me? How dare she make all those empty promises and then leave me alone here to drown? I *needed* Jackie and Aaron, and they weren't here for me. They hadn't been here for me ever since I'd left. What kind of friends were those?

And why had I just been going along with it?

I grabbed my phone. Jongjin wouldn't answer me, but maybe Jackie and Aaron would.

You guys have been ignoring me and I'm sick of it. I'm sick of being treated like I don't exist and I'm sick of you pretending to be my friends when you've forgotten me ever since I left.

I was so angry that I typed it out and sent it within thirty seconds. Those were the words that had been crashing around my head for ages; they spilled out in my rapid typing.

I took deep, huffing breaths as I waited for their response. If they didn't answer within two hours, I was going to block both of them and force them out of my life for good.

I turned off my phone, the screen going black. I refused to wait there for a typing icon to appear—refused to be the desperate one still clutching on when they'd let go, dependent on them, needy and at their mercy.

I started pacing the room again, turning sharply in the tiny space.

I didn't expect anyone to answer right away—but the notification went off. Heart pounding, full of stress, I checked the message.

I think we should video call.

I looked at it for a few seconds, then took a deep breath to calm my queasy stomach. **Fine.**

I took my laptop off the dresser next to my bed and opened it up, sitting cross-legged against my pillow. My hand was shaking as I adjusted the screen. This would be the first time I'd see their faces since I left.

After a few minutes of setting up, they appeared. First Aaron—sitting at the desk in his dark bedroom—and then Jackie, outside somewhere, the background a wash of intense green. They looked exactly like I'd remembered them, hadn't changed at all. The sight almost made me melt, but I channeled all my emotions into anger.

"Hi," I said stiffly.

"Hi," Aaron repeated nervously, scuffing his hand through the side of his hair, his typical anxious habit I knew so well. I used to think it was endearing, but now I found it irritating.

"Hi," Jackie said at nearly the same time. She also looked nervous.

I didn't even know them both anymore. Who *were* these people?

I waited for them to say something.

"We're sorry, Leyla," Aaron said, scuffing his hand through his hair again, gaze drifting anywhere but at me.

I didn't say anything.

He continued. "It's just... we weren't sure how to tell you."

"Tell me what," I said flatly.

"Well... the thing is... right after you left, me and Jackie realized how we felt about each other and started dating," said Aaron.

What?

"It just kind of happened," Aaron continued. "It was just the two of us, and...."

And I was conveniently out of the way. The minute I'd left everything had changed.

"And we didn't know what to do!" Jackie said. "We didn't know whether to tell you or not, or whether you'd feel left out, or it would upset you...."

"So you just didn't talk to me at all?"

"We *tried!*" Jackie said. "But it was so hard and awkward! Trying to act like nothing had changed...."

...When everything had changed. They were right. We'd never be the same three group of best friends we once were. So they'd decided to drop me.

But maybe things could've been different. Either of them could have told me how they felt when I was still there, but they hadn't. And they could've told me right when they became boyfriend and girlfriend, and I could've at least *tried* to celebrate. They hadn't even given me a chance.

"Why didn't you just *tell* me?" I said.

"We thought maybe you'd guess," Jackie said, eyes downcast, fingers playing with some sort of plant next to her.

I suddenly became aware of her surroundings. "Wait—you're in Aaron's front yard. Aren't you? That's his front yard. You were *together* at his house when I texted. Having lots of fun, I guess. Probably laughing at me for being so stupid."

"No—no, we weren't laughing!" Jackie said, sounding like she was about to cry. I didn't have the patience for it. How dare they play "the good guys" when they'd ignored me ever since I'd come to California, for no good reason? When I needed them the most? When they'd caused me so much hurt and confusion?

"Okay, whatever," I said. "But the next time you video call—actually, there won't be a next time—at least don't bother trying to pretend you're in two different places. Obviously you do think I'm stupid if you don't think I'll recognize the place I've been hundreds of times." Fury was pouring off me like smoke. "And one day I hope you meet someone who treats you like trash, so you can know how it feels like."

"Leyla, we didn't mean to!" Jackie cried.

"I don't care!" I shouted. "Go cry on Aaron's shoulder, then. You can both stand there and whine about what a bad person I am."

Aaron opened his mouth to say something angrily, but I slammed the laptop shut so hard that something went *crack.*

I threw it down on the bed with a noise of irrepressible frustration, left there in the silent room alone, and then I walked down the stairs and outside, trembling with adrenaline and rage.

The driveway was empty where Jongjin had once stood.

It was just as hot as ever, the sunlight baking on my skin, but I started to run. I ran like something was chasing me, blood hot. I was seething, about to explode, throwing all my energy into pounding the concrete sidewalk as fast as possible. No time to think—no time to slow down—just running.

I built up speed, furiously. I was barely aware of my surroundings as I sprinted, except for the puffing of my breath and the sweat running down my forehead. My body screamed in protest but I pushed harder, farther, faster, until my lungs felt like they were going to collapse from lack of air. My throat stung and I swallowed with difficulty, gasping in breaths as my shoes slammed into the sidewalk, but still I wanted to face the sky and roar with anger.

Until my shoe caught on something, my tired body uncoordinated, and I tripped.

I hit the concrete hard, crashing into it. My hands just barely managed to catch me to keep my face up and pain shot up my wrists and scraped palms.

I lay there for a brief second, stunned, and then I pushed myself up. "Ow," I whimpered, blinking my stinging eyes.

The rough concrete was hot and burned my skin, radiating through my clothes. I pulled my legs up closer to my body and looked at the hole I'd torn in the knee of my jeans, skin scratched. My palms were red, but everywhere else I was bruised. I staggered upright, smarting and sore, wiping tears from my eyes with the back of my hand. Every ounce of anger had been knocked out of me with my fall, leaving me empty and sad and in pain.

I cried as I slowly walked back home. I cried because it hurt, I cried because I was alone, I cried because my heart felt like it had cracked into pieces. Shattered beyond repair, with three vicious blows of a hammer—Amanda, Jongjin, and my former best friends.

No one was out at this time of day, in the afternoon. I cried like no one was watching, because no one was. I clutched my heart with my stinging palms, choking on sobs, stumbling clumsily home.

"Jongjin," I whispered, voice thick and wet. "Jongjin, where are you...."

It was so burning and oppressive outside, in the unrelenting sun. My head felt hot. I found my way back in a daze, then fell into a chair inside, being blasted with the cool air conditioning and turning on a fan.

I cleaned myself up and then lay on my floor in the dark with the blinds pulled down, not moving, not doing anything at all. Hardly even thinking.

I fell asleep that way.

It was too easy to sleep in the next days, weeks—I didn't even know how long it had been. Time blurred together. When I slept I could forget about everything. I could just escape. And yet I still made myself shower, made myself get up because I had to.

My friends had already been shutting me out, so the silence on that end—I'd blocked both of them—was something I was used to. I didn't want to hear from them. But Jongjin's absence hurt more and more.

My days had become a flat gray monotony—walking past Amanda's empty room, trying to watch television to distract myself, just lying there on the sofa.

"Are you okay?" The same question.

"I'm fine." The same lie.

The pain didn't seem to get better, but rather worse. I started to go to bed later and later at night, usually eating some sort of comfort food—cinnamon rolls, chips, boxed mac'n'cheese with spicy gochujang, s'mores, tteokbokki snacks.

Tonight it was a bubbling pot of budae jjigae. Creamy, caloric American cheese melted like satin over ramyun, red spicy broth, umami-rich mushrooms, and slices of salty hot dog, all sprinkled with bright green onions. Everything was dyed red with chili flakes and chunks of tangy kimchi.

Every hot bite of chewy ramyun and intense flavor sent warmth spreading inside me, and the overwhelming spiciness set my mouth on fire, numbing the pain of my emotions. The savory, fiery heaviness soothed my soul. I sighed as I ate it, feeling calmer, though still with that sorrowful ache in my chest that had refused to go away ever since I'd come to accept that Jongjin wasn't coming back.

I knew he wouldn't. But I still couldn't crush that last tiny bit of irrational hope. Maybe it was the only thing holding me together now. I still checked my phone, but every day less and less often, dully, knowing nothing would be there.

I'd never been more alone than I was now. I sipped the last bit of orange-red broth, slightly creamy as some of the cheese had melted into it, as the glowing numbers on the kitchen clock turned to 1:30.

I finished it off with a spoonful of *the* ice cream, which had been waiting unopened ever since I'd bought it. As the gentle vanilla and caramel sweetness flooded my mouth, freezing cold, I could close my eyes and imagine myself in the dark aisle with Jongjin, before the lights had turned on. I was there, with him beside me, the person I'd felt a connection to before I'd even known who he was, eating ice cream straight from the tub with a plastic spoon.... And then when I'd bought this carton the next day, in remembrance, he'd shown up and recognized it in surprise.

I'd been so happy....

I could almost imagine his voice, almost pretend that I'd open my eyes and really be there, back in time.

Was Jongjin purposely trying to break my heart? Why didn't he answer? Why didn't he do *something?*

If he wanted us to break up, or didn't think we could work, then he should've had the guts to just say so. Why just vanish?

Maybe he'd already planned to cut it off and blame it on JNP taking his phone, hoping I lost interest, but I'd ruined his plan by giving him all the rest of my contact information.

No, that soft voice said inside me. *You know him... he wouldn't do that....*

I thought I'd known him. I thought I'd known Jackie and Aaron.

I pushed up the sleeve of my soft, overlarge pajama shirt to reveal the bright yellow wristband. I'd worn it ever since the two of us had gotten matching ones on the last day we'd ever seen each other, right before he'd saved me from Milo. Every day I'd tried to work up the motivation to take it off, to forget it and Jongjin, but somehow *couldn't.*

My fingers grabbed the rubber, ready to tear it off, ready to throw it across the room....

I couldn't bear to do it.

I let my sleeve fall over the wristband again. It was the only piece of Jongjin I had left.

Ping!

I froze. My phone was across the room, plugged in on the coffee table. I could see the glow of the screen in the darkness, which then went out.

I got up and looked at it. It wasn't a text message, but a notification for a Tr3sure live.

My mouth felt dry and I was suddenly nervous. I swallowed, then clicked it and fell on the sofa.

It was *all* of them—all five of them. Seeing Jongjin after so long was a complete shock. His handsome, oh-so-familiar features were like a little punch in the heart, making me unable to breathe. I fumbled for my earbuds and put them in, feeling sick with longing, frustration, and rejection.

There he was, sitting there in the dance practice room with the others, apparently at ease with nothing else to do, with so much *better* things to fill his time than say even a passing word to me. His bronze-brown eyes flicked to the camera, but they looked different. I'd remembered them warm, glowing, soft, vulnerable... he looked more closed-off, cautious. The typical sparkle wasn't there when he smiled.

And yet he looked okay. He didn't look broken. He didn't look sad. He looked *good,* even.

He was good at faking that. Maybe he was good at faking a lot of things.

It was how good he looked that made me start to hate myself. He was over there not even thinking about me, doing just fine, and I was here *wrecked.* I looked like a mess, I *was* a mess. Listening to sad music, too depressed sometimes to do anything at all but just lay on my floor, eating to make myself feel better, thinking about him every moment.

I was aware of the rubber bracelet on my wrist as I fell backward on the pillows, holding my phone above my head. My eyes were drawn almost against my will to Jongjin's wrists.

They were covered by the cuffs of his sleeves. But even if they hadn't been... of course he wouldn't be wearing it. I was stupid for even considering it. What would he care?

Jongjin looked at the camera and spoke, his smooth voice both pleasurable and painful to my ears. He was speaking in Korean, but it was simple hellos.

"So," Tae-X said in English, clapping his hands together, "California was awesome." He looked back at the rest of the members, obviously expecting them to jump in and add more.

Jongjin smiled at the camera, something strange in his generic expression. "We had a great time," he said, in English. "I want to thank all you American fans for coming to see us, and being excited we were there. Each world tour makes me want to do another one."

I was frozen watching the phone, completely unmoving, looking at his plastic expression, hearing his plastic voice, his plastic words.

"My favorite part was the food," chimed in Sun Chi-Ho, making the others grin.

"I'd love to visit Brazil next," Jongjin continued. "I really hope to go there."

Acting like nothing had happened. Like he'd never met me, completely unchanged. Like I was just a speck in his memory he barely remembered now. On to the next thing.

I yanked out my earbuds angrily, throwing them to the floor, then turned my phone to black and buried my face in the pillows, the last bit of hope I had now crushed.

종진
JONGJIN
31

We got off the plane in Seoul, Korea, being greeted by a mass of wildly screaming fangirls. The five of us—Tr3sure—strode down the shiny airport floor, surrounded by bodyguards as flowers and bouquets were tossed all around us.

"*JONGJIN!*" was screamed the most. I gave a smile and a nod, trying not to show the way I was broken on the inside.

"Why aren't you flirting?" Tae-X asked me under his breath. "Where did the flirtatious Jongjin go?"

"He got stuck in a pharmacy after someone crashed into him, spilling butter everywhere," I said in a voice just as low.

A rose smacked me right in the middle of my chest. I stopped, hesitated, then picked it up and held it in my fingers. All around us, the screaming grew to an almost painful, high-pitched frenzy as girls went berserk. I glanced back at the crowd and then kept going as Manager Son put a hand on my shoulder and shoved me along.

I still held the rose as we climbed silently into the black van, cut off from the rest of the world as one of the managers shut the door. Through the dark, glossy, one-way window I watched bodyguards trying to hold some girls back who were attempting to run after us.

Of course, the effort was pointless. We were like birds now, safely trapped back inside our cages. Too valuable to let fly.

The traffic was so thick that it took until noon to get back to the chrome-silver JNP building, rising into the sky right in the heart of Seoul. While the rest of Tr3sure headed to unpack their things in the dorm, I walked, as if in a dream, to the rooftop. Endless stairs, each step making one name flash through my mind. *Leyla.*

The door to the rooftop was unlocked. I strode out onto the pale concrete, shedding my jacket in the intense summer sun and rolling up the sleeves of my button-up shirt. I still held the rose—the maroon lipstick-red rose, thorns on the slender stem pressing into my fingers.

I sat down on the rooftop and rested my arms on the middle bar of the railing, legs slipping under the lower bar, letting my dress shoes dangle out over the expanse. My heart beat extra fast at the dangerous thrill of being up so high.

If I couldn't reach Leyla, what would she think? The answer was imminent. She would think that I was ignoring her, just like her friends ignored her. Maybe she would give me the benefit of the doubt for a while, but how long?

I could locate her house, from the map images. But if that was the only route I had, then all that remained was to send a letter. That would take weeks. Maybe months.

She would think it impossible that I wouldn't be able to contact her in any way, even through Seojung, Tae-X, Laon, and Sun Chi-Ho. She wouldn't think that her contact information had been discovered and literally burned.... Was she angry with me? Had she given up on me already? I didn't *have* weeks or months.

I thought of my stolen phone, in Manager Jeon's pocket or in his desk, maybe. How many missed texts and calls were accumulating on it? How many times would she try before she gave up?

The sun beat down on my face. Even this high up, like a king in a palace overlooking his city, the air still smelled like car exhaust, hot pavement, sewer, cigarette smoke, and savory food.

And roses. I held it up to my face and started slowly pulling off petals.

"She still loves me... she doesn't love me anymore...."

The deep red velvet, lusciously soft and rich in hue, floated down into the busy city of Seoul, among the silver, glittering buildings, the black road with crisp white crosswalk lines. Rose petals disappeared among the cars, the pedestrians, the bicycles; fading out of sight among the intense noonday sun that cast a glare on every shiny surface.

I was afraid to finish the rose. I tossed it behind me, still with the tightest center bud intact.

So I started to sing. Softly, to myself. One of the songs that had gotten me accepted as a trainee.

"Though not for now... maybe someday... like the seasons... we can be together...."

I wasn't able to finish that without my voice breaking. I grumpily blinked away the water in my eyes. I hadn't cried for two years, since Tr3sure's debut. I shouldn't be about to start now.

I wished Leyla could be here to sit with me on the rooftop, to see everything. July in Korea—all simmering heat, humidity and crashing monsoon rain; cold jjolmyeon, caramel bingsu, and fried chicken. We could experience everything together.

I wanted my 20th year to be full of her.

I settled on humming the song, swallowing the lump in my throat as I looked out at the horizon, the endless expanse of buildings and people. There were thousands of people probably just in the radius that I could see, and none of them were her; none of them would ever, *could* ever, replace her.

"What are you doing out here?" said a voice from behind me. "You're going to get heatstroke."

I groaned. "Am I not allowed to experience mild discomfort for even five minutes?"

Seojung ignored me. There was a pause, and then he said, "You're not unpacking with us."

Did he expect me to act like everything was normal and fine?

When I didn't say anything, he said, "We were going to order some cold noodles. Since the comeback and tour diets are over."

"I'll have whatever you're having," I said.

Of course they'd be ordering in. Not like in California where no one knew me and I could buy my own food. Here, we had to hide in our shiny silver tower that was JNP Entertainment.

At least we could eat normal food in peace.

"We also have a dance practice right after," Seojung added.

Of course.

☆ ♡ ☆

After dance practice for several hours, I walked to our dorm, exhausted. Manager Jeon had shown up and insisted that we dance longer and harder than normal. Trying to distract us or break us, I didn't know.

It had been aimed at me, since I had a solo spotlight part that I'd been forced to repeat, over and over.

Manager Yoo and Son had also dropped by to watch. They folded their arms and nodded approvingly as I did my choreography yet again, muscles screaming, whole body burning up, tiredness taking the crisp edge away from the moves.

"Jongjin's vital to Tr3sure," Manager Yoo said, commanding voice carrying clearly to everyone in the room. "He's the face, the voice, of the group and ultimately of JNP Entertainment."

I didn't have the energy or the breath to think or say anything. The music wound down to a close, but Manager Jeon had said, "Again."

Now I was back in the dorm. Sweat dripped off my forehead and onto the desk as I pulled out a sheet of paper and a pen and started writing to Leyla.

My hand trembled with fatigue as I started, English script larger and clumsier than my own Korean one. *My precious Leyla.* I started explaining, summarizing what had happened, asking her to send back a letter with her phone number and all her contact information so we could talk again. I gave her all of mine—email, secret social media accounts, everything—so that as soon as she got the letter she could contact me immediately. I apologized, but I was having a hard time thinking. The paper looked fuzzy.

Before I knew it I was on the floor, having slid out of my chair and hit my head on the ground. Laon was shouting panicked in my ear and a hand shook my shoulder; cold water was splashed in my face.

I sat up, dizzy.

"They ran him to the ground." That was Tae-X's deep, authoritative voice, stinging with anger.

A piece of candy was pushed between my lips. As the sugar melted on my tongue, I immediately felt more alert.

"I'm fine," I mumbled, staggering to my feet as Tae-X and Seojung grabbed me under the arms and hauled me to the sofa, pushing me back down again. Sun Chi-Ho appeared at my elbow with some cold water and I sipped it after the candy was gone.

"I'm okay," I said, in response to Sun Chi-Ho's very worried stare.

Sun Chi-Ho looked towards Seojung, doubt in his eyes. "Uncle Seojung?"

"He'll be fine," Seojung sighed. "He's just been pushed too hard. He should recover with some rest, sleep and food. Don't you worry about it."

"Yeah, he'll be fine," Tae-X said, pushing his hand up into his neon-orange hair. He gave Sun Chi-Ho a weary smile.

Bless them. Sun Chi-Ho was still the marshmallow the four of them tried to protect against the world.

Laon was watching me with blazing, bright, intense eyes as he stood next to the sofa. "Should we get you checked on so that none of us have to be concerned?"

Laon did end up summoning our in-building medic. It was just as the others had said. I was simply pushed too hard, and was fatigued and exhausted, not to mention having low blood sugar from the hours of constant exercise with not enough food.

The medic also called in Manager Son. "He needs a break," he said.

Manager Son's reply was nervous. "I'm not in charge of the schedule. But it's packed. I think even a few days off is not going to happen."

I watched them both from the sofa, drinking my electrolyte beverage and eating a 7-Eleven dosirak lunch that Laon had pulled from the fridge.

The medic sighed. "It doesn't have to be a long break. For the short-term, he can get by with just a few extra hours."

"We can do that," said Manager Son, sounding relieved. "JNP has been using this strategy since Tr3sure debuted, to great success."

"Great success for JNP," I said dully once the medic had left, shutting the door behind him. "Not us."

Manager Son shook my shoulder. "Ya, brighten up. Look at the big picture. If another member drops out, it'll be fine without them, but if you drop out, Tr3sure won't exist."

"It *won't* be fine without them." My hand clenched on the bottle of my drink as I stared straight ahead of me. "You don't even give them a chance. Everything they do is determined by the script."

"I don't write the script," he reminded me uncomfortably. His voice changed to a consoling tone. "I'll see if I can get you all a treat. How about that? How about that, eh? And maybe talk to the people who organize the public appearances and shows and see if we can get Seojung, Laon, Tae-X, and Sun Chi-Ho some more screen time."

I saw the four of them glance at each other, not looking very excited. JNP management had been talking about this for years, but not much had ever been done about it.

Manager Son patted me on the shoulder and left. As soon as he did, Laon flopped down next to me on the sofa.

"I don't mind not having lots of screen time, actually," he said quietly. "What, so I can just end up like you? I don't want to be in your place."

Stabbing words that had truth to them.

"Me neither," Tae-X murmured. Sun Chi-Ho made a noise of agreement.

"I don't think any of us can envy you right now," Seojung said, intense dark eyes sweeping across all of us. "Who wants this? Who wants to pay this price?"

"Leyla," I whispered, staring straight ahead. "They took Leyla from me."

My voice cracked with the truth of those gut-wrenching words. *They'd taken Leyla from me.* That was the price. The ultimate price.

What was I to do? I could only send her a letter, and in several weeks' time—if I was lucky—it would arrive to her, explaining everything.

Hoping she wasn't so hurt and angry she threw it away without reading it. Hoping she didn't look at those words and call me a liar. Hoping she hadn't had time to reconsider the idea of us and decided to move on.

"Shouldn't you be resting?" Tae-X cried as I stood up.

"I can't," I said. "I have a letter to write."

☆ ♡ ☆

The days, and then weeks, passed slowly. Every moment that slid by increased my desperation.

It was like I was being suffocated, being squeezed, until my air ran out. I was dying on the inside. She haunted my every movement, my every thought. Now that I was off the comeback tour diet and was allowed to eat, I was never hungry. I barely touched food.

Everything felt... empty. There was a huge hole in my life where Leyla should be. I tried to keep my chin up, tried to stay positive, but I was sinking.

I *needed* her. I'd never felt so understood and loved by anyone.

The first chance I had to contact her started with a Tr3sure group live. If I could just somehow even *hint* to her that I was being stopped against my will....

But this was our first live video in a while, and Managers Son and Jeon were behind the camera, watching, breathing down our necks.

Making sure I behaved.

They underestimated the chance that I didn't care about the consequences.

We started the video with the usual pleasantries. Tae-X started the script, talking more directly to our American fans as he switched to English.

"So," he said, clapping his hands together, "California was awesome." He looked back at the rest of us, our cue.

The lines flowed easily off my tongue, like they had for two years. "We had a great time," I said, taking care to pronounce the English words. It was supposed to be for the American fans, but if Leyla was watching... "I want to thank all you American GOLD for coming to see us, and being excited we were there. Each world tour makes me want to do another one." Heart racing, I started to open my mouth again, to say *something* just in case she was watching. But Sun Chi-Ho jumped in too fast.

"My favorite part was the food!" said Sun Chi-Ho. We all smiled. Like we were supposed to.

"I'd love to visit Brazil next," I continued, hyperaware of the feel of the yellow rubber bracelet on my wrist. Dare I show it, and risk the managers taking it away? "I really hope to go there."

Laon opened his mouth, his breath shifting as he was about to speak, but I jumped in before he could. "I love visiting GOLD," I said, desperation clawing at my throat. "In fact, in America, there are some fans I'm sorry I didn't get to spend some more time with."

Everyone behind the camera *froze*. Son's and Jeon's eyes were popping. The cameraperson's eyebrows raised. Beside me, Tae-X suddenly squeezed my leg, hard.

"That's right!" Seojung said effortlessly with a smile. "We're always sorry to go." He gave the camera a hot, elegant wink.

We jumped back on track from there. As soon as we turned off the video, Manager Jeon turned towards me. "That wasn't on the script!" he bellowed. "Did you want to start rumors?"

Even Manager Son was seething mad. "What do you think you're *doing?*" he cried. "You could *ruin* Tr3sure!"

The others had gotten up and stretched their legs; Seojung was leaning against the wall, sipping his water languidly. Tae-X looked worried, Laon just avoided everyone's gaze, and Sun Chi-Ho was looking back and forth from me to the managers.

"It better not happen again, got it?" said Manager Son, poking me in the chest and tilting up his head to look at me, since he was several inches shorter.

"It won't," I said in a low voice, despondent.

Because that was my only chance. I'd done it, the best I could. I just had to hope that she'd see it, and understand....

I wasn't allowed to do any video lives for the next several weeks, and instead was overloaded with pre-filmed content to be released over the next several weeks. It kept me constantly busy, but still, my heart ached so much it was almost physically painful.

After being run ragged by the exhausting amount of work each day, I would try to stay cheerful for Sun Chi-Ho, Tae-X, Laon and Seojung, but I couldn't. The four of them would be laughing together in the dorm as they got ready for bed, talking animatedly, but I would be sad, distant from them, separated. Like a shadow of my old self. Every time I tried to fake a smile, I remembered Leyla seeing right through it, which just made all my feelings stronger and the smile harder to force.

It was also harder to sleep. I would often pass out on the bed from sheer exhaustion of the day, but then wake up in the middle of the night, without having dreamt at all.

Tonight was like that.

My eyes had opened to stare at the black underside of Tae-X's bunk. The bedroom was completely dark; across the room, curtains were pulled over the floor-to-ceiling windows to block the city lights. The sliver of light I could see through the crack looked bluish and melancholy, and I realized now I could hear a gentle, uneven pattering, the tapping of rain at the window.

Occasionally a raindrop would strike the glass with a harder *thwack* than the rest, making it hard to drift back off. But I wouldn't have anyway. I was too awake.

I sat up, blankets falling off my shirtless torso, as I swung my legs over the side of the bed and looked out at that crack, the tiny sliver of the outside world. No one else moved in the room, sound asleep, as I quietly stood up and went to the window, opening the heavy curtain.

My other hand went to the List in my pajama pants pocket. Jeon hadn't bothered to confiscate it that day. Now it was extremely worn, soft and falling apart.

It was my most prized possession. A love letter.

Because I was shirtless, I could easily see the yellow rubber bracelet on my right wrist. I never took it off, even though it was always hidden underneath the cuffs of my sleeves during the day.

Cool air radiated off the glass of the window and onto my skin. I could just barely see the ghost of my reflection; I looked too thin, muscles too sharp, the cost of not eating.

I let the curtain fall again, playing with the yellow bracelet as I padded silently over to the closet in my bare feet. I pulled on a white dress shirt, not bothering to button it up, letting it hang loosely open as I walked to the next room, gently shutting the door behind me so as not to wake up the others.

The floor-to-ceiling living room window was curtainless, completely bare. I stood in front of it, watching the rain patter faster and faster until it created a steady humming of noise. The crystal-clear drops ran down the glass, and I touched one or two with my fingertips, which were still shiny from the scar of my burn. I wished I could actually feel the cool water.

Leyla would just be waking up right now, or maybe already had been awake for hours.

It was like my slowly leaking, punctured oxygen tank had finally run out. I was alone and isolated, but I had left *her* even more alone. I'd told her I'd be there for her, I'd tried to protect her, but I'd failed.

Failed. I was a failure at the one thing in the world I wanted more than being an idol. I'd failed Leyla.

"I'm so sorry," I whispered. "I'm *so sorry.*"

The air in here suddenly felt stale, the walls suddenly much closer. I gazed at the outside, trapped behind the glass, in my suffocating gilded cage.

I couldn't stand being in here anymore. I spun around, still quietly, and went to the door, slipping on my dress shoes without any socks. Then I unlatched the door with a sharp *snap* and stepped into the hallway.

The stairs to the roof were dimly illuminated by lights near the floor, parallel on either side, going up to infinity. I followed the path, heels clicking on the metal, slowly, until I reached the door.

When I pushed it open, I was hit square in the chest with a huge gust of cool wind. It billowed my open shirt, rushing upwards through my hair and filling my lungs with precious breath.

Cold, steady rain was swept into me, carried by the wind. There was no cover here, no overhang to take shelter beneath. I walked over the wet concrete to the middle of the roof as lightning flashed in the sky over Seoul—brilliant, pure, illuminating everything. Rain dripped over my skin and clothes.

Up here, I was finally free—but I wasn't full. I wasn't content. I was just as empty and full of pain as before.

I deserved this.

I deserved this pain, because I'd left Leyla all alone.

My shirt was plastered to my skin now, the rain intensifying, getting harder, faster. In my chest, my heart ached so much it physically hurt.

And for the first time in two years, I cried.

Actually cried. As I stood there, hands behind my back, my shoulders shook with the weight of my silent sobs.

Lightning cracked through the horizon and the thunder ripped it apart. I unleashed a roar, screaming into the howling abyss of wind, unable to hear my own voice in the soul-shaking *boom* of thunder that trailed off into a growl. I bent over, screaming my heart out, as the monsoon rain crashed against the gray sky. It pounded the rooftop, wrathful and violent, streaming down the slick surfaces and making it almost impossible to see.

I fell to my knees as the wind battered me and the thunder rumbled through my chest, reverberating.

It was just like that night—the night when everything changed. The one I couldn't go back from, would never choose to go back from—no matter the cost. Even if Leyla never wanted to see me again. Even if I pursued her and she would never let herself be caught. The amount of beauty, of color, of *life* that had flooded every corner of my being was like nothing I'd ever experienced. After nine years of pouring all of my energy and very soul into the industry that consumed everything I'd given it, Leyla had reclaimed my soul. Like having sunshine on my face after nine years of darkness. It had been long enough that I'd forgotten what it felt like, but she'd reminded me.

She'd come crashing into my life—literally.

Every step of the way, it was like fate had tried to bring us together. My very soul cried out for hers, hungering. I loved her laughter and her tears, her voice and her silence, just the presence of her. She was unlike anyone I'd ever met—or would ever meet again.

She was *everything* to me.

And I didn't know how this was going to end.

I stayed there on my knees, shoulders shaking, the icy shards of rain pounding every bit of my exposed skin. I tilted my face up to the sky and accepted it, lost in the chaos, at one with it. As the wind swirled around me, pushing and shoving and making me sway, I felt a slight nudge at my leg. I looked down. It was a rose—a dried out and now sodden red rose, blown into me.

She still loves me... she doesn't love me anymore....

Tears ran down my face as I picked it up, hand cradling the bud. I was still afraid of its answer.

Without Leyla, my entire world had been washed gray and colorless, just like the endless city expanse in front of me, the violent rain unrelenting in its pummeling. Was this going to be the rest of my life?

I pressed my lips to the rose and then tossed it upwards in the air, where the powerful wind immediately snatched it up and carried it away in its jaws, far, far beyond the JNP Entertainment building.

I stayed there for hours. My body grew cold and numb in the icy rain, but I didn't leave. Eventually, as the storm slowed and the rain trickled to a gentle pattering, I curled up on the ground, hollowly watching the drops splash to the concrete.

"JONGJIN!"

Someone was shouting my name—I'd fallen asleep. In a panic, I shoved myself up blearily, completely disoriented.

It was barely dawn. Weak yellow sunlight shone on puddles all around me. The sky was cloudy and everything was fresh. I blinked and looked around.

Seojung was frozen near the door, staring at me. It had been him who'd shouted my name. I staggered to my feet as he stalked towards me.

"What are you doing out here?" he snapped. "Laon is downstairs looking for you."

"I just—the rain—I fell asleep—"

"When I saw you I thought you'd *died!*" Seojung yelled, grabbing me by the collar and pulling me towards him, my face inches from his snarling one.

"I'm sorry!" I said, completely stunned and off-balance.

His ink-black eyes bored into mine for one very long moment before he shoved me away. "We're going back to the dorm. There's something you need to see."

I combed my fingers through my straggling hair and buttoned my still-damp shirt as we headed down the stairs. I had to rush to keep up with Seojung, who wouldn't tell me what was happening or going on until we'd reached the dorm. He pulled out his desk chair and sat me down in front of the computer screen of his laptop.

"I saw this as soon as I woke up," he said. "Read."

It was an article from a tabloid news site. I frowned and leaned forward. The article started:

Byun Jongjin always puts on a smile for his Tr3sure members and for GOLD, but the truth is that he's tired and needs a break. As the most popular member, since the debut, JNP has been pushing him too hard....

"Wh—who did this?" I asked, my voice coming out hoarse. My eyes raked downward.

Confidential sources reveal that Byun Jongjin has asked JNP for a small hiatus or break multiple times, unable to even celebrate on his birthday. Even though JNP refuses, Byun Jongjin still smiles because he wants to make us happy.

And then the picture. Me. No makeup, revealing the obvious dark shadows under my eyes and exhaustion on my face, looking with almost a kind of weary longing towards the horizon as the sun rose over the ocean. It was a shot that told a story.

I remembered that moment. I remembered....

"Sun Chi-Ho," I whispered in shock.

Sun Chi-Ho had taken that photo.

And he'd leaked it.

레일라
LEYLA
32

My phone rang, and I frowned. I wasn't used to people calling me nowadays, now that Jongjin....

I refused to let my mind finish that sentence.

I was outside a café in the shade at a little table, drinking an iced coffee with some origami papers spread out in front of me. It was late in the afternoon, the air hot and the sun golden, without the hint of a breeze. I'd gotten dressed up today so I looked very presentable. I even had some cheap sunglasses I was trying to pretend were fancy.

I was *trying* to get over him. I was *trying* to have fun and be happy without him. As far as I was concerned, I was on the rebound, and Amanda had told me the best way to get over an ex was "to live so that they'll be jealous when they see you enjoying yourself so much and looking so hot".

Well, it was impossible he'd ever accidentally run into me, but maybe the same principle remained.

It was probably better than lying on my floor, too depressed to move.

My phone was still ringing; the caller ID read *Carolyn.* I picked it up with a sigh. "Hello?"

"Have you seen what's going on?" she shrieked, sounding shocked, not even bothering to say hello.

"Seen what?" I said, confused.

"JNP Entertainment on the hot seat? The huge scandal with Jongjin?"

My heart gave a jolt at his name.

"Fans are in a frenzy! They're protesting with signs in front of the building, taking over social media and boycotting the entire label!" She took a breath. "The internet's exploding! You know what's going on, right? You and him are friends, right?"

"He... hasn't talked to me for a while," I said carefully. "I don't know anything about it."

"Oh." She sounded disappointed. "I hoped you'd have some inside information. Sorry to bother you."

And she hung up.

I put my phone down on the table and took a sip of my drink, leisurely looking around at the people walking by, green potted plants and baking concrete. Then I picked up an origami paper and started to fold it, slowly.

I didn't need to know what was going on. I was living for myself, nobody else. Why would I care?

I didn't care. Exactly.

I continued to fold my paper very methodically, taking a while to smooth out every sharp corner.

Oh, whatever. I grabbed my phone and looked up JNP. News articles and images flooded the screen.

Leaked Photo of Superstar Byun Jongjin Reveals JNP Scandal

The Dark Side of JNP Entertainment

Jongjin Overworked, Sad

JNP Entertainment Apologizes for Mistreatment of Byun Jongjin

And the photo. The photo made my whole body go still. It was Jongjin—no makeup, showing the heavy shadows under his eyes, his expression wistful and tired and forlorn. And yet his face was so beautiful, so intimate to me. I could remember exactly what it was like to kiss him, the vulnerability in his soft bronze-brown eyes before his gentle lips met mine. To be that close... to see every eyelash, every tiny detail in his skin....

I remembered his sad voice over the phone, whispered and clumsy. *"Leyla?"*

I desperately swiped past the photo, cheeks going hot with emotion. My longing for him was like an anvil on my chest, painful and hard to breathe.

I sucked in a deep, steadying breath that was a little shaky, and clicked on one news section, skimming the article.

Carolyn was right. Fans had flooded the area around the JNP building holding signs, angry and refusing to leave. JNP was being ripped into on every website, video compilations were accumulating of "Every Time JNP Tried to Hide Mistreatment of Jongjin and Tr3sure," and fans were refusing to watch any JNP videos or support any JNP artists.

Cornered by the fans, JNP had no other choice but to release an official statement sugarcoating and apologizing—and saying they'd give Jongjin, and the rest of Tr3sure, a two-week hiatus every year.

I gaped at that. A *two-week hiatus.* Every year. That was more than he'd ever asked for.

Who had released that photo? Was it tabloid reporters? But the article had referred to information that could only have been obtained from an inside source. And why had they done so? Had they really wanted to help Jongjin?

Whoever it was, they'd pushed JNP to the limit. The company had gone from taking away his phone and posting bodyguards at his door, without even one day off, to letting him free for weeks.

Whoever released the photo had played the ultimate, and perhaps only, trump card. They'd outsmarted JNP and beat them at their own game, all while keeping Jongjin in positive public light.

I breathed a silent thanks to whoever had been brave enough to risk their own position to help Jongjin—if that really was what they wanted.

I wanted to still be angry at Jongjin. I wanted to tell myself he was such a jerk that he deserved what he'd got before, and resent the fact that life was getting better for him—life was getting better without me.

But I was happy for him. In my sad way, I was happy that he was happy.

It was getting hot out here. I picked up my cup and swirled around the coffee, ice cubes bumping against each other as I stared forlornly into the middle of it, lost in my own head. Lost in bronze-brown eyes that I still loved.

"A two-week hiatus," I mumbled. "Wherever you are, I hope you're happy."

He must have been. He must have been thrilled.

I went home, filled with bone-crushing sadness tempered with a sweetness that somehow only made the pain worse, like a sharp arrow pierced right through my heart.

As soon as I stepped through the door, I saw Dad down the hall at the kitchen counter. I dropped my bag underneath the peg that Amanda's bag should've occupied and went to go join him.

He was sifting through the mail. "Letter for you," he said without looking up.

"Letter?" I said, confused. "From who?"

His brow furrowed. "I forgot how to pronounce it. Anyway, it was from Korea. Where the boy you liked went back to."

I stopped breathing, completely frozen.

Dad looked at me, seeming slightly concerned at my reaction. "I put it on your bed, if you want it."

"Korea?" I managed.

He nodded.

"Thanks," I forced out in a gasp, and then I walked up the stairs.

Walked. When I wanted to run. I forced myself to take each step at a time, feeling almost dizzy, the whole world surreal.

This was when I found out whether there was still something left for us to salvage or if it was goodbye forever.

The letter had been laid on my bed, waiting for me. I stared at it. My eyes widened as I took it slowly, gingerly, in my hands; the thin envelope, battered from coming so far, felt light and precious and fragile.

My name had been written very deliberately and with great neatness on the front—with a little heart next to it.

"Byun Jongjin," I whispered fiercely, eyes glossy, "this better be what I hope it is."

He better not break my heart. It couldn't stand any more breaking.

For a second I just held the beautiful envelope, sucking in a long, slow breath.

Then I opened it and unfurled the paper inside, smoothing it out on the table gently, carefully.

At the very top were a bunch of social media and messaging accounts—a thousand different ways to contact him.

It began *My precious Leyla.* I pressed my hand to my mouth, trying to stifle the sobs, as I read everything. *Everything.* My eyes raced over his scribbled explanations, the truth growing clearer with every word. He hadn't forgotten about me. He'd tried to reach me. So many things had happened and he'd done his best to fight them but in the end, he'd still lost me.

At the bottom, a little spaced out from the rest of the text, was the end.

You said you don't like change, but for me, change saved my life. I think it was destiny that brought us together that night. When I met you, nothing was ever the same. You saw the real me and you were all I ever wanted.

You asked me, before, about what I wanted to do after Tr3sure. All of my new dreams have you in it.

I don't know if this letter is too late. I don't know if you want to go, but if you do, and if you ever think of me, know that you are always welcome to come back. I'll always be here, waiting for you.

You're my only one.

Byun Jongjin

I swallowed the lump in my throat, the page blurring in front of me. "I love you," I said, crying. "I love you. I don't care where I am, as long as you're there."

종진

JONGJIN

33

"SUN CHI-HO!" I shouted, tackling him, laughing and grinning and unable to contain my excitement. "SUN CHI-HO, YOU CLEVER, BRAVE, BRILLIANT—"

"You're messing up my hair!" he cried. But he was grinning too, wrestling me back as we both fell on the sofa.

"Two *weeks!*" I said. "Two entire weeks!"

I broke apart and gripped him by the shoulders, suddenly serious as I looked into his eyes.

"Thank you," I said.

He smiled that cute little smile back at me. "I just wanted to help you," he said quietly. "I don't think you're as good at fooling me as you think you are."

And then Laon tackled me from behind and the five of us were jumping around the living room in a circle, arms around each other's shoulders, whooping and shouting and celebrating.

Seojung broke free to run to the kitchen, coming back with five shot glasses and a can of watermelon soda. He popped open the tab with a hissing noise and poured us each a fizzing, bubbly, light pink glass.

"To brothers," Seojung said as we picked them up, and then we clinked them together.

"Sun Chi-Ho," Tae-X said after he swallowed, "how did you know you wouldn't get caught? If JNP finds out who leaked the photo and some of the information in the article...."

Sun Chi-Ho shrugged. "I was really careful. I just had to do something. I think... it was worth taking a chance."

I hugged him, and the others piled on.

"Are you crying?" Tae-X said, trying to stare into my face.

I pushed him away. "YA, shut up. I'm not crying."

But I was so filled with happiness I could burst. The only thing left now....

I jumped up and ran to my computer—since Jeon still had my phone—and checked my messages.

My heart *stopped*.

Hey, I guess we have a lot of catching up to do :)

"What is it?" Tae-X was calling.

"It's Leyla!" I said. "It's *Leyla!*"

☆ ♡ ☆

It was a summer I would never forget. Between talking and video calling Leyla every day, laughing with my Tr3sure brothers as we went out and explored parks and restaurants on our days off (because JNP had given us more than just the two week break in the official statement, wanting to seem even more generous "behind-the-scenes"), getting to sing new songs, and planning for a South American tour, I was busy but had never been happier. My heart was full to bursting. I even got to see my parents more, visiting home and eating all I could as my mom liked to cook huge feasts whenever I came home. I took selfies in the streets with fans, went swimming with Sun Chi-Ho and Laon, and hung out with my friends from other groups. Tr3sure worked on our next comeback and ate gimbap and takeout along with our green smoothies and salads, dancing and practicing choreography. Leyla was there to cheer me on for all of it, though I wished she could visit.

Ice cream was still off-limits, but I did eat some occasionally. Just occasionally.

It felt good to be in Korea—to be home. I wanted Leyla to see everything. I wanted to cook with her in the dorm's tiny kitchen, to go on secret dates with her in disguise, to show her the backstage of a concert.

But I knew those days would come. Sooner than later, if my plans worked out.

For the first time in my life, I felt like I was truly living out my dreams.

레일라
LEYLA
34

The summer was, unexpectedly, the best one of my life.

Between talking constantly with Jongjin (often right before one of us fell asleep at night), meeting new people through Carolyn's group of friends, setting off little fireworks, listening to music, and just *living*—I was filled to the bursting with happiness.

Amanda visited more often now, bringing bakery goods with her, and we'd sit on the driveway under the palm trees and the moon and dusky sky and eat them, talking and laughing. We even jumped on the trampoline for old times' sake. Carolyn and I spent time going to K-pop shops and trying Korean restaurants, and Dad and I did some family trips to the beach.

When July turned to August and September, I didn't mind going to school. I still had mixed feelings about California—it didn't have as much green as I would've liked—but it was the home of Dad and Amanda, and the place where I'd met the love of my life, Jongjin. For that, it would always have a special place in my heart.

Milo was no longer welcome with Carolyn and her friends, because I'd told her what had happened that day in front of the burger shop and the whole story, and she'd believed me. For that, I was eternally grateful. I couldn't ask for a better friend.

Milo left me alone, acting like I didn't exist, but gossip had it that he whipped around nervously whenever he saw a tall Korean man with dress shoes.

The guy who'd called me "rude and ugly" so long ago either graduated or transferred to a different school—because I never saw him again.

As for Jackie and Aaron, I'd finally unblocked them, but our relationship was tentative. They'd abandoned me when I'd needed them most; that was a serious breach of trust. But life was messy. Things happened. I wasn't angry with them, even though I wasn't sure I could ever open my heart to them again.

Life was good. The school year was even enjoyable, filled with friends and crazy fun and the comforting, routine grind. The only thing that dampened my happiness was Jongjin's absence. I missed him, missed being able to hug him, missed seeing his eyes sparkle.

It was near New Year's when an envelope arrived for me in the mail with a Korean postmark. I had just strolled into the kitchen to grab a handful of Chex mix when Dad held it up.

I tore into it immediately, then looked down at it in disbelief.

Dad saw the stunned expression on my face. "What is it?"

"A ticket to Incheon, South Korea."

종진

JONGJIN
SIX MONTHS LATER

The most beautiful girl I had ever seen was walking towards me.

She hadn't noticed me yet—she had in earbuds and was hauling a rolling suitcase, glancing around as her glasses slid a little down her nose.

We were in a section of the airport that was absolutely packed with a crush of people of all different nationalities, and I knew I was almost unrecognizable in my hat, sunglasses, and complete fashion change.

When her gaze flicked towards me, I held up my hand in a finger heart.

She slowed, staring at me, and then recognized me. She gave a little *scream* and ran towards me, letting go of her suitcase. I held out my arms, staggering underneath her enthusiasm as she jumped on me and hugged me tightly with both her arms and her legs. I laughed, spinning her around as I hugged her back, tighter than I ever had before, never wanting to let go.

Leyla released her legs, but still kept her arms around my neck as she looked up at my face. Her cheeks were wet with happy tears and I kissed them off, so happy to see her that I forgot any sense of public manners.

She reached up and pulled my sunglasses an inch down my nose, revealing my eyes. I kept my arms around her. She was so soft, so precious.

"I missed you," she said.

I was smiling so much my face hurt. "I missed you too," I said in a low voice. With all the conversations we'd had, my English had become fluent. "But you're mine for the next two weeks."

She laughed. "And next time, maybe you can come visit me in America."

"I definitely will," I said. My breath caught as I looked into her beautiful eyes. "What are the chances that I'd go to get ice cream in America that late at night, and the backup generator failing when the power went out, and you crashing into me? We're meant for each other!"

"It's destiny," she said, reaching up on tiptoes to give me a quick kiss on the mouth.

"Exactly," I said, my insides feeling like they were lit up with a bright glow of overflowing, abundant happiness. "What more could I want?"

Here are a few of Jongjin's favorite songs:

IYAH by **Kang Seung Yoon**
Wave by **ATEEZ**
Trap by **HENRY**
Power Up by **Red Velvet**
Rain by **TAEYEON**
N/S by **Stray Kids**
Anti-Romantic by **TXT**
Polaroid Love by **ENHYPEN**
Jamais Vu by **BTS**
Yours by **Raiden X CHANYEOL (Feat. LeeHi, CHANGMO)**

LUCY GOLD is an author who loves Korean food, reading, writing, anime, and —of course— K-pop music. She was born on New Year's Eve, making her Korean age two years 'ahead' instead of just one. You can reach her on Instagram— @lucygoldkpop.

LIKED **BEHIND THE IDOL**? TRY LUCY GOLD'S **BIAS** OR ITS GERMAN EDITION, **MORE THAN A STAR**

www.ingramcontent.com/pod-product-compliance
Lightning Source LLC
Chambersburg PA
CBHW050316110726
47899CB00007B/2263